ARCHIE GOES TO WORK

One good glance and I liked the job. The girls. All right there, all being paid to stay right there, and me being paid to move freely about and converse with anyone whomever, which was down in black and white. Probably after I had been there a couple of years I would find that close-ups revealed inferior individual specimens, Grade B or lower in age, contours, skin quality, voice or level of intellect, but from where I stood at nine-fifty-two Wednesday morning it was enough to take your breath away. At least half a thousand of them, and the general and overwhelming impression was of—clean, young, healthy, friendly, spirited, beautiful and ready. I stood and filled my eyes, trying to look detached. It was an ocean of opportunity.

TOO MANY WOMEN

Too Many Women

by Rex Stout

A Nero Wolfe Mystery

BANTAM BOOKS
TORONTO • NEW YORK • LONDON • SYDNEY • AUCKLAND

TOO MANY WOMEN

*A Bantam Book / published by arrangement with
The Viking Press, Inc.*

PRINTING HISTORY

Viking edition published October 1947

Detective Book Club edition published February 1948

Bantam edition published October 1949
New Bantam edition published November 1955

2nd printing ....December 1955	5th printing ....December 1972
3rd printing ....May 1967	6th printing ....August 1975
4th printing ......August 1968	7th printing ......August 1985

ISBN 0-553-25066-3

Published simultaneously in the United States and Canada

---

*Bantam Books are published by Bantam Books, Inc. Its trademark,
consisting of the words "Bantam Books" and the portrayal of a
rooster, is Registered in U.S. Patent and Trademark Office and in
other countries. Marca Registrada. Bantam Books, Inc., 666 Fifth
Avenue, New York, New York 10103.*

PRINTED IN THE UNITED STATES OF AMERICA

O   16   15   14   13   12   11   10   9   8   7

1.

IT WAS THE same old rigmarole. Sometimes I found it amusing; sometimes it only bored me; sometimes it gave me a pronounced pain, especially when I had had more of Wolfe than was good for either of us.

This time it was fairly funny at first, but it developed along regrettable lines. Mr. Jasper Pine, president of Naylor-Kerr, Inc., 914 William Street, down where a thirty-story building is a shanty, wanted Nero Wolfe to come to see him about something. I explained patiently, all about Wolfe being too lazy, too big and fat, and too much of a genius, to let himself be evoked. When Mr. Pine phoned again, in the afternoon, he insisted on speaking to Wolfe himself, and Wolfe made it short, sour, and final. An hour later, after Wolfe had gone up to the plant rooms, just to pass the time I dialed the number of Naylor-Kerr, Inc., managed to get through to Mr. Pine, and asked him why he didn't come to see us. He snapped that he was too busy, and then he wanted to know, "Who are you?"

I told him I was Archie Goodwin, the heart, liver, lungs, and gizzard of the private detective business of Nero Wolfe, Wolfe being merely the brains. He asked sarcastically if I was a genius too, and I told him no indeed, I was comparatively human.

"I could run down now," I said.

"No." He was curt but not discourteous. "I'm filled up for today. Come tomorrow morning at ten o'clock. Better make it ten-fifteen."

2.

Those pyramids of profit down in the Wall Street section, sticking straight up nine hundred feet and more, are tenanted by everything from one-room midgets to ten-floor super-giants. Though the name of Naylor-Kerr, Inc., was vaguely familiar to me, it was not a household word, and I lifted the brows when I learned from the lobby directory that it paid the rent for three whole floors. The executive offices were on the thirty-sixth, so up I went. The atmosphere up there was of thick carpets, wood panels and plenty of space, but as for the receptionist, though she was not really miscast she was way past

1

the deadline, having reached the age when it is more blessed to receive than to give.

She received me at ten-fourteen, and at ten-nineteen I was escorted down a corridor to the office of the president. Naturally he had a corner room with batteries of big windows, but I had to admit that in spite of more panels and carpets and the kind of office furniture you see in Sloane's window, it gave me the impression of a place where somebody got some work done.

Mr. Jasper Pine was about the same age as the receptionist, a little short of fifty maybe, but on him it looked good. Except for his clothes, with the coat obviously cut for the stoop of his shoulders, he had more the appearance of a foreman or a job boss than a top executive of a big corporation. In the middle of the room he shook hands as if he were comparatively human too, and, instead of fencing himself off behind his desk, assigned us to a couple of comfortable chairs between two windows.

"My morning's a little crowded," he told me in a deep voice that sounded as if all it needed was more breath to reach Central Park, and he could furnish the breath when necessary. I was sizing him up, not knowing then whether the job was a lead pencil leak in the supply room, which would have been beneath our notice, or wife-tailing, which was out of bounds for Nero Wolfe. On the phone he had refused to specify.

"So," he was going on, "I'll sketch it briefly. Looking over some reports recently, I noticed that our employee turnover here in the home office, exclusive of the technical staff, was over twenty-eight per cent for the year nineteen forty-six. That was excessive. I decided to look into it. As a first step I had a form drawn up and two thousand copies of it multigraphed, and sent a supply of it to all heads of departments, with instructions that one be filled out for each person who had left our employ during nineteen forty-six. The forms were to be returned direct to me. Here's one that came from the head of the stock department." He extended a hand with a paper in it. "Take a look at it. Read it through."

It was a single sheet, letter size, with a neat job of multigraphing on one side. At the top it said:

RETURN TO THE OFFICE OF THE PRESIDENT
BY MARCH TENTH

The blank spaces had been filled in with a typewriter. First came the name of the ex-employee, which in this case was

Waldo Wilmot Moore. Age: *30. Unmarried.* Home address: *Hotel Churchill.* Employment began: *April 8, 1946.* Hired through: *Applied personally.* Job: *Correspondence checker.* Salary: *$100 weekly.* Rises: *To $150 weekly September 30, 1946.* Employment ended: *December 5, 1946.*

Other spaces had been filled in, about how well he had done his job, and his relations with other employees and his immediate superiors, and so forth, and then at the bottom came what was of course the key question. Reason for ending employment (give details). There were three inches of space after it, plenty of room for details, but for Waldo Wilmot Moore only one word had been thought necessary and there it was:

Murdered.

3.

So apparently it wasn't a lead pencil leak.

I looked at Jasper Pine. "An excellent idea," I said enthusiastically. "These reports will show you where the weak spots are, and you can take steps. Though Moore's case was probably an exception. I don't suppose many of the twenty-eight per cent got murdered. Incidentally, I keep track of murders for business reasons, and I don't remember this one. Was it local?"

Pine was shaking his head. "Moore was run over by a car, a hit-and-run driver—here in New York somewhere uptown. I believe that is called manslaughter, not murder, which requires malice aforethought. I'm not a lawyer, but I looked it up when this report—when I saw this." He made a gesture of impatience. "The hit-and-run driver was not found. I want Nero Wolfe to find out if there is any basis for the supposition that it was murder."

"Just curiosity?"

"No. I took it up with the head of the stock department, who made that report, because I didn't think it desirable to have it in our files, stating that one of our employees had been murdered, unless that was actually the case. Also I wanted to know what reason he had, if any, to make that statement. He refused to give any reason. He agreed with my definition of murder and manslaughter, but he refused to change the report or to make another report using a different word or phrase. He insisted that the report is correct as it stands. He refused to elaborate. He refused to discuss it."

"Goodness." I was impressed. "That ought to be a record. Four refusals to a corporation president from a mere head of a department! Who is he? Mr. Naylor? Or Mr. Kerr?"

"His name is Kerr Naylor."

I thought for a second he was injecting comic relief, but the look on his face showed me quite the contrary. He was taking time out to light a cigarette, and it was easy to see that the purpose of the maneuver was to hide embarrassment. The president was unquestionably embarrassed.

After a good puff he coughed explosively and explained, "Kerr Naylor is the son of one of the founders of this business. He was named Kerr after the other founder. He has had a—uh, varied career. Also he is my wife's brother. He actually controls a large block of the corporation's stock, but he no longer owns it because he gave it away. He refuses to be an officer of the company, and he refuses to serve on the Board of Directors."

"I see. He's a dyed-in-the-wood refuser."

Pine made the gesture of impatience again. He did it with a little fling of a hand, and it was abrupt but not domineering. "As you see," he said, "the situation is not simple. After Mr. Naylor's refusal either to justify the report or to change it, I was inclined just to let the matter drop and merely destroy the report, but I mentioned it to two of my brother executives and to a member of the Board, and they were all of the opinion that it should be followed up. Besides that, news of the report, with that word on it, has got around among the employees of the department, presumably through the stenographer who typed it, and there is a lot of unhealthy gossip. This man Moore was the type—I'll put it this way— he was the type that stirs up gossip in the circle he lives in, and now, nearly four months after his death, here he is stirring it up again. We don't like it and we want it stopped."

"Oh. You said you wanted Mr. Wolfe to find out if there was any basis for using the word murdered. Now you want the gossip stopped. You'd better pick which."

"It amounts to the same thing, doesn't it?"

"Not necessarily. If we find out he was murdered and the finding percolates, the gossip gauge will go right through the ceiling, not to mention other possible results."

Pine glanced at his wristwatch, reached to an ash tray to ditch his cigarette, and stood up. "Damn it," he said, with more breath but not more noise, "do I have to explain that the situation is made more complicated by the fact that it was Mr. Kerr Naylor who signed that report? This is a damn nuisance and it's taking my time that ought to be spent working! His father, old George Naylor, is still living and is Chairman of the Board, though he turned over his stock to his children long ago. This is the oldest and largest company in its field, the largest in the world, and it has built up a reputation and a tradition. It has also built up—uh, complexities. The directors and executives now managing its affairs—of whom I am one—want this thing looked into, and I want to hire Nero Wolfe to do the looking."

"You mean the corporation? Wants to hire him?"

"Certainly!"

"To do what? Wait a minute, can I put it this way? We're either to make that word on that report good, or we're to make this Mr. Kerr Naylor eat it. Is that the job?"

"Roughly, yes."

"Do we get credentials for around here?"

"You get all reasonable co-operation. The details will have to be arranged with me. More time gone. It will have to be handled with discretion—and delicately. I had an idea that a way to do it would be for Nero Wolfe to get a job in the stock department, under another name of course, and he could—what's the matter?"

"Nothing. Excuse me." I stood up. The notion of Wolfe fighting his way down to William Street every morning or even with me driving him, and punching a time clock, and working all day in the stock department, had been too much for my facial control.

"Okay," I said, "I guess I know enough to put it up to Mr. Wolfe. Except about money. I ought to warn you that his charges have not joined in the postwar inflation because they were already so high that a boost would have been vulgar."

"This company never expects good work for low pay."

I told him that was fine and got my hat and coat.

4.

A coolness had sprung up between Wolfe and me. These coolnesses averaged about four a week, say, a couple of hundred a year. This particular one had two separate aspects: first, my natural desire for him to buy a new car opposed to his pigheaded determination to wait another year; and second, his notion of buying a noiseless typewriter opposed to my liking for the one we had.

It happened that at that moment there were other coolnesses swirling around in the old brownstone house, on West Thirty-fifth Street not far from the Hudson River, which he owned and used both for a residence and an office. Four of us lived there, counting him, and we were all temporarily cool. Wolfe had somewhere picked up the idea of putting leaves of sweet basil in clam chowder, and Fritz Brenner, the cook and house manager, strongly disapproved. A guy in New Hampshire who was grateful to Wolfe for something had sent him an extra offering, three plants of a new begonia named Thimbleberry, and Wolfe had given them good bench space up in the cool room, and Theodore Horstmann, the plant nurse, who thought that everything that grew except orchids was a weed, was fit to be tied.

So the atmosphere around the place was somewhat arctic, and on my way down in the elevator the thought struck me that this Naylor-Kerr or Kerr Naylor or Pine-Kerr Naylor business might be used as an excuse to go somewhere out of the cold for a few days. Why couldn't it be me who got a job in the stock department? Grabbing a taxi from under the chins of two other prospective customers, I considered it. Just any job, one that happened to be loose, didn't seem practical. A little friendly conversation with the elevator starter had informed me that the line of Naylor-Kerr, Inc., was Engineers' Equipment and Supplies, and I knew all of nothing about them except maybe overalls. Anyway, the job would have to be one that would let me roam around and rub elbows, or it might take months, and I didn't want months. It would be hard enough to maneuver Wolfe into letting me try it for a week, since he needed me every hour and might need me any minute, for anything and everything from opening the mail to bouncing unwanted customers or even shooting one, which had been known to happen.

Liking the idea, and being afraid of the dark when it comes to anything resembling murder, I told the taxi driver I had had a vision and asked him to go to the address of the Homicide Squad on West Twentieth Street. There by good luck I found that Purley Stebbins, my favorite sergeant, was on hand, and he obligingly got what I wanted with only three or four growls. A phone call to a brother sergeant downtown brought the information that the death of Waldo Wilmot Moore had occurred around midnight on December 4. The body had been discovered by a man and wife on Thirty-ninth Street a hundred and twenty feet east of Eleventh Avenue. The wife had phoned in while the man stood by, and a radio

car had arrived on the scene at one-nineteen A.M. on Decem-
5. It was a DOA, dead on arrival, with Moore's head crushed
and his legs broken. The car that hit him had been found the
next morning, parked on West Ninety-fifth Street near Broadway. It was hot, having been stolen the evening of the fourth
from where it was parked on West Fifty-fourth Street. Its
owner had been checked up and down and backwards and
forwards, and was out of it. No witnesses to the accident had
been found, but the post-mortem report, plus laboratory examination of various particles clinging to the tires and fender
of the stolen car, had satisfied everybody as to what had happened. It was filed as a routine hit-and-run and was still open.
After the phone call Purley went through a door, and came
back in a couple of minutes and told me that Homicide still
had it and was working on it.

"Yeah," I grinned at him, "I can imagine it—conferences,
minute clues subjected to severe scrutiny, ten of your best
men turning over stones all the way—"

Purley pronounced a word. Having granted my slightest
wish, he sneered, "Come and take my desk and do it. Now
give. Who's your client?"

I shook my head. "About that noise you use for a voice,
I know how you got it. Your mother had a longing for nutmeg
graters when she was carrying you. It might be, say, an insurance company."

"Nuts. No insurance company pays Nero Wolfe prices.
Who invited you in?"

"Nothing for now." I got erect. "Somebody had a dream,
that's all. If and when anything for the teeth is brought on,
we'll see that you get a bite. Much obliged, and give my
love to your boss."

But I had a chance to do my own love-giving. On my way
out there he was, striding in from the entrance, Inspector
Cramer himself, concentrated and in a hurry.

He saw me, stopped short, and demanded, "What do you
want?"

"Well, sir," I said pleadingly, "I thought with my experience if you had a vacancy anywhere, I'd be willing to start
as a patrolman and work my way—"

"Natural-born clown," he said personally. "Is it the Mere-
dith case? Has Wolfe crashed the gate—"

"No, sir, Mr. Wolfe would regard that as impertinent. As
he was saying only yesterday, if ever Mr. Cramer—"

He was on his way. I looked reproachfully at his broad
manly back and then headed for the street.

Seated at my desk in the office, I put the phone back in the cradle and told Nero Wolfe, "The bank says that Naylor-Kerr is good for anything up to twenty million."

Wolfe, seated behind his own desk, heaved a sigh and then was silent. I had given him the story complete, in a dry factual manner with no flavor or coloring on account of the coolness previously mentioned. His inclination, naturally, was to turn it down, since he was always annoyed at any hint of a prospect that he might have to use his brain, but I doubted if I would have to ride him hard on this because it looked like easy money and we could always use it.

He sighed again.

I spoke, still dry. "I suppose the best bet is that Pine killed Waldo Wilmot Moore himself and is keeping up appearances. What for being unknown to us, but surely not to everybody. Anyway, we would be paid by the corporation, not him. His suggestion that you get a job in the stock department under another name shows that he has given the problem a great deal of thought. You could call yourself Clarence Camembert, for instance, or Percy Pickerel. If they gave you too much to do you could bring things home and I'd be glad to help. They could pay you by weight—say, a dollar a pound a week. As you stand now, or at least sit, close to three hundred and forty pounds, it would come to an annual salary—"

"Archie. Your notebook."

"Yes, sir." I got it and flipped to a new page.

"A letter to Mr. Pine, president and so on. Mr. Goodwin has reported his conversation this morning with you. I accept the job of investigating, on behalf of your company, the death of your former employee, Waldo Wilmot Moore. It is understood that the purpose of the investigation is to establish, with satisfactory evidence, the manner of his death —whether by accident or by the deliberate action, with intent, of some person or persons. The job does not, as I understand it, extend to the disclosure of the identity of the murderer— if there was a murder—nor to procurement of proof of guilt. Should such extension be desired, you may notify me. Paragraph.

"The procedure promising quickest results, I think, will be for you to put Mr. Goodwin on the company payroll as a personnel expert. You can plausibly explain his presence as a part of your campaign to reduce your employee turnover. Thus he can spend his days there, moving freely about and conversing with anyone whomever, without causing comment or increasing the gossip you deplore. I suggest that you make his salary two hundred dollars weekly. Paragraph.

"My fee will of course be determined by the amount of time spent on the case and the amount and kind of work required. No guarantee is given. No retainer is necessary unless you prefer it that way, in which case the check should be for two thousand dollars. Sincerely."

Wolfe, who always straightened up to some extent to dictate, leaned back again. "After lunch you can go down and give that to him."

If I had been cool before I was a glacier now. "Why lunch?" I demanded. "Why should I eat?"

"Why not?" His eyes went open. "What's the matter?"

"Nothing. Not a thing. But what I start I like to finish, and this may take weeks. There are one or two other little matters that need attention around here, and there's a bare possibility that you may find it slightly inconvenient when you buzz me or call me or grunt at me, as you do on an average of ten times an hour, and I'm not here. Or, perhaps, that hadn't occurred to me, perhaps you're figuring on a replacement?"

"Archie," he murmured. His murmur is Wolfe at his worst. "I agree with someone, I forget who, that no man is indispensable. By the way, you may have noticed that I suggested the same salary as you receive from me. You can either endorse their checks over to me for deposit in my bank, and take my checks weekly as usual, or just keep their checks as your pay, whichever is simpler for your bookkeeping."

"Thank you very much." I made no attempt to speak further. His deliberate use of the plural, checks, instead of check, three times, therefore got exactly the effect he intended it to. I got out paper and carbon and inserted them, and started on the typewriter in a way that left no possible doubt whether it was noiseless or not.

Coolness.

I started work as a personnel expert for Naylor-Kerr, Inc., the next day, Wednesday morning, March 19, the next to last day of winter.

I knew just what I had known after my first call on Pine, and no more. Tuesday afternoon, when I took him Wolfe's letter, he was co-operative about letting me ask questions, but he couldn't supply many answers. He liked Wolfe's idea on procedure, and proved he was a good executive by starting immediately to execute. That was simple. All he had to do was call in an assistant vice-president, introduce me, tell him about me, and instruct him to put me on the payroll and present me personally to all heads of departments. That was accomplished Tuesday afternoon, the presentations being made in the office of the assistant vice-president, to which the department heads were summoned. I found an opportunity to drop the remark that after looking over the reports and records I thought I would start in the stock department.

Wednesday morning I was on the job in the stock department on the thirty-fourth floor. It handed me a surprise. I had vaguely supposed it to be something on the order of an overgrown hardware store, with rows of shelves to the ceiling containing samples of things that hold bridges together and related objects, but not at all. Primarily, as far as space went, it was a room about the size of the Yankee Stadium, with hundreds of desks and girls at them. Along each side of that area, the entire length, was a series of partitioned offices, with some of the doors closed and some open. No stock of anything was in sight anywhere.

One good glance and I liked the job. The girls. All right there, all being paid to stay right there, and me being paid to move freely about and converse with anyone whomever, which was down in black and white. Probably after I had been there a couple of years I would find that close-ups revealed inferior individual specimens, Grade B or lower in age, contours, skin quality, voice, or level of intellect, but from where I stood at nine-fifty-two Wednesday morning it was enough to take your breath away. At least half a thousand of them, and the general and overwhelming impression was of—clean, young, healthy, friendly, spirited, beautiful, and ready. I stood and filled my eyes, trying to look detached. It was an ocean of opportunity.

A voice at my elbow said, "I doubt very much if there's a virgin in the room. Now if you'll come to my office . . ."

It was Kerr Naylor, the head of the stock department. I had reported to him on arrival, as arranged, and he had introduced me to a dozen or so of his assistants, heads of sections. All but two of them were men. One of them I had regarded with special interest was the head of the Correspondence Checking Section, since Waldo Wilmot Moore had been a correspondence checker, but I was careful not to give him any extra time or attention there at the start. His name was Dickerson, he could easily have been my grandfather, and his eyes watered. I gathered from our brief talk that the function of a correspondence checker was to mosey around, pounce and grab a letter when the whim seized him, take it to the checker's office, and give it the works on content, tone, policy, style, and mechanical execution. So it could safely be assumed that his popularity quotient around the place would be about the same as that of an MP in the army, and that was bad. It presented the possibility that any letter-dictator or stenographer in the department might have felt like murdering Moore, including those who had lost their jobs—and the turn-over had been twenty-eight per cent. For one man to sort out the whole haystack, a straw at a time, was not my idea of the pursuit of happiness, but it did have its good points as suggested above.

Kerr Naylor's office was also a corner room, but was considerably more modest in every respect than the president's, two floors up. One whole wall was behind ceiling-high filing cabinets, and there were piles of papers around on tables and even two of the chairs. After we were seated, him at his desk and me at one end of it, I asked him:

"Why do you refuse to hire virgins?"

"What?" Then he tittered. "Oh, that was just a remark. No, Mr. Truett, this office has no prejudice against virgins. I merely doubt if there are any. Now how do you want to begin?"

His voice matched his appearance. The voice was a thin tenor, and while he was not a pygmy they had been all out of large sizes the day he was outfitted. Also they had been low on pigments. His skin had no color at all, and the only thing that made it reasonable to suppose there was anybody at home inside it was the eyes. They too were without color, but they had a sharp dancing glint that wasn't just on the surface but came from behind, deep.

"This first day," I said, "I guess I'll just poke around and get my directions straight. No virgins at all? Who has picked all the flowers? You might as well call me Pete. Everybody does."

The name I had chosen to be introduced by was Peter Truett, liking the implication of the first syllable of the Truett. Pine had thought my own, Archie Goodwin, might be familiar to someone. I went back to virgins again because I wanted to keep the talk going to get acquainted with this bird. But apparently it had really been just a remark and the virgin question had not come to a boil in him, as it often does with men over fifty, for he ignored it and said:

"As I understand it you are going to study the whole employee problem, past, present, and future. If you want to start with a specific case and spread out from there, I suggest the name of Waldo Wilmot Moore. He was with us last year, from April eighth to December fourth—a correspondence checker. He was murdered."

The glint in his eyes danced out at me and went back in again. I kept my own face under control, in spite of his splashing it out like that, but it is only natural and proper for anyone to betray a gleam of interest in murder, so I let one show.

My brows went up. "Gosh," I said, "no one told me it had gone that far. Murdered? Right here?"

"No, no, not on the premises, up on Thirty-ninth Street at night. He was run over by a car. His head was smashed flat." Mr. Naylor tittered, or maybe it wasn't a titter but only a nerve untwisting somewhere in the network. "I was one of those requested to come and identify him, at the morgue, and I can tell you it was a strange experience—like trying to identify something you have known only as a round object, for instance an orange, after it has been compressed to make two plane surfaces. It was extremely interesting, but I wouldn't care to try it again."

"Could you identify him?"

"Oh, certainly. There was no question about that."

"Why do you say murdered? Did they catch the guy and hang it on him?"

"No. I understand that the police regard it as an accident —what they call a hit-and-run."

"Then it wasn't murder. Technically."

Naylor smiled at me. His neat little mouth wasn't designed

for anything expansive, but it was certainly meant for a smile, though it went as quick as it came. "Mr. Truett," he said, "if we are to work together we should understand each other. I am rather perceptive, and it would probably surprise you to know how much I understand of you already. One little fact about me, I have always been a student of languages, and I am extraordinarily meticulous in my choice of words. I detest euphemisms and circumlocutions, and I am acquainted with all the verbs, including those of the argots, which mean to cause the death of. What did I say happened to this man Moore?"

"You said he was murdered."

"Very well. That's what I meant."

"Okay, Mr. Naylor, but I like words too." I had a strong feeling that no matter what his reason had been for tossing this at me right off the bat, if I fielded it right I might at least end the inning, and possibly the game, that first morning. I tried. I grinned at him. "I have always been fond of words," I declared. "I never got worse than B in grammar, clear to the eighth grade. Not that it's any hide off of me, but since we're speaking of words, when you say Moore was murdered I take it to mean that the driver of the car knew it was Moore, wanted him dead or at least hurt, and aimed the car at him. Doesn't it come down to that?"

Naylor was looking up at the wall behind me. His eyes stayed that way, with no glint showing because they were upraised, until I twisted my neck to see what he was looking at. All that was there was a clock. I untwisted back to him, and his gaze came down to my level.

He smiled again. "Twenty minutes past ten," he said resentfully. "I understand, Mr. Truett, that Mr. Pine has hired you to survey our personnel problems. What do you think he would say if he knew you were sitting here at your ease, prolonging a discussion of a murder which has no possible connection with your job?"

The damn little squirt. The only satisfactory way to field that one would have been to pick him up and use him for a dust rag. Under the circumstances that satisfaction would have to be postponed. I swallowed it, stood up, and grinned down at him.

"Yeah," I said, "I'm a great talker. It was nice of you to listen. Why don't you put through a voucher in triplicate, or however you do it, docking me for an hour? I deserve it, I really do."

I left. If the "uh, complexities" that Pine had mentioned

13

included a desire on the part of his brother executives and him to tie a can to Kerr Naylor's tail, I was all for it. He sure was tricky and mean. He had me so sore that I went from his office straight to the main arena, took a random course through the labyrinth of desks, glancing in all directions at faces, shoulders, and arms, and took my time picking one who had probably been a Powers model and got fired because she made all her colleagues look below standard.

I sat on the corner of her desk and she looked up at me with the clear blue eyes of an angel and a virgin.

I leaned to her. "My name is Peter Truett," I told her, "and I've been hired as a personnel expert. If your section head hasn't told you about me . . ."

"He has," she said, in a sweet musical voice, a contralto, which is my favorite.

"Then please tell me, have you heard any gossip recently about a man named Moore? Waldo Wilmot Moore? Did you know him when he worked here?"

She shook her head. "I'm awfully sorry," she said, sweeter than before if anything, "but I only started here day before yesterday, and I'm leaving on Friday. Just because I can't spell! I never could spell." Her lovely fingers were resting on my knee and her eyes were going straight to my heart. "Mr. Truman, do you know of any job where you don't have to spell?"

I forget exactly how I got away.

7.

I had been assigned a room of my own, about the right size for an Irish setter but not big enough for a Great Dane, about midway of the row of offices that ran along the uptown side of the arena. It contained a cute little desk, three chairs, and a filing cabinet with a lock to which I had been given the key. Apparently there were nothing but shanties across the street, since the window had space outside, and if you took it at a slant there was a good view of the East River.

I went there and sat.

It seemed I had breezed into something with insufficient consideration of strategy and tactics. As a result I had already pulled two boners. When Kerr Naylor had unexpectedly jumped the gun by shoving Moore and murder at me, I should have shrugged it off as a man with a single-track stomach and no appetite for anything but personnel problems. And when he side-stepped and caught me off balance, I should have backed clear up and looked it over, instead of getting peeved and spilling Moore's name to a vision of delight that couldn't spell. I was too exuberant.

On the other hand, I certainly didn't intend to spend a week or so just getting myself established as a personnel expert. I sat there through two cigarettes, thinking it over, and then went and unlocked the filing cabinet and got out a couple of the folders I had stowed there. On one of them the tab said STOCK DEPARTMENT—STRUCTURAL METALS SECTION, and on the other STOCK DEPARTMENT—CORRESPONDENCE CHECKERS SECTION. With the folders under my arm, I emerged to the arena, crossed it by a main traffic aisle, and knocked at the door of an office on the other side. When a voice told me to come in I entered.

"Excuse me," I said, "you're busy."

Mr. Rosenbaum, the head of the Structural Metals Section, was a middle-aged, bald-headed guy with black-rimmed glasses. He waved me on in.

"So what," he said without a question mark. "If I ever dictated a letter without being interrupted I'd lose my train of thought. No one ever knocks around here, you just bust in. Sit down. I'll ring later, Miss Livsey. This is the Mr. Truett mentioned in that memo we sent around. Miss Hester Livsey, my secretary, Mr. Truett."

I was wondering how I had ever missed her, even in that colossal swarm outside, until it struck me that a section head's secretary probably had her own room. She was not at all spectacular, not to be compared with my non-speller, but there were two things about her that hit you at a glance. You got the instant impression that there was something beautiful about her that no one but you would ever see, and along with it the feeling that she was in some kind of trouble, real trouble, that no one but you would understand and no one but you could help her out of. If that sounds too complicated for a two-second-take, okay, I was there and I remember it distinctly.

She went out with her notebook and I sat down.

"Thanks for letting me horn in," I told Rosenbaum, taking papers from the folder. "It won't take long. I just want to ask a few general questions and one or two specific ones about these reports. You people have certainly got this thing organized to a T, with your sections and subsections. It must simplify things."

He agreed that it did. "Of course," he added, "it gets mixed up sometimes. I'm Structural Metals, but right now I've got thirty-seven elephants in stock, over in Africa, and I can't get any other section to take them. My basic position is that elephants are nonmetallic. I may have to go up to Mr. Naylor to get rid of them."

"Hah," I said triumphantly, "so that's where your stock is, Africa! And elephants. I've been wondering. With that settled, let's tackle personnel. Speaking of which, I noticed that your secretary, Miss Livsey, didn't seem to be wading through bliss. I hope she's not quitting too?"

That proved she had had that effect on me as described, my going out of my way to mention her name, with no reason at all.

"Bliss?" Rosenbaum shook his head. "No, I guess she isn't. The man she was engaged to died a few months ago. Got killed in an accident." He shook his head again. "If it's a part of your job to make our employees happy, I'm afraid you won't get to first base with Miss Livsey. She's a damn good secretary too. If I had that hit-and-run driver here I'd—do something to him."

"I'd be glad to help," I said sympathetically. I riffled the papers. "The man she was engaged to—is he among these? Did he work here?"

"Yes, but not in my section. He was a correspondence checker. It was an awful blow for her, and she stayed away —but here I go again, you're not here to listen to me gab. What are your questions, Mr. Truett?"

Since I had quit being exuberant I decided not to press it, only it did seem that wherever I went I met Waldo Wilmot Moore. We got down to business. I had questions ready that I thought were good enough to keep me from being spotted as a phony, and I stayed with him a good twenty minutes, which seemed ample for the purpose.

Then I went down the line to the office of the head of the Correspondence Checkers Section. The door was standing open and he was there alone.

Grandpa Dickerson was by no means too old or too watery-eyed to know the time of day. As soon as the preliminary courtesies had been performed and I had sat down and got the folder opened, he inquired, perfectly friendly:

"I'm wondering, Mr. Truett, why you start with me?"

"Well—you're not the first, Mr. Dickerson I've just had a session with Mr. Rosenbaum. Incidentally, there's a special problem there: are elephants personnel?"

But he wasn't having light conversation. "Even so," he said, "I have the smallest number of employees of any section in the department. Only six men, whereas other sections have up to a hundred. Also, I have had no turnover for nearly eight years, except one case, a man who got killed and was replaced. I'm quite willing to co-operate, but I really don't see what you can do with me."

I nodded at him. "You're perfectly right—from where you sit. From the standpoint of general personnel problems you're out. But your section is something special. Everybody in the place regards your six men as dirty lowdown snoops, and you're the Master Snoop."

It didn't feeze him. He merely nodded back at me. "How do you propose to change that?"

"Oh, I don't. But it certainly ties it in with personnel difficulties. For instance, the man that got killed. Don't you know there has been talk around that his death wasn't an accident?"

"Nonsense! Talk!" He tapped on his desk blotter. "Look here, young man, are you intimating that the functioning of this section has been the cause, directly or indirectly, of the commission of a crime?"

"Yes."

His jaw trembled, and then came open and hung open. I was restraining myself from taking my handkerchief and wiping his eyes.

"That's not the way to put it," I said with emphasis, "but it was you who put it that way. I would say it more like this, that the talk about that man's death is certainly one of the personnel problems around here, and Mr. Naylor himself suggested that I might use it as one of my starting points. Do you mind my asking a few questions about him? About Moore?"

"I resent any insinuation that the operation of this section has resulted in any injustice or has been the cause of any legitimate desire to retaliate." His jaw was back under control.

"Okay. Who said anything about legitimate? Desires to retaliate come in all flavors. But about this Moore, how did he rate with you? Was he a good worker?"

"No."

"No?" I was matter-of-fact. "What was wrong with him?"

The old man's jaw trembled again, but it didn't come open. When he had it in hand he spoke. "I have been in charge of this section ever since it started, over twenty years ago. Last April I had five men under me, and I regarded that as adequate. But a new man was hired and I was told to put him to work. He was incompetent, and I so reported, but my report was ignored. We had to put up with him. On several occasions his mistakes would have discredited the section if we had not been alert. It made it harder for all of us."

I thought to myself, my God, here we go again. I was trying to get started narrowing it down, and here were six more added to the list, Dickerson himself and five loyal checkers, who might have been irritated into killing Moore for the honor of the section. Now everybody was in except Kerr Naylor himself.

"But," I objected, "what about the hiring regulations? I understand there is no over-all personnel control and each department head rolls his own in theory, but in practice the section heads have the say. Who hired Moore and saddled you with him?"

"I don't know."

"How could you help knowing?"

Dickerson used his own handkerchief on his eyes, which relieved the tension a lot for me. I hoped he would keep the handkerchief in his hand, but he deliberately and neatly returned it to his pocket.

"This," he said, "is a very large concern, the largest in the world in its field, and beyond all comparison the best. Naturally the authority is tightly organized. No one on this floor is my superior except the head of the department, Mr. Kerr Naylor, the son of one of the founders. Therefore any exercise of authority can be brought to bear on me only through Mr. Naylor."

"Then it was Naylor who hired Moore?"

"I don't know."

"But it was Naylor who said you needed another man and wished Moore on you?"

"Certainly. The line of authority is as I have described it."

"What else can you tell me about Moore besides his incompetence?"

"Why, nothing." Dickerson's look and tone indicated that he regarded my question as silly. Obviously, if a man was incompetent that settled it; nothing else about him mattered one way or another. But it appeared that he was willing to concede that even a competent man must eat. He pulled a watch from his vest pocket, looked at it, and stated, "My lunch hour starts at twelve, Mr. Truett."

8.

Outside Dickerson's office I turned left, toward the far end of the arena, and then was struck by an idea and came to a halt. Turning the idea over, and seeing that it had no visible defects on either side, I faced around and headed in the other direction. When I got to Rosenbaum's door I found it closed again, but since he had said no knocking I turned the knob and entered. My intention was to ask him where his secretary's room was, but I didn't carry it out because she was there in a chair at the end of his desk with her notebook.

She didn't turn her head at my entrance. Rosenbaum gave me a glance and said unemotionally, "Hello again."

"I just had a logical train of thought," I told them, "and I wanted to find out what Miss Livsey thinks of it."

She looked at me. Nothing had changed in her in the hour that had passed. It was still obvious that no one on earth but me could understand her or help her.

"It goes like this," I explained to her. "My job here requires that I have talks with units of the personnel, as many as possible. I should do that with a minimum amount of interference with the work of the department. You are a unit. If we eat lunch together and do our talking then, there will be no interference with your work. I'll pay for the lunch and put it on expense."

Rosenbaum chuckled. "That's a good approach," he said appreciatively. He spoke to his secretary. "Since he thought that all up just for you, Hester, the least you can do is let him buy you a sandwich."

She asked him, in a voice that could have been a pleasure to listen to if there had been any lift to it, "Do I owe it to anybody?"

"Not to me," he declared, "but maybe to yourself. Mr. Truett sounds as if he might be capable of making you smile. Even if only a wan and feeble smile, why not let him try?"

She turned to me and said politely, "Thank you, I think not."

There was certainly something about her, and I frankly admit I was getting a good start at being jealous of Waldo Wilmot Moore, even dead. He had found some way of propagandizing this wren to the point of agreeing to marry him.

Her eyes were back on her notebook. Rosenbaum, his

lips bunched, was gazing at her and shaking his head philosophically. I might as well not have been there, so I removed myself. My hand was on the knob, with my back to them, when her voice came:

"Why did you ask one of the girls if she had heard any gossip about Mr. Moore?"

Talk about grapevine. Less than two hours had gone by! I turned.

"There, see? Didn't I say I didn't want to interfere with your work? You could have asked me that over anything from roast duckling to a maple sundae."

"All right, I will. I go at one o'clock. We can meet in the lobby, William Street side, near the mailbox."

"That's the girl. Save a smile for it." I went.

So I had it all glued on, a lunch date with Hester Livsey, but it peeled off—though it wasn't her fault or mine either. I returned to my own little room, put the folders back in the cabinet and locked it, and stood at the window to look at the river and sort things out. All I got out of that was the realization that so far there was nothing to sort. Of course, I thought sarcastically, if I was Nero Wolfe I would have finished up here by noon and gone home to drink beer, but as it is, about all I've accomplished is to start the grapevine rustling. That really got me. In two short hours, and with no meal period for opportunity! Where it branches out from, I thought, is the restroom. If I could borrow a skirt and blouse and spend thirty minutes in the restroom I would have all I needed for a final report. Out on the river two tugboats nearly hit and one of them scooted off like a ripple skipper.

When the buzz sounded I jerked around, startled, it was so loud in the little room. I wasn't sure what it was, but the best guess was the phone, so I went to the desk and took it up and said hello, and came within an ace of adding, "Archie Goodwin speaking." I bit it off, and a tenor voice asked my ear:

"Hello, Mr. Truett?"

"Right. Speaking."

"This is Kerr Naylor. I'd like you to lunch with me if that's convenient. Could you step down to my office?"

I told him I'd be glad to, and hung up. A glance at my wrist showed me ten to one. I lifted the phone again, and when I got a voice I asked to be connected with Miss Hester Livsey, Stock Department, Structural Metals Section. In a second the voice said, "Extension six-eight-eight please ask by extension number whenever possible," and after a short wait another voice said, "Miss Livsey speaking."

"Peter Truett," I told her. "This is the unluckiest day I've had since my rich uncle changed doctors. Mr. Kerr Naylor just phoned me to have lunch with him. I can meet you as arranged and come back after lunch and quit my job."

"I don't want you to quit your job," she declared. "I've been thinking about you. Go with Mr. Naylor, of course. My room is next to Mr. Rosenbaum's, the one on the left."

But it didn't set me up any, on account of the motive, which I was fully aware of. I got my hat and coat and went along to the corner office, where Naylor met me at the door. I took my hat and coat because, although the assistant vice-president had told me I would rate eating lunch in the executives' section of the Naylor-Kerr cafeteria on the thirty-sixth floor, my hunch was that the son of the founder didn't patronize it. The hunch was right. He had his hat on and his topcoat over his arm. We went to an elevator, and from the lobby on the ground floor he steered us out the back way, down a block and around a corner, and to a door which had painted on it in green lettering, FOUNTAIN OF HEALTH. That could mean only one thing, and I grimly told my stomach it was in the line of duty as we entered, made our way to a table against the wall, got seated, and accepted menus from a waitress. There it was, roots and leaves and coarse fodder, with such names as EPICURE'S BOWL and BRAN AND CARROT PUDDING. My reaction was so strong that I was barely aware that Naylor was talking. With the waitress there waiting for us to name it, he was saying something like:

". . . so I tried it once about five years ago, and I've been lunching here ever since. I find it makes an enormous difference, physically, mentally—and even spiritually. There's a purity about it. It keeps a man light and clean. What will you select, Mr. Goodwin?"

I heard that all right.

9.

It was like the tricky little squirt to choose that moment for it, with the waitress, who knew him, there by us, making it as awkward as possible for me. So he thought. But I merely elevated the menu so it came between his eyes and my face, to get a little privacy, and turned my brain loose on the problem. Manifestly there was no point in trying to make a grab for the cat. After an interval, not a long one, I handed the menu to the waitress and told her to bring me three apples and a glass of milk. Then I asked him politely:

"Were you saying something? I'm afraid I wasn't listening."

He gave the waitress his order and let her go.

"I was speaking of diet," he snapped, "and you heard me. It isn't to be expected, Mr. Truett, that you'll like this food at first. No one does. But after a while you will wonder how you ever liked anything else."

"Yeah. When I like it I'll whinny. You ought to make up your mind who you're treating to lunch, though. Goodwin or Truett?"

"I much prefer Goodwin." He smiled at me. "That was my chief reason for inviting you to lunch, to tell you that the only way to deal with me is directly and forthrightly. Also to give you a message for Mr. Nero Wolfe. Tell him, please, that you have badly bungled this job. This morning when I mentioned the murder of a former employee of my department, you should have displayed no interest in the matter."

"I see. Much obliged. So that aroused your suspicion and you investigated." I looked at him admiringly. "You certainly stepped on it. Where did you start from?"

"Now, now," he scolded me and shook his head. "You're extraordinarily transparent, Mr. Goodwin, and I must say it's a surprise to me—and a disappointment. It would have been gratifying to find a good man, a good mind, starting to work on that murder. I would have watched you with the keenest interest and expectation— Those aren't the best apples." He frowned at the waitress. "Haven't you any Stayman Winesaps?"

It seemed they hadn't. When she had served us and was gone I started peeling an apple. It is not my custom to peel apples, but I figured it would outrage him. That was wasted effort, since he ignored it and waded in with a fork on a big bowl of a raw unholy mess, which he had ordered by name: TODAY'S VITANUTRITA SPECIAL. With his small mouth he had to feed it in dribs, chewing with a straight one-two beat and skipping two chews for each drib going in.

"Here's an idea," I said amiably. "You can't count on me to give that message to Mr. Wolfe. Why don't you drop in on him this evening after dinner and give it to him yourself?"

"I would be glad to." He chewed. "But not this evening." He chewed. "Three evenings a week, Wednesday, Thursday, and Friday, I play chess at the Midtown Chess Club." He chewed. "Saturday I'm going to the country, to spend the week-end looking at birds." He chewed. "I should be delighted to do that on Monday."

"Okay, I'll fix it up." I started on another apple, not bothering to peel it. "But by that time I may be all through here. In my opinion, and I hope Mr. Wolfe will agree, there's only one thing to do: tell the police about it and let them start up the machinery. An accusation of murder is entirely too ticklish, especially for a bungler like me."

He stopped chewing to ask, "Who has made such an accusation?"

"You have."

"I have not. I have merely stated that Moore was murdered. The police? Pooh. They started their machinery the moment the body was discovered, but they have let it stop. Your intention, of course, was to force me into making disclosures by threatening to get the police after me. My dear Mr. Goodwin, I'm afraid this affair is far beyond the range of your abilities. A week ago I called upon Deputy Commissioner O'Hara, whom I have known for years, and stated to him that Moore was murdered. Naturally he wished me to elaborate, and naturally I refused. I told him that all I could furnish was the bare fact, that the procurement of evidence and apprehension of the criminal were functions of his department."

Naylor tittered. "I really believe that for some moments the Deputy Commissioner was tempted to have the third degree tried on me. At the end he merely regarded me as a babbler." He resumed on the Vitanutrita.

My impulse was to finish the milk, shove the third apple in my pocket, beat it to Thirty-fifth Street, and tell Wolfe that Kerr Naylor was a malicious chattering hay-eating beetle and that was all there was to it. Various considerations restrained me, two of which were that Naylor-Kerr, Inc., was good for any amount up to twenty million, and that I now knew where Miss Livsey's room was.

"Okay," I said, completely friendly, "threats are out, disclosures are out, and chess and bird-looking will keep you from calling on Mr. Wolfe before Monday. Meanwhile, I noticed that on that report to Mr. Pine, the one about Moore, where it asked how he got hired, you put, 'Applied personally.' Who did he apply to, the head of that section, Mr. Dickerson?"

That was the first dent I made in the beetle's shell. It didn't make him drop his fork, or even start the glint in his eyes dancing, but he went on conveying and chewing far beyond

23

the limit of politeness. It was plain that he was finding it necessary to decide what to say.

He swallowed and spoke. "He applied to my sister."

"Oh. Which sister?"

"I have only one." The glint became perceptible. "My sister, Mr. Truett, is a remarkable and interesting woman, but she is far more conventional than I am. Each of us was given one-quarter of the stock of the corporation by our father, who wished to get rid of his burdens and responsibilities. I turned mine over, without compensation, to certain old employees of the business, because they had earned it and I hadn't. I don't like to own things to which other people might conceivably assert a claim, especially a moral claim. Legal claims don't interest me. But my sister, being more conventional, kept her stock. That was lucky for her husband, Jasper Pine, whom I believe you have met, as otherwise it is unlikely that he would have become president of the corporation."

"And Moore got his job through your sister?"

The glint did a jig. "You have a talent, Mr. Goodwin, for making statements in the most distasteful manner possible. My sister likes to do things for people. She sent Moore to me, and I spoke with him and had him interviewed by Dickerson, and he was given a job in that section. Now how about some pudding? And some Pink Steamer? Hot water with tangerine juice."

He was through as an information bureau. From there on the only thing that appealed to him as a topic of conversation was the food, and questions about Moore or murder or sister were simply ignored. He irritated me most when he was ignoring. I gave up and sat and watched him sip Pink Steamer.

When we got back to the building on William Street I parted from him in the lobby, went to a phone booth and dialed the number of the *Gazette*, and asked for Lon Cohen. He knew more facts than the Police Department and the Public Library combined.

When he was on I told him, "It's your turn on the favors. What about a Mrs. Jasper Pine? When born she was called Naylor. Her husband is president of a big engineers' supply firm with offices downtown. Ever hear of her?"

"Sure, she's meat."

"What kind of meat?"

"Oh, that means anyone who might make a meal for a journalist some day, strictly as news. So far she has kept herself off the menu, except for paragraphs on the right inside pages, but not a sheet in town has lost hope."

"What keeps the hope going?"

"Where are you phoning from? Wolfe's office?"

I tutted at him. "Didn't I tell you my name? That's all right, I'm in a booth."

"Okay. The subject of your inquiry is a befriender of young men. Not promiscuous. Discriminating, but chronic. She has plenty of dough, is well preserved, and presumably not a fool or she would have lost her balance long ago. I would advise you to try for it—how old are you, thirty? Just about right for her! You have the looks, and you could brush up on manners—"

"Yeah. You'll get ten per cent. I don't suppose you could get hold of a list of my predecessors she has befriended?"

"Well, we wouldn't have one, we're not that thorough. Do you think this paper would nose into people's private af— Say! Wait a minute! You and Nero Wolfe and your homicides. I'll try word association on you, damn it, what was that name? Murray? No. Moore?"

"Mr. Cohen," I said in awe, "you have nailed the head on the hit as usual. Compared to you John Kieran is a blank page. Moore was killed by a hit-and-run on Thirty-ninth Street the night of December fourth. Do tell me he was being or had been befriended."

"I do."

"By Mrs. Pine?"

"Restate the question. Even from a booth I don't like names on anything as fragile as this."

"By the subject of my inquiry?"

"Yes."

"Would you mind spreading it out?"

"Sure, it looked as if the meat might be on its way to the table, that was all. With him mowed down like that in the dead of night, and with that connection he had, we felt we owed it to the community to cover all angles in an effort to prevent any breath of scandal—"

"My God. Go on."

"So we did, and I suppose the cops did too, but it was a washout. The details are hazy by now, but it was definitely nothing doing for the presses. I remember this, the most obvious line only got us to a starve-out. The husband had certainly not done a desperate deed to retrieve his honor, or for vengeance. Moore was nothing but number—I don't know— seven or eight—and besides, he had been ditched months before and the current befriendee was—I forget his name, it doesn't matter. And the husband had known all about it for years. That was absolutely established by our research department. You must be smothering in that booth. I've got to go to work. I do so by demanding that you come clean, for the record if possible. Who has hired Wolfe?"

"Not yet," I told him. "You'll get it as soon as it's ripe if it hasn't got worms. You know us, we return favors with interest. If I pay you a visit could I talk with whoever worked on it?"

"You'd better phone ahead."

"I will. Thanks and love from all of us."

I ducked out through the lobby to the street, down the block to a place I had spotted, bought three ham sandwiches and a quart of milk, and transported them to the building and up to my place of employment on the thirty-fourth floor. There in my room I ate my lunch without being disturbed. By the time it was all down I had arrived at a couple of decisions, the first one being that it was just as well I hadn't obeyed my impulse to walk out of the Fountain of Health with nothing to show for my trouble but an apple.

10.

Having two things to do, it would have been in character for me to save the best till the last, and I had it programmed that way, but it didn't work. The idea was to phone Jasper Pine to arrange to run up to see him at three o'clock, but when I tried it all I got was the word from a Mr. Stapleton that Mr. Pine would not be available until four-fifteen. That compelled me to shift. But before making a call on Miss Livsey I thought it would be well to get in a piece of equipment I needed, so I did what I had been told to do when the occasion arose, called Extension 637 and said I needed a stenographer. In two minutes, not more, one entered with a notebook. She was nothing like my nonspeller, but neither was she any evidence against my theory that there was a strong preference at Naylor-Kerr for females who were easy to look at.

After I had got her name I told her, "I have nothing against you, quite the contrary. The trouble is I don't want you, just your typewriter. Could you bring it in here and let me use it?"

From the look on her face it might have been thought I had asked her to bring Mr. Kerr Naylor in handcuffs and set him on my lap. She tried to be nice about it, but what I had asked for was not done and could not be done. I let her go and went to work on the phone, and it wasn't too long before I had a typewriter, with paper and other accessories. Then I emerged to the arena, crossed to the other side, found the door next to Rosenbaum's on the left standing open, and entered.

I pushed the door shut, crossed to a chair near the end of her desk, and sat down. Her room was twice as big as mine, but there was just as little free space in it on account of the rows of files. The light from the window filtering through the top layer of her fine brown hair made it look as if someone had crowned her with a wreath of shiny silk mesh. She gave the typewriter a rest and let me have her full face.

"It was simply stinking," I said. "Mr. Naylor eats oats and shredded bark."

No smile for that, but she nodded. "Yes, he's famous for that. Someone should have warned you."

"But they didn't, including you. Are you crowded for time?"

"No, I only have eight or nine more letters." She glanced at her wrist. "It's only three o'clock."

"Good." I tipped my chair back, with my hands in my pockets, to show how informal I was. "I guess the best way to start is just to follow the routine. How long have you been working here?"

"Three years. Well—two years and eight months. I'm twenty-four years old, nearly twenty-five. I get fifty dollars a week, and I can do over a hundred words a minute."

"That's wonderful. What are the three things you dislike most, or like least, about your job?"

"Oh, now, really." Still no smile, but there was a little curving twist to her lips. "May I ask one?"

"Go ahead."

"Why did you invite me to lunch?"

"Well—what do you want, candor?"

"I like it."

"I do too. One look at you, and I seemed to be paralyzed all over, as in a dream. The two sides of my nature were fighting for control. One, the base and evil side, wanted to be alone with you on an island. The other side wanted to write a poem. The lunch thing was a compromise."

"That's pretty good," she said, with some sign of appreciation but not enthusiastically. "If that's candor, let's have some double talk. Why? You wanted to ask me about Waldo Moore, didn't you?"

"What makes you think so?"

"Why, my lord. You practically broadcast it! Asking that girl about him—it was all over the place in no time."

"Okay, so I did. What did I want to ask you about him?"

"I don't know, but here I am, ask me."

"You shouldn't be a stenographer," I said admiringly. "You should be a personnel expert or a college president or a detective's wife. You're perfectly correct, it would be difficult for me to question you about Moore without giving you a hint of where I got on and what my ticket says. So I won't try. You and Moore were engaged to marry, weren't you?"

"Yes."

"'A long time?"

"No, just about a month, a little less."

"And of course his death was an awful blow."

"Yes."

"Would you mind telling me in a general way what kind of a guy he was?"

"Why—" She hesitated. "That's a strange question. He was the kind of guy I wanted to marry."

I nodded. "That settles it for you," I agreed, "but I've only known you about twenty minutes, altogether, so it leaves me hazy. You understand, of course, that this is just you and me talking. I represent no authority of any kind and your tongue is yours. Had he been married before?"

"No."

"How long had you known him?"

"I met him soon after he came to work here."

"What was he—tall, short, handsome, ugly, fat, thin—"

She opened a drawer of her desk and got her handbag, took a leather fold out of it, and opened the fold and handed it over.

So she was still carrying his photograph. I gave it a good look. To my eyes he was nothing remarkable one way or another—about my age and build, high forehead, lots of hair worn smooth over his dome. He could have been catalogued as the kind of specimen seen buying motorboats in ads, if it hadn't been for the chin, which started back for his throat too soon.

"Thanks," I said, handing it back to her. "That clinches it that he didn't make a play for you as a last resort. First, you are not a last resort. Second, he was apparently nice to look at. I suppose that was the opinion of those who knew him?"

"Yes. Every woman who saw him was attracted to him. There wasn't a girl in the place who wouldn't have been glad to get him."

I frowned at her. That didn't sound like my Miss Livsey,

that vulgar boasting, but I had never assumed that she was without any defect at all. I followed it up.

"Then a lot of them must have been after him. Unless you reject the theory that girls have been known to chase—"

"Of course they do. They did."

"Did it make him very mad?"

"No, he loved it."

"Did it make you mad?"

She smiled. However, it was not precisely the sort of smile Rosenbaum had had in mind. I smiled back at her.

She asked, "Now we're getting down to it, aren't we?"

"I don't know," I said. "Are we?"

As soon as her words were out she had caught her lower lip with her teeth. After holding on for a moment, not long, the teeth let go. "That was silly," she declared. "No, I don't think it made me mad. In a way I enjoyed it and in a way I didn't. Go ahead."

I took my hands from my pockets and clasped them back of my head and regarded her. "I would like very much to go ahead, Miss Livsey, if I only knew which way. Say we try another door. Have you ever had any reason to suppose or suspect that Moore's death was anything but a hit-and-run accident?"

"No," she said bluntly.

"But there's been gossip about it, hasn't there?"

"There certainly has."

"What started the gossip?"

"I don't know what started it back in December, when it happened—I guess it just started itself, the way gossip does. Then it died down, it stopped entirely as far as I know, that was quite a while ago, and just last week it started up again."

"Do you know what started it again?"

She looked at me, made sure she had her eyes into mine, and asked, "Do you?"

"I'll say yes if you will."

"It's a go. Yes."

"Same here. Have you any idea why he put that word on that report?"

"No. I don't know and I can't imagine. I know I'd like to—" She bit it off.

"What?"

She didn't say what. She didn't say anything. She was visibly, for the first time in my three encounters with her, having feelings about something. I wouldn't have called her cold, that word simply didn't fit her and never would, but even the name of Moore and talking of him had put nothing you could call emotion into her face or voice. Now she was letting something show. She didn't exhibit anything as trite as quivering lips or eyes blinking to keep tears back, but a sort of loosening of her face muscles indicated that some strict discipline had met more than it could handle.

Suddenly and abruptly she got up, crossed to me, and put her hand, her open palm, on top of my head and patted it several times. I got more the impression of a melon being tested to see if it was firm than of a woman caressing a man, but that might have been only my modesty. I didn't budge.

She backed up a step and stood looking down at me, and my clasped hands let my head go back so as to meet her look.

"It's a funny thing," she said, half puzzled and half irritated. "I used to be able to handle men any way I wanted to. I'm not bragging, but I really could. I knew how to get anything I wanted from men, you know, little things, you know how girls are—and now I want something from you, and look at me! It isn't you either—I mean there's nothing wrong with you, you're quite good-looking and there's nothing wrong with you at all. I don't know whether you're a policeman or what you are, but whatever you are you're a man."

She stopped.

"Every inch," I agreed warmly. "I could suggest better how you ought to go about it if I knew what you want. First tell me that."

"Well, for one thing, I want to keep my job here."

"Done. I'll attend to that in my report. Next?"

Her voice muscles were loose too now. "That's ridiculous," she stated, not offensively. "I don't know who you are or what you are, but I do know you're trying to find out something about the death of the man I was going to marry, and it's getting to be more than I can stand. I want to forget all about it, I want to forget about him—I do, I really do! You don't know what hundreds of girls together in a place like this—you don't know what they can be like when they get started talking—it's horrible, just horrible! Why Mr. Naylor started it going again—I don't know. I can't stand it much longer and I'm not going to, but I like it here and I have to have a job—I like my work and I like my boss, Mr. Rosenbaum—"

She went to her chair and sat down, with her two fists resting on the desk in front of her, and addressed not me but the world.

"Oh, damn it!"

"I still don't know," I protested, "what you want from me."

"Certainly you know." She almost glared at me. "You can stop the talk. You can show that Mr. Naylor is nothing but a silly old fool. You can settle it, once and for all, that Waldo was killed by a hit-and-run driver and that's all there is to it!"

"I see. That's what you want."

Her eyes had come back to me, and mine were at a slant to meet them. We went on looking at each other, and I had a distinct feeling, whether shared by her or not I didn't know, that we were beginning to get acquainted. When a girl has patted a man's head, and sat and let him look for ten seconds or more, and looked back at him, with no words exchanged, she can no longer maintain the attitude that he is a complete stranger.

"I'm not a policeman," I said. "Whatever I am, I can't settle it how and why he got killed, because that was settled nearly four months ago, the night of December fourth. It's all down somewhere, all settled, and all I can do is try to dig up enough of it to satisfy everybody concerned. It helps to know that you're already satisfied."

"You're working for Mr. Naylor," she declared, her tone and look indicating that in all her long association with me she would never have supposed me capable of sinking so low.

"No." I was emphatic. "I'm not."

"You're really not?"

"Really and positively."

"But then—" She stopped, frowning at me but not for me. "But he has talked to you about Waldo, hasn't he?"

"He has indeed. He's a great talker."

"What did he say?"

"That Moore was murdered."

"Oh, I know that." The frown was still there. "He put that on the report. The whole floor knows about it, which was what he wanted, that was why he had a floor girl type the reports instead of his secretary. What else did he say?"

"About Moore, nothing of any importance. He just says murdered. It's an eeday feex."

"What else did he say about anything?"

"Oh, my God. That eating cooked vegetables brought on the war. That a man who eats meat—"

"You know perfectly well what I mean!" She was actually scolding me. "What did he say about me?"

"Not a peep. Not a single word. He made only one remark that could possibly be construed as a reference to you. This morning, standing out there at the end of the arena, he said

31

he doubted if there was a virgin in the room, but since you have your own office it probably didn't apply to you."

The question of virginity apparently wasn't troubling her. She insisted, "He really hasn't mentioned me?"

"Not yet." I looked at my wrist, let the front legs of my chair come down to the floor, and stood up. "You have your letters to do, and I have some chores myself. I'm sorry it can't all be settled the way you want it right now, I honestly am sorry. You say you really want to forget all about Moore?"

"Yes! I do!"

"Okay, we'll keep that on the agenda."

11.

The first chore on my list consisted of manual labor, with the typewriter in my room as the tool for it, so I went there and started to work.

I had asked, among other items, for some coated stock, letter size, and while the stuff they had sent was nothing to brag about, I inspected it again and decided it would serve. It was a quarter to four, only half an hour till my date with Jasper Pine, and therefore I had to step on it. Making a club sandwich of three sheets of the coated stock and two of carbon paper, I inserted them in the machine and typed in the upper right-hand corner in caps:

REPORT FROM THE
OFFICE OF NERO WOLFE
March 19 1947

Four spaces down, in the middle, I put:

CONFIDENTIAL TO
NAYLOR-KERR, INC.
914 William Street
New York City

There wasn't time to do it up brown, giving all the little details, the way it should be done for most clients to make them feel they're getting something for their dough, but I made it fairly comprehensive and in my opinion adequate. It conveyed the information the Kerr Naylor had introduced Moore's name in the first three minutes, that he had invited me to lunch and flushed me by calling me by my right name, that he insisted Moore had been murdered but refused to furnish any specifications of anything, that he had agreed to go to see Wolfe, that he said he had told Deputy Police Commissioner O'Hara that Moore had been murdered, and that he also said that Moore had been recommended for employment by his sister. In addition to all that on Naylor my report had a summary of my talk with Dickerson, the head of the Correspondence Checkers Section, a statement that word had got around in the department that I was investigating Moore's death, and a one-sentence paragraph to the effect that I had talked with one Hester Livsey, who had been engaged to Moore, without any result worth mentioning. The only incident the report passed up entirely was my brief interview with the non-speller, which didn't seem to me to be relevant—and of course the phone call to Lon Cohen at the *Gazette*, which seemed to be a little too relevant.

Through at the typewriter, I signed the original, folded it and stuck it in my pocket, and did likewise with one of the carbons. The other carbon I didn't fold. I went and unlocked the filing cabinet, opened the drawer I was using, removed all the folders, and with my handkerchief gave a good wipe to the inside of the metal drawer, sides and ends and bottoms. As I replaced the folders, which were made of green slick-surfaced cardboard, I wiped each one, all four surfaces. Inside the third folder from the top, on top of the papers that were already in it, I placed the second carbon of the report I had just typed, and on top of the report I carefully deposited four grains of tobacco which I had removed from the end of a cigarette. I put them in four selected spots and gently lowered the cardboard of the folder onto them. Closing the drawer, I wiped the whole front of the cabinet, and then I was confronted with a question which I would have liked to consider a little if it hadn't been twelve minutes past four and me due upstairs in three minutes. Should I just leave it unlocked, or leave the key there in the lock? I voted for the former and tuck the key in my pocket.

I hotfooted it to the outside hall and the elevators, and, as I got off at the thirty-sixth floor, found myself faced by another question which I should have had an answer all ready for but had overlooked in the rush. For the veteran receptionists in the lobby of the executive offices, who was I? The day before, calling on Pine, I had been Goodwin. Was I now to be Truett and expect her to look straight at my intelligent face and think it credible that I didn't know my own name?

Impossible. I walked up to her desk and told her that Mr. Goodwin had an appointment with Mr. Pine for four-fifteen.

Then I had to sit and wait over ten minutes. Usually I am a good waiter, unruffled and relaxed, but that time it irritated me because I could have done a much better job of wiping if I hadn't hurried. However, it couldn't be helped, and I sat till I was summoned.

Pine looked tired, busy, and harassed. He stayed behind his desk and started talking before I got across to him.

"I can only give you a few minutes," he said brusquely. "I already had a full schedule and things are piled up. What is it?"

I handed him the original of the report and stayed on my feet. "Of course you could take it and read it later, but I thought maybe—"

I chopped it off because he had started reading. He raced through it, three times as fast as Wolfe ever reads, and then went back and gave some of the paragraphs a second look.

A sharp glance came at me. "I knew Mr. Naylor had called on the Deputy Commissioner of Police."

"Sure," I conceded heartily. "You didn't mention it, but a man can't mention everything. Which reminds me, I've got a little problem. When Mr. Wolfe reads a copy of this, you see I know him pretty well, the first thing he'll ask will be whether you knew Mr. Naylor's sister had asked him to give Moore a job, and if so why you didn't tell me." I thought it was more diplomatic to say "Mr. Naylor's sister" than to say "your wife." I was going on, "Of course if you don't—"

"Certainly I knew," he snapped. "What has that got to do with it?"

"Nothing, so far as I know." I was conceding everything. "But I need your advice. As I say, I know Mr. Wolfe. He'll tell me to get Mr. Naylor's sister on the phone, and ask her to come to his office to see him, and if and when she won't come he'll tell me to go to see her, and I'll have to go. What would you advise me to do?"

"You work for Wolfe, don't you?"

"Yes."

"Then do what he tells you to."

"Okay, thanks. You have no suggestions or instructions?"

"No." Pine made his little gesture of impatience. "If you mean I might want to protect my wife from annoyance, you will learn why it is unnecessary when you meet her. What I want to know is how did Mr. Naylor learn your identity? Can you tell me?"

"If I could," I said, "it would be in that report. I'd like to know too. There are two possible ways. My picture has been in the paper a couple of times. It could be that he—or someone else had told him—remembered it well enough to recognize me, but the odds against it would go up into six figures. I like the other way better. How many people around here know about me? The receptionist outside, and who else? I believe you mentioned discussing it with two of your brother executives and a member of the Board of Directors."

I could tell by the look on his face that he was not lost at sea. He liked the other way better too, and he was checking off names. The "—uh, complexities" were turning up again, and he wasn't getting any pleasure out of them.

"Not the receptionist," he said grimly. "I spoke to her myself about it. Miss Abrams has been with us twenty years, and there's no question about her." He was getting some satisfaction from the assurance that there was one around he could trust.

"Then . . . ?" I asked meaningly.

He nodded, more to himself than to me. "I suppose so," he muttered. He put the report on his desk, just so, nice and square, and gazed down at it, with his palms pressed together, the fingers out straight, rubbing slowly back and forth. "I suppose so," he repeated gloomily but not despairingly. His face jerked to me. "I'll give that some consideration. Disregard it. What about this young woman Moore was hoping to marry—what's her name?" He fingered to the last page of my report. "Hester Livsey. Did she furnish any—uh, information?"

"Nothing to speak of, no. I'll try her again—that is, if I'm to go on. Do you want me to come back tomorrow?"

"Certainly. Why not?"

"I just thought, since Naylor's on to me, and probably by tomorrow noon everybody else will be too—"

"That doesn't matter. Come by all means. I have no more time now, but ring me in the morning around ten. We've started this and we're going through with it." He reached for a fancy phone thing, a kind I hadn't seen before, and told it he was ready for a Mr. Whosis, a name I didn't catch.

I bowed out.

Quitting time at Naylor-Kerr was five o'clock. It was four-fifty-six as I went back down the corridor of the executive offices. On the elevator I said, "Thirty-four," not on account of any scruple about chiseling the company to the tune of

35

four minutes' time, but because my hat and coat were in my room.

There was no sign that any visitors had called during my brief absence. Closing the door, I opened the drawer of the cabinet to give things a look, and found that the particles of tobacco were all present and accounted for. I stood by the window a while, going over the developments in my mind, including the talk with Pine, and considered the desirability of phoning Wolfe to suggest that it might be a good plan for me to intrude on Mrs. Jasper Pine before her husband got home from work. I probably would have done that if it hadn't been for the coolness previously mentioned. Under the circumstances I voted no.

Outside my door I stopped short and surveyed the scene. It was a real shock. The place looked absolutely empty, in spite of all the hundred of desks and chairs and miscellaneous objects. The girls were gone, and what a difference it made! I stood and gazed around, making one or two quick changes in my philosophy. I decided that until you single one out and she gets personal to you, a hundred girls, or a thousand girls, are just a girl. So it wasn't accurate to look at that empty room and say to yourself, the girls have gone; the way to say it was, the girl has gone. Nursing a strong suspicion that I had hit on something that was profound enough for three magazine articles or even a book, I made my way to the elevators and down to the street. A taxi in that part of town at that time of day wasn't to be thought of, so I went to the corner and turned right on Wall Street, headed for the west side subway.

Since I have been in the detective business for over ten years and have done a lot of leg work, naturally I have both tailed and been tailed many times, and when I'm on a case and on the move outdoors it is almost as automatic with me to keep aware of my rear as it is for everybody to glance in the traffic direction before stepping down from a curb. It rarely happens that I have a tail without knowing it, but it did that time. She must have been in ambush in the downstairs lobby with an eye on the elevators, and followed me crosstown. I am not a loiterer, so she had probably had to trot to keep up. The first I knew of it, there in the home-going throng on the sidewalk, I felt a contact that was not merely a bump or a jostle; it was a firm and deliberate grip on my arm.

I stopped and looked down at her. She was at least nine inches below me. She kept the arm.

"You brute," I said. "You're hurting me."

She looked good enough to eat.

12.

"You don't know me, Mr. Truett," she said. "You didn't notice me today."

"I'm noticing you now," I told her. "Let go my arm. People will think I'm the father of your children or I owe you alimony."

That may have been a mistake. It set the tone for my association with her, or at least the beginning of it, and the good view I was having of her made it my responsibility. With her black eyes saying plainly that they had never concealed anything and didn't intend to, her lips confirming it and approving of it, and all of her making the comment on geometry that a straight line is the shortest distance between two points but you can't prove it by me, she was obviously the kind of female that gets nicknamed. In Spain or Italy it would be something like The Rose Petal, and where I live it would be something like The Curves, but the basic idea is the same. That kind is often found in the neighborhood of trouble, or vice versa, and perhaps I should have given that a thought before setting the tone.

Passers-by glancing at us meant nothing to her. The only passer-by she would have been interested in was one she didn't intend to let pass.

"I want to talk to you," she stated. She had dimples, so tiny that the angle of light had to be just right to see them.

"Not here," I said. "Come on." We moved together. "Did you ever ride on the subway?"

"Only twice a day. Where are we going?"

"How do I know? I didn't know we were going anywhere until you just told me. Maybe ladies' night at one of my clubs." I came to a sudden halt. "Wait here a minute. I have to make a phone call."

I stepped into a cigar store, waited a minute or two for a phone booth to be vacated, slid in, and dialed the number I knew best. I knew it wouldn't be answered by Wolfe himself, since four to six in the afternoon was always reserved for his visit with the orchids up in the plant rooms. It wasn't.

"Fritz? Archie. Tell Mr. Wolfe I won't be home to dinner because I'm detained at the office."

"Detained—what?"

"At the office. Tell him just like that, he'll understand."

I went back to the sidewalk and asked The Curves, "About how long a talk do you think we ought to have?"

"As long as you'll listen, Mr. Truett. I have a lot to tell you."

"Good. Dinner? If we eat together I'll see that it gets paid for."

"All right, that would be nice, but it's early."

I waved that aside and we aimed for the subway.

I took her to Rusterman's. For one thing, it was the best grub in New York outside of Wolfe's own dining-room. For another, the booths along the left wall upstairs at Rusterman's were so well partitioned that they were practically private rooms. For another, Rusterman's was owned and bossed by Wolfe's old friend, Marko Vukcic, and I could sign the check there, whereas if I took her where I must part with cash Wolfe would have been capable of refusing to okay it as expense on the ground that I should have taken her home to eat at his table.

By the time we were seated in the booth I had collected bits of preliminary information, such as that her name was Rosa Bendini and she was assistant chief filer in the Machinery and Parts Section. I had also reached certain conclusions, among them being that she was twenty-four years old, that she had never been at a loss in any environment or circumstances, and that she was eligible as evidence in support of Kerr Naylor's remark about virgins.

She said she didn't care for cocktails but loved wine, which of course got her an approving glance from Vukcic, who had spotted me entering and had himself escorted us upstairs—honoring not me, but his old friend Wolfe. Then she evened up by turning him down flat on Shad Roe Mousse Pocahontas and preferring a steak. I trailed along with her to be sociable. When we had been left to ourselves she lost no time opening up.

"Are you a cop, Mr. Truett?"

I grinned at her. "Now listen, girlie. I'm easy to pick up, as you discovered, but I'm hard to take apart. You said you had a lot to tell me. Then we'll see what I have to tell you. What makes you think I might be a cop?"

"Because you asked about Waldo Moore, and the only thing about him any more is how he got killed, and that's a thing for a cop, isn't it?"

"Sure. It's also a thing for anyone who is interested. Let's put it that I'm interested. Are you?"

"You bet I am."

"In what way?"

"I'm just interested. I don't want to see anybody get away with murder!" There was a quick blaze in her eyes, one flash, up and out. She added, "He was a friend of mine."

"Oh, was he murdered?"

"Certainly he was!"

"By whom?"

"I don't know." With sudden accurate movement, but nothing impetuous about it, she covered my hand, there on the tablecloth, with both of hers. Her fingers and palms were warm and firm, and neither too moist nor too dry. "Or maybe I do. What if I do know?"

"Well, considering your character as I know it, I suppose you'd be a good girl and tell papa."

She kept my hand covered. "I wish," she said, "you had taken me where we could be alone. I don't know how to talk to a man until after he has had his arms around me and kissed me. Then I know what he's like. I could tell you anything then."

I sized her up. If I had let myself get cooped up in a booth at Rusterman's with a chronic nymph and that was all there was to it, at least I could preserve my dignity by not letting it cost me anything but twenty bucks or so of Wolfe's money. But I doubted if that was it. My analysis indicated that she simply had her own definite opinion of what constituted human companionship, and I wasn't prepared to argue with her.

I slid out clear of the table, got upright, drew the curtain across the entrance to the booth, got on my knees on the seat beside her, and enfolded her good. Her lips, like her hands, were warm and firm, and neither too moist nor too dry. She not only had her theory about companionship, she was willing to submit it to a thorough test, which is more than some people will do with their theories.

When it was obviously time to go I backed off, went and pulled the curtain open, and got back into my seat. As I did so the waiter entered with our baked grapefruit. When he had it arranged and left us she asked:

"What were you doing in Hester Livsey's room? What you just did with me?"

"There you go again," I protested. "You said you had a lot to tell me, not to ask me. How do you know Moore was murdered?"

She swallowed some grapefruit. "How did I know it would be all right if you held me and kissed me?"

"Anybody would know that from looking at me. Thanks for the passing mark, anyway. You couldn't tell Moore was murdered just by looking at him, with his head smashed flat. Even the cops and the city scientists couldn't."

Her spoon had stopped in mid-air. "That's an awful thing to say."

"Sure. Also it's fairly awful to say a guy was murdered, especially when he was your friend. How good a friend?"

She ate some grapefruit, but, as it seemed to me, not to gain time for deciding what to say, but just because she felt like eating. After three more sections had been disposed of she spoke.

"I called him Wally, because I didn't like Waldo, it sounds too intellectual, and anyway I often use nicknames, I just like to. My husband's name is Harold, but I call him Harry. Wally and I were very close friends. We still were when he—got murdered. Didn't I say I could tell you anything?" She spooned for grapefruit.

"Your husband?" I turned the surprise out. "Bendini?"

"No, his name is Anthony, Harold Anthony. I was working at Naylor-Kerr when I was married, nearly three years ago, and I didn't bother to change my name there. I'm glad I didn't, because he'll let me get a divorce sooner or later. When he got out of the Army he seemed to think he had left me put away in moth balls. Wally would never have been silly enough to think that about me. Neither would you."

"Never," I declared. "Does your husband work at Naylor-Kerr?"

"No," he's a broker—I mean he works for a broker, on Nassau Street. He's educated, some college, I can never remember which one. I haven't been living with him for quite some months, but he isn't reconciled to losing me, and I don't seem to be able to persuade him that we're incompatible, no matter how much I explain that it wasn't true love, it was just an impulse."

She put her spoon down. "Let me tell you something, Mr. Truett. I really and truly loved Wally Moore. One way I know I did, I have never been jealous of anyone in my life, but I was with him. I was so jealous of all his other girls I would think of ways they might die. You wouldn't think I could be like that, would you? I wouldn't."

My reply was noncommittal because the waiter arrived with the steak. After he had served it, with grilled sweet potatoes and endive and the wine, and left the reserve there on our table over a brazier of charcoal, I picked up my knife and fork but was interrupted by Rosa.

"This looks wonderful. I'll bet that curtain's stuck so you couldn't close it again."

I went and closed the curtain. This time she left her seat too, and we had companionship standing. All the time it lasted the warm inviting smell of the steak came floating up to us, with a tang in it that came from the poured Burgundy, and the combination of everything made it a very pleasant experience.

"We mustn't let it get cold," I said finally.

She agreed, with good common sense, and I pulled the curtain open for air.

That wrecked most of the remaining barriers. By the time the meal was finished I had enough to fill six pages, single-spaced. She gave me most of it in straight English, but on the two or three points where she merely implied I am supplying my own translation. Beginning with the day he started to work, Waldo Wilmot Moore had gone through the personnel of the stock department like a dolphin through waves. There could be no conservative estimate of the total score he had piled up, because there had been nothing conservative about it. I got the impression that he had tallied up into the dozens, but Rosa was probably exaggerating through loyalty to his memory, and only four names stood out—and two of those were men.

GWYNNE FERRIS, according to Rosa, was a perfect bitch. Being a born beckoner and promiser, she had tried her routine on Moore, had been caught off balance, and had had her beckoning and promising career abruptly terminated, or at least temporarily interrupted. She was about Rosa's age, in her early twenties, and was still a stenographer in the reserve pool after nearly two years.

BENJAMIN FRENKEL, a serious and intense young man who was assistant head of a section, and who was generally re-garded as the third-best letter dictator in the whole depart-ment, had been beckoned and promised by Gwynne Ferris until he didn't know which way was south. He had hated Waldo Moore with all the seriousness and intensity he had, or even a little extra.

HESTER LIVSEY was a phony, a heel, and a halfwit. Moore had kidded her along and had never had the faintest intention of marrying her. He would never have married anyone, but she was too dumb to know it. For a while she had actually be-lieved that Moore was her private property, and when she had learned that he was still enjoying the companionship of

Rosa, not to mention any others, she had gone completely crazy and had not recovered to date.

SUMNER HOFF was something special, being a civil engineer and a technical adviser to the whole stock department. He had been the hero—or the villain, depending on where you stood—of the most dramatic episode of the whole Moore story. On a day in October, just before quitting time, at the edge of the arena outside Dickerson's office, he had plugged Moore in the jaw and knocked him into the lap of a girl at a near-by desk, ruining a letter she was typing. He had implied, just before he swung, that what was biting him was a checker's report Moore had made on a letter he had dictated, but according to Rosa that was only a cover and what was really biting him was Moore's conquest of Hester Livsey. Sumner Hoff had been after Hester Livsey, strictly honorable, for over a year.

I was beginning to understand why Pine had said that Moore was the type that stirs up gossip.

For nearly two hours, sitting there working on the steak and its accessories, and another bottle of wine, and then pastry and coffee and brandy, Rosa told me things. When she got through I had a bushel of details, but fundamentally I didn't know anything I hadn't known before. It was no news that Moore had made various people sore in his capacity as a correspondence checker, or that his own section head hadn't liked him or wanted him, or even that he was death on dames. All Rosa had done was fill in, and when we got right down to it, how did she know Moore had been murdered and who did it, all she had was loose feathers. She knew he had been murdered because she knew who wanted him dead. Okay, who? On that she reminded me of the old gag about which one would he save, his wife or his son? She would have rooted for Hester Livsey if it hadn't been for Gwynne Ferris, and she would have rooted for Ferris if it hadn't been for Livsey. As for the actual circumstances of Moore's death, she had plenty of gossip, unshakable opinions, and a fine healthy set of suspicions and prejudices, but no facts I didn't already know.

I wasn't greatly disappointed, since in the detective business you always draw ten times as many blanks as you do paying numbers, but with all her pouring it out I had an uneasy feeling that she might have something I wasn't getting. It was plausible that she had waylaid me just to give me moral support and a friendly shove in what she regarded as the right direction, she was quite capable of that, but by the time we finished with the brandy I had decided that she was also capable of hiding an ace. And I seemed to be stymied. So I told her:

"It's only a little after eight. We could go somewhere and dance, or take in a show, or I could get my car and we could ride around, but that can wait. I think for tonight we ought to concentrate on Wally Moore. Did you ever hear of Nero Wolfe?"

"Nero Wolfe the detective? Certainly."

"Good. I know him quite well. As I said, I'm not a cop, but I'm sort of a detective myself, and I often consult Nero Wolfe. His office is in his house on Thirty-fifth Street. What do you say we go down there and talk it over with him? He knows how to fit things together."

She had got completely relaxed, but now she darted a glance at me.

"What is it, just a house?"

"Sure, with a room in it he uses for an office."

She shook her head. "You've got me wrong, Mr. Truett. I wouldn't go into a house I'd never been in with a man I didn't know well enough to call him by his first name."

The girl interpreted everything in terms of companionship. "You've got me wrong," I assured her. "If and when I ask you to enjoy life with me it won't be on the pretense that we've got work to do. I doubt if I'll feel like it until you get this Wally Moore out of your system. That might even be why I want to go and discuss it with Mr. Wolfe."

She wasn't stubborn. Fifteen minutes later we were down on the sidewalk, climbing into a taxi. In that quarter-hour I had signed the check, drawn the curtain again for a decent interval, and phoned Wolfe to tell him what was coming.

In the taxi she was nervous. Thinking it would be a good idea to keep her relaxed, and anyway I had drunk my half of the wine and brandy, I courteously got hold of her hand, but she pulled it away. It irritated me a little, because I felt sure that what made her balky was not the idea of discussing murder with Nero Wolfe but the prospect of entering a strange house with me. It seemed a little late in the day for a Puritan streak to show. As a result, however, my faculties resumed their normal operations, and therefore I became aware, at Forty-seventh Street and Tenth Avenue, that we had an outrider. Another taxi had stuck to our rear all the way across town, and turned south on Tenth Avenue behind us. The driver was apparently not the subtle type. Since Rosa had seen fit to build a fence between us, I said nothing about it to her.

When we turned right on Thirty-fifth Street our suffix came along. By the time we rolled to the curb in front of Wolfe's house there wasn't even a hyphen between us. I paid the driver from my seat, and my giving Rosa a hand out to the sidewalk, and the emergence from the other cab of a big husky male in a topcoat and a conservative felt hat, were simultaneous.

As he started toward us I addressed him, "I didn't quite catch the name."

He snubbed me and spoke to her, coming right up to her and ignoring me entirely. "Where are you going with this man?"

Masterful as he was, it by no means withered her. "You're getting to be a bigger fool every day, Harry," she declared, extremely annoyed. "I've told you a thousand times that it's none of your business where I go or who with!"

"And I've told you it is and it still is." He was towering over her. "You were going in that house with him. By God, you come with me!" He gripped her shoulder.

She squirmed, but not a panicky squirm; he was probably squeezing her flesh into her bones. With his build he could have tucked her under one arm. Grimacing from it, she appealed to me.

"Mr. Truett, this is that husband I was telling you about. He's so big!"

Implying I was helpless. So I spoke to him. "Listen, brother, here's a suggestion. We'll only be in there three or four hours, that ought to do it. You wait here on the stoop and when she comes out you can take her home."

I suppose it was badly phrased, but husbands who try to go on steering when the car is upside down in a ditch always aggravate me. He reacted immediately by letting go of her shoulder, which was a necessary preliminary to his next move, an accurate and powerful punch aimed for the middle of my face.

Ducking out of its path, my thought was that this would be simple, since he didn't know enough about it to go for something more vulnerable and easier to get at than a face, but I was wrong. He knew plenty about it, and evidently, also think- it would be simple, hadn't bothered about tactics. When I merely jerked my head sideways to let the punch go by and planted a left hook with my weight behind it just below the crotch of his ribs, thereby informing him that I knew the alphabet, he became a different man.

Within a minute he had landed on my body three times

and underneath my jaw once, and I had become aware that, with his extra fifteen or twenty pounds, he had the advantage in every way but one: he was mad and I wasn't. Believing as I do in advantages, so long as you don't do anything you aren't willing to have done back at you, I carefully chose moments to use a little precious breath on remarks.

When he missed with a right swing and had to dance back a step to recover I told him, "Three hours with her . . . seems like three minutes . . . huh?"

When I sneaked in a swift short punch and had the other one coming up and he had to clinch, I muttered, "In a month or so I'll be through with her anyway."

At one point, just after he had jolted me good with a solid one over the heart, I thought he was doing some conversing himself. I distinctly heard a voice say, "You might as well pay me now. He shouldn't try to talk. You can't talk and fight both."

Then I realized at the edge of my mind that it wasn't him. The taxi drivers were leaning against the fender of the cab I had paid for, enjoying a free show. I resented that, and, knowing I was in no position to resent anything, shoved it out of the way. The husband apparently had oversized lungs. With no gong to announce intermissions I was beginning to wish I had learned to breathe through my ears, but he didn't even have his mouth open. He just kept coming. I told him, "Even if you put me to sleep . . . I'll wake up again . . . and so will she . . . not three hours . . . three days and nights . . . and it'll be worth it . . ."

With his right he started a haymaker for my head practically putting his left in his pocket. He had done that once before, and I had been a tenth of a second too slow. My best punch is a right to the body, the kidney spot, turning my whole weight behind it exactly as if I meant to spin clear on around. When the timing and distance are just right it's as good as I've got. That one clicked. He didn't go down, but it softened the springs in his legs, and for an instant his arms were paralyzed. I was on him, in close, sawing with both elbows, my face not six inches from his, and when I saw he was really on the way and perfectly safe for two full seconds, I backed out a little and let him have two more kidney punches. The second one was a little high because he had started down.

I stood over him with my fists still tight and became aware that I was trembling from head to foot and there was nothing I could do about. I heard the voice of one of the taxi drivers:

"Boy, Oh boy. Pretty as a picture! I felt them last two myself."

I looked around. That block was never much populated, and at that time of day was deserted. We hadn't done any yelping or bellowing. Not a soul was in sight except the two drivers.

"Where's the lady?" I asked.

"She beat it like a streak when he slammed you up against my car." He aimed a thumb west. "That way. And I don't want no argument with you. What the hell, Mac, you're good enough for the Garden!"

I was still trying to catch up on my breathing. The husband rose to an elbow and was evidently on his way up. I spoke to him.

"You goddam married wife-chaser, the second you're on your feet you get more of the same, or even on one foot. Do you know who lives in this house? Nero Wolfe. I was taking her to see him on business. Now she's gone, and damned if I'm going in with nothing, so I'll take you. Besides, you ought to get brushed off and drink a cup of tea."

He was sitting up, looking the way I felt. "Is that straight?" he demanded. "You were bringing her here to see Nero Wolfe?"

"Yes."

"Then I'm sorry. I apologize." He scrambled to his feet. "When it comes to her I don't stop to think. I could use a drink and I don't mean tea, and I'd like to take a look in a mirror."

"Then up that stoop. I know where there's a mirror. Your hat's there in the gutter."

One of the drivers handed it to him. I followed him up the seven steps and let us in with my key. We hung our things in the hall, and I steered him on to the office. Wolfe was there behind his desk. He took the husband in with a swift glance, then transferred it to me and demanded:

"What the devil are you up to now? Is this the young woman who dined with you?"

"No, sir," I said. I was feeling battered but self-satisfied, and I had my breath back. "This is her husband, Mr. Harold Anthony from the financial district, a college man. He tailed her from her office, and tailed her and me clear here, and he thought I was bringing her as a plaything for you. Evidently he knows your reputation. He aimed for my face and missed, on the sidewalk out in front. He has taken lessons and it took me ten minutes or more to nail him, which I did

46

with three kidney punches. He was down flat. Is that correct, Mr. Anthony?"

"Yes," he said.

"Okay. Scotch, rye, or bourbon?"

"Plenty of bourbon."

"We have it. Mr. Wolfe will ask Fritz to bring it. The bathroom is this way. Come along."

Wolfe's voice came behind us, "Confound it, where is Mrs. Anthony?"

"No soap," I told him from the bathroom door. "You'll have to stifle your desires for tonight. She went for a walk. Her husband is substituting for her."

13.

A few feet from the end of Wolfe's desk is a roomy and comfortable red leather chair, and next to it on one side is a solid little table made of massaranduba, the primary function of which is as a resting place for checkbooks while clients write in them. Harold Anthony sat in the chair, with a bottle of bourbon at his elbow on the little table, while Wolfe kept at him for over an hour.

Mr. Anthony had a conviction: the stock department of Naylor-Kerr was a hotbed of lust and lechery where the primitive appetites germinated like sweet potato sprouts.

Mr. Anthony had a record: since he had got out of the Army in November he had bopped four assorted men whom he had detected in the act of escorting his wife somewhere, and one of them had gone to a hospital with a broken jaw. He did not know if one of them had been named either Wally or Moore.

Mr. Anthony had an alibi: the evening of December 4 had been spent by him in a bowling alley, with friends. They had quit around eleven-thirty and he had gone home. When Wolfe observed that that would have left him plenty of time to get over to Thirty-ninth Street and run a car over Moore, he agreed without hesitation but added that he couldn't have had the car, since it had been stolen before eleven-twenty, at which time the owner, coming from the theater, had arrived where he had parked the car and found it gone.

"You appear," Wolfe commented, "to have followed the accounts of Mr. Moore's death with interest and assiduity. In newspapers?"

"Yes."

"Why were you interested?"

"Because the papers had pictures of Moore, and I recognized him as the man I had seen with my wife a few days before."

"Where?"

"Getting into a taxi on Broadway, downtown."

"Had you spoken with him?"

"Yes, I said something to him, and then I cooled him off."

"Cooled? By what process?"

"I knocked him halfway across Broadway and took my wife."

"You did?" Wolfe scowled at him. "What's the matter with your brain? Does it leak? You said you didn't know whether one of your wife's escorts, the ones you bombarded, was named Moore."

"Sure I did." The husband was not disturbed. "What the hell, I didn't know then you were going into it."

He was really two different persons. Sitting there with a couple of men, drinking good bourbon, he had poise and he knew the score. I would hardly have recognized him as the wild-eyed infuriated male moose who had lost all self-control at the sight of me helping an assistant chief filer from a taxicab, if it hadn't been for a band-aid covering a gash on his face. The gash was the result of my having neglected to remember, for a brief moment, that cheekbones are hard on knuckles.

At the beginning, after he and I had finished in the bathroom and returned to the office, he had been suspicious and cagey, even with bourbon in him, until he was satisfied that I really had been bringing Rosa there on business. Then, when he learned that the business was an inquiry into the death of Waldo Wilmot Moore, it took him only a minute to decide that his best line was full and frank co-operation if he wanted any help from us in keeping his wife out of it as far as possible. At least that was the way it looked to me, and by the time we got to his alibi for December 4 I was almost ready to regard him as a fellow being.

Around a quarter to ten he left, not because the bottle was empty or Wolfe had run out of questions, but because Saul Panzer arrived. I let Saul in, and as he headed for the office the husband came out, got his things from the rack, and grunted and groaned without any false modesty as he got into his coat. He offered a hand.

"Christ, I'll be a cripple for a week," he admitted. "That light of yours would dent a tank."

I acknowledged the compliment, closed the door after him, and returned to the office.

Saul Panzer, who was under size, who had a nose which could be accounted for only on the theory that a nose is all a face needs, and who always looked as if he had shaved the day before, was the best free-lance operative in New York. He was the only colleague I knew that I would give a blank check to and forget it. He had come to make a report, and, judging from the ground it covered, Wolfe must have got in touch with him and put him to work that morning as soon as I had left the house.

But that was about all you could say for it, that it covered lots of ground. He had talked with squad men who had worked on the case, had gone through three newspaper files, had been shown the record by Captain Bowen downtown, and had even seen the owner of the car; and all he had harvested was one of the most complete collections of negatives I had ever seen. No fingerprints from the car; nobody had any idea what Moore had been doing on Thirty-ninth Street; no one had seen the car being parked, afterwards, on Ninety-fifth Street; not a single lead had been picked up anywhere. The police knew about Moore's friendship with Mrs. Pine, and his romantic career at Naylor-Kerr, and a few other things about him that were news to me, but none of them had turned on a light they could see by. It was now, for them, past history, and they had other things to do, except that a hit-and-run manslaughter was never finished business until they collared him.

"One little thing," said Saul, who wasn't pleased with himself. "The body was found at one-ten in the morning. An M.E. arrived at one-forty-two. His quick guess was that Moore had been dead about two hours, and the final report more or less agreed with him. So we have these alternatives: first, the body was there on the street, from around midnight until ten after one, with nobody seeing it. Second, the M.E. report is a bad guess and he hadn't been dead so long. Third, the body wasn't there all that time but was somewhere else. I mentioned it downtown, and they don't think it's a thing at all, not even a little one. They have settled for either number one or number two, or a combination. They say Thirty-ninth Street between Tenth and Eleventh might easily be that empty from midnight on."

Saul turned his palms up. "You can pay me expenses and forget it."

"Nonsense," Wolfe said. "I'm not paying you, the client is. A tiger's eyes can't make light, Saul, they can only reflect it. You've spent the day in the dark. Come back in the morning. I may have some suggestions."

Saul went.

I yawned. Or rather, I started to, and stopped. It is true that wine always makes me yawn, but it is also true that the aftereffect of a series of socks on my jaw and the side of my neck makes me stop yawning. I swiveled my chair around with a swing of my body, not bothering to put my hand on the edge of my desk for an assist. A simultaneous protest came from at least forty muscles, and, since Harry was no longer there, I groaned without restraint.

"I guess I'll go to bed," I stated.

"Not yet," Wolfe objected. "It's only half-past ten. You have to go to your job in the morning and I haven't heard your report." He leaned back and closed his eyes. "Go ahead."

And three hours later, at half-past one in the morning, we were still there and I was still reporting. I have never known him to be more thorough, wanting every detail and every little word. My face felt stiff as a board, and I hurt further down, especially my left side, but I wasn't going to give him the satisfaction and pleasure of hearing me groan again, and I didn't. After I had given him everything he kept coming back for more, and when it was no longer possible to continue that without making it perfectly plain that he was merely trying to see how long it would take me to collapse on the floor there in front of him, he asked:

"What do you think?"

I tried to grin at him, but I doubt if I put it over.

"I think," I said, "that the crucial point in this case will come in about a month or six weeks, when we'll have to decide whether to stop and send in our bill or go on a while longer. It will depend on two things—how much we need the money, and how much Naylor-Kerr will pay for nothing. That's the problem that confronts us and we must somehow solve it."

"Then you don't think Mr. Moore was murdered."

"I don't know. There are at least two hundred people who might have murdered him. If one of them did, and if there were any possible way of finding out which one, naturally I have my favorites. I have mentioned Pine. I like the idea of him because it is always gratifying to call a bullheaded bluff, and if it was him he certainly tried one when he hired you. But if he's the sort of bird who takes it in his stride when his

ife keeps two-legged pets on account of her owning stock in
he company that pays his salary, what would ever work him up
o murder? Anyhow, she had given Moore the boot. My real
avorite is Kerr Naylor."

"Indeed."

"Yes, sir. On account of psychology. Wait till you see him
Monday. His last ten incarnations he was a cat, and he always
eld the world's record for mouse-playing. Add that to the
ell-known impulse of a murderer to confess, and what have
ou got? Although it has all been filed away as a hit-and-run
ith the hit-runner not found and not likely to be at this
te day, he has got that impulse, so he tells the world, in-
luding a Deputy Commissioner of Police, that it was murder.
hat satisfies the impulse without costing him anything, and
so it carries on the tradition of his cat ancestry. Baby, what
n! In this case the mouse is the people in his department,
he president of the firm and the Board of Directors, the cops
—everybody but him. Yep, he's my favorite."

"Any others?"

I started to wave a hand but called it back on a word from
y shoulder. "Plenty. Dickerson, for the honor of the Section.
Rosenbaum, hipped on Miss Livsey and wanting to save her
rom a two-bit Casanova. And so on. But this is all academic.
We might reach some kind of a conclusion, but what if we do?
he waves have washed all the footprints away, and as I said
efore, all we'll be able to solve is the question when to quit
nd render a bill. The only consolation is that I'll get a wife out
f it. I'm going to make Miss Livsey forget Waldo."

"Confound it." Wolfe reached for his beer glass and saw
hat it was empty, lifted the bottle and found it empty too,
nd glared at both of them. "I suppose we'd better go to bed.
Are you in pain?"

"Pain? Why? I thought we might sit and talk a while. This
s a very difficult case."

"It may be. Tomorrow I'd like to see Mrs. Pine. She can
ome at eleven in the morning, or right after lunch. You can
rrange it through Mr. Pine." He gripped the edge of his desk
vith both hands, the customary preliminary to getting to
is feet.

The phone rang. I swiveled my chair, not groaning, and
ifted the instrument.

"Nero Wolfe's office, Archie Goodwin speaking."

"Oh, Mr. Goodwin? My husband has told me about you.
This is Cecily Pine, Mrs. Jasper Pine."

"Yes, Mrs. Pine."

"I just got home from a theater supper, and my husband told me about your inquiry regarding Waldo Moore. I would like to help, if I can in any way, and I don't think these things should be put off, so I'll drive down there now. I have the address."

I tried to keep my voice friendly and sociable. "I'm afraid it would be better to make it tomorrow, Mrs. Pine. It's pretty late, and Mr. Wolfe—"

But he ruined it. He had got on his extension, and broke in, "This is Mr. Wolfe, Mrs. Pine. I think it would be better to come now. An excellent idea. You have the address?"

She said she had and would leave right away, and only had to come from Sixty-seventh Street. Wolfe and I hung up.

"It's unfortunate," Wolfe said. "You should be in bed, but it may be necessary for you to take notes."

"I'm not sleepy," I said through my teeth. "I was hoping she would call."

14.

Considering what I knew of her, I could hardly believe my eyes when I opened the door and let her in. Probably I had unconsciously been expecting something on the order of Hedy Lamarr as she would be with the wrinkles of age, and therefore the sight of her pink smooth-skinned wholesome face and her medium-sized housewife's chassis, a little plump maybe, but certainly not fat, gave me a shock.

"You're Archie Goodwin," she said in a low-pitched educated voice.

I admitted it.

She was openly staring at me, and advanced a step to see better. "What on earth," she asked, "has happened to your face? It's all red and bruised!"

"Yeah. I got in a fight with a man and he hit me with his fist. Both fists."

"Good heavens! It looks simply awful. Have you got any beefsteak?"

I did not believe, considering everything, that she was speaking from experience. She had simply read about it. I told her that it wasn't bad enough to rate beefsteak at ninety cents a pound, adding pointedly that all I needed was a good long night's sleep, and ushered her into the office.

Wolfe was on his feet, having probably got up to stretch.

Mrs. Pine crossed to him to shake hands, declined the red leather chair because she preferred straight ones, accepted the one I placed for her, let me take her coat of platinum mink or aluminum sable or whatever it was, and sat down.

"You really ought to do something for your face," she told me.

The funny thing was that her harping on it didn't irritate me. She gave me the distinct impression that it really made her feel uncomfortable for me to be uncomfortable, and how could I resent that? So we discussed my face until Wolfe finally dived into an opening.

"You wanted to see me, madam, did you?"

She turned to him, and her manner changed completely, possibly because he didn't have bruises and red spots.

"Yes, I did," she said crisply. "I thoroughly disapprove of what my husband has done, engaging you to investigate the death of Waldo Moore. What good can it possibly do?"

"I'm sure I don't know." Wolfe was leaning back, with his forearms paralleled on the arms of his chair. "That's a question for your husband. If you don't like his engaging me you should persuade him to disengage me."

"I can't. I've been trying to. He's being extremely stubborn about it, and that's why I came to see you."

Good for Jasper, I thought, but who the hell stuck a ramrod down his spine?

Mrs. Pine went on. "I suppose, of course, my husband has committed himself—or rather, the firm. If you withdraw from it, now, there'll be no difficulty about that. I'll pay whatever it comes to."

"What good would that do you?" Wolfe inquired testily. I won't go so far as to say that he never liked women, but he sure didn't like women who picked up the ball and started off with it. "Your husband would hire someone else. Besides, madam, while I like to charge high prices for doing something, I haven't formed the habit of charging for doing nothing, and I won't start with you. No. Obviously you're accustomed to getting what you want, but there must be some other way of doing it. What is it you want?"

Mrs. Pine turned to me. For a second I thought she was going to revert to my face, but instead she asked, "What's he like, Archie? Is he as stubborn as he sounds?"

The Archie came from her perfectly natural. "From him," I told her, "I would call that almost flabby."

"Good heavens." She regarded Wolfe with interest but with no sign of dismay. "I presume," she said abruptly, "you know that Waldo Moore was at one time a close friend of mine?"

Wolfe nodded. "I have been told so. By Mr. Goodwin. He got his information from a newspaperman. Apparently it is known."

"Yes, of course. That's the advantage of not trying to hide things; things that people know about are taken for granted. But permitting people to know about them, and permitting them to be publicly discussed in newspapers—that's a very different thing. Do you suppose for a moment, Mr. Wolfe, that I'm going to sit and do nothing while you make pictures for tabloids out of my private life? While you make a public sensation out of the death of Waldo Moore?"

"Certainly not, madam." Wolfe was still testy. "It's quite plain that you aren't going to sit and do nothing. You aren't now. You've come here to see me at half-past two in the morning. By the way, you must have asked that same question of your husband. What did he say?"

"He says it will not become a public sensation. He says that all he is after is to stop the gossip at the office and make it impossible for my brother to start it again. But I don't care to run that risk and I don't intend to."

"What does your brother say? Have you discussed it with him?"

That pricked her skin. Since I had not yet been told to take notes I was able to give her face my full attention, and that was the first sign it showed of needing to go into conference. She pressed her lips together and said nothing. It occurred to me that it seemed to run in the family, since at my so-called lunch with Kerr Naylor the first and only time he had paused to think had been when his sister had been inserted into the conversation.

She finally spoke: "I don't know what is in my brother's mind—not exactly. He won't tell me, though he usually does. He is a—very peculiar man. He dislikes my husband and all of the other top men in the company—all except one or two."

Wolfe grunted. "Does he dislike you?"

"Why, no. No!"

"Then why doesn't he stop his flummery about murder when you ask him to?"

"He doesn't—" She stopped, then went on, "That's interesting, I hadn't thought of it that way, but my brother says exactly what my husband says, that there's no danger of it's becoming public. But I don't care what they say, there's still a risk, and I have always believed in doing anything within reason to avoid unnecessary risks. If my husband and my brother are both going to act like spoiled brats—actually making idiots of themselves in my opinion—then I'll have to take things into my own hands."

She looked at me, and immediately became a different woman. "It seems a little chilly in here, Archie. May I have my coat?"

I thought no wonder, since she was still dressed for the theater, with nothing above the bra line but skin. For her age, which must surely have been mine plus ten, the skin was absolutely acceptable. I got the coat and draped it over her shoulders, and she smiled up at me for thanks, and I went and upped the thermostat a notch.

She resumed on Wolfe. "The best way, I thought, would be to deal directly with you. Perhaps you're quite right—if you simply quit, as I asked, my husband would engage someone else. Then why not let him have what he wants? Apparently he wants you to investigate, and my brother does too, so why not? You will be paid whatever has been agreed on, and in addition I will give you my personal check, and you can't possibly object that I am paying you for nothing, because you will give me your guarantee that the investigation will not—let's see—that no publicity will result. It doesn't matter how we put it so long as we understand what we mean. The check could be for—ten thousand dollars?"

Wolfe was shaking his head at her. "For heaven's sake," he muttered incredulously. "Do you realize you're offering to pay me to keep a secret?"

Her eyes widened. "I am not! What secret?"

"I don't know. Yet. But your husband—or his firm, in which you are the largest stockholder—is paying me to discover something, and you want to pay me to conceal it if and when I discover it. You called your husband and brother idiots, but what do you call yourself? You offer ten thousand dollars. You assume that I am capable of double-dealing. If I am, why should I stop there? Why not a hundred thousand, a million? Madam, you're an imbecile."

She ignored the complaint and was concentrating on the logic. "That's silly," she said scornfully. "Would I have come to you like this if I hadn't known your reputation? That would be blackmailing, and you're not a crook!"

Wolfe was speechless, which was one more piece of evidence that he didn't understand women half as well as he did men. I got her with no trouble at all. Her position was simply that if he double-crossed Naylor-Kerr, Inc., there would be nothing crooked about it because that was what she wanted, whereas if he double-crossed or blackmailed her he would be a snide, a louse, and a blackguard; and she knew his reputation, and he wasn't.

Seeing there was no meeting of minds and one wasn't likely, I put in, "Look, Mrs. Pine, it won't work that way, really it won't. You can't bribe him or threaten him."

She gazed at me, and evidently I wasn't Archie any more, at least not at the moment.

"I haven't tried to threaten him," she stated.

"I know you haven't. I just put that in."

She looked at Wolfe, and then back at me. "But—" She was inspecting an idea. "It should be possible to have his license revoked. With the taxes I pay and the people I know, I should be able to do that. Doesn't a detective have to have a license?"

That nearly made me speechless too, but somebody had to keep up our end. "He sure does," I told her, "and I'm one too. You might try that, Alice, but I doubt if you'll get anywhere."

"My name is Cecily."

"I know it is. I meant Alice in Wonderland. You remind me of her."

"That's a wonderful book," she declared. "I read it over again just recently, Are you men partners?"

"No, I work for him."

"I don't see why. I don't see how you can stand him. How much would it take for you to go into business for yourself?"

"Pfui," Wolfe interposed. "This is tommyrot. You would find, madam, if you made the slightest effort, that I am a reasonable man. Do you want a suggestion from me?"

"I don't know," she said reasonably. "Tell me what it is first."

"It's this. You'll never accomplish anything with this sort of cackle—not with Mr. Goodwin or me. Anyway, even if I accepted your ridiculous offer, you might be wasting your money. Your assumptions may not be sound. Evidently you assume that if we do a competent job of investigating Mr. Moore's death it is certain, or at least highly probable, that a public scandal will result. What makes you so sure of that?"

She looked at him appreciatively. "That's quite clever," she said generously. "If I really were sure and told you why, it would be a great help to you. But I'm not sure at all. I just don't want to run the risk."

"Do you share your brother's opinion that Mr. Moore was murdered?"

"Certainly not. It was an accident."

"Had you seen Mr. Moore that day? The day he was killed?"

"No. I hadn't seen him for months." She laughed. It came from her throat on out, as if something had really struck her as funny. "He was going to get married! To a girl at the office named Livsey, Hester Livsey. He phoned me one day to tell me about it. Of course you can't realize how grotesque that was because you didn't know him."

"Did you advise him not to marry?"

"Heavens, no. It wouldn't have done any good. If I had known the girl I might have given her some advice, but not Waldo." Mrs. Pine turned to me. "Is this a habit of his, Archie? He said he had a suggestion for me, and instead he cross-examines me."

"Yeah," I agreed. "He doesn't do it deliberately. His mind jumps the track."

"The suggestion," Wolfe told her, ignoring me, "is a contingent one. It's no good unless you've been telling the truth. If you have no knowledge of facts the disclosure of which would cause a sensation, and all you're after is insurance against a risk, why not trust to my discretion? I have some, and I would gain neither pleasure nor profit from starting a public uproar unnecessarily. Why not help me get it over with? Its kernel is your brother's tenacity, his fondness for the notion of murder—or at least for the word. I suppose you know your brother better than anyone else does. Why not help with him? Why not start now by telling us about him? For instance, I understand that you asked him to give Mr. Moore a job. Did he have any objection to that?"

It was a fair try, but it didn't work. Apparently Wolfe hadn't noticed that she was allergic to talk of her brother, but that doesn't seem likely, since he notices everything. At any rate, it was no go. She didn't abruptly end the interview—on the contrary, she seemed quite willing to sit and chat all night—but she was utterly disinclined to furnish us with a biography of her brother. The most specific statement Wolfe could drag out of her was that her brother was peculiar, and she had already told us that, and we knew it anyway.

Finally Wolfe got hold of the edge of his desk, pushed his chair back, and stood up. Mrs. Pine arose too, and I went and helped her on with her coat.

In the hall, with my hand on the knob of the front door,

she stood where I couldn't open it without banging her toe, and told me sympathetically, "I hope your face is better tomorrow."

"Thanks. So do I."

"And you didn't answer my question about how much it would take for you to start your own business."

"That's right, I didn't. I'll figure it up."

"Do you like symphony concerts?"

"Yes, some, when I'm lying down. I mean on the radio." She laughed. "Anyway, it's nearly April. Boating? Golf? Baseball?"

"Baseball. I go as often as I can get away."

"It's a wonderful game, isn't it? Yankees or Giants?"

"Both. Either one, whichever's in town."

"I'll send you season tickets. Frankly, Archie, I think my brother is crazy. Don't tell Mr. Wolfe I said that."

"I never tell him anything."

"Then that's our first secret. Good night."

I escorted her out, down the stoop and to the curb, but didn't get to open the car door for her because her chauffeur was already attending to that. As I reascended the steps I was telling myself that I mustn't forget to phone Lon Cohen in the morning and inform him that the job was practically mine but nothing doing on his ten per cent because I was landing it strictly on merit.

Back in the house I made a beeline for the stairs, taking no chances, but found it desirable to mount one step at a time. My room was two flights up. On the first landing I turned and yelled back down, "I'm going up and figure how much it will set her back to furnish my office! Good night!"

15.

The next morning, Thursday, the arena of the stock department was a different place as far as I was concerned. Whenever I showed my face, coming and going, the change could be seen, felt, and tasted. Wednesday morning I had been a combination of a new male, to be given the once over and labeled, and an intruder from outside who could be expected to regard the lovely little darlings merely as units of personnel. Thursday morning I was a detective after a murderer. That's what they all thought, and they all showed it. Whether Kerr Naylor had started another ball rolling, or whether it was just seepage from various leaks, I didn't know, but the reaction that greeted me wherever I went left no doubt of the fact.

The bits of tobacco in the folder had not been disturbed. That was no great disappointment, since I had no good reason to suppose that anyone in the place was sitting on tacks, and I left the set-up intact. At ten o'clock I got Jasper Pine on the phone and gave him a report of the Mr. and Mrs. Harold Anthony episode.

I also said, "Your wife came to see us last night."

"I know she did," he replied, and let it go at that. It was a fair guess that his position was that there was no point in asking what she had said because she had already said everything to him about everything. When I told him that the whole department apparently had me tagged as a bloodhound, he said grimly that in that case I might as well act like one and gave me the run of the pasture.

My first gallop was out of the pasture entirely, up to the Gazette office to see Lon Cohen, having first called him. I had a healthy curiosity not only about Pine's attitude toward his wife's fondness for pets, but also about her and Moore. Wanting the lowdown, I came away, after a session with Lon and talks with a couple of legmen, satisfied that I had it. Either Pine had years ago adopted the philosophy that a wife's personal habits are none of a husband's business, and really didn't give a damn, and Mrs. Pine had completely lost interest in Moore early in 1946, except to see that he got a job, or the Gazette boys were living in a dream world, which didn't seem likely.

I bought them a lunch at Pietro's and then returned to William Street. There was nothing in my office for me, no message from Wolfe or Pine or even Kerr Naylor, and the drawer of the cabinet hadn't been touched. I was still without a bridle and could pick my own directions. Across the arena to Miss Livsey's room was, I thought, as good as any.

Her door was open and she was inside, typing. I entered, shut the door, lowered myself onto the chair at the end of her desk, and inquired, "What thoughts have you got about Rosa Bendini?"

"What on earth," she inquired back, "have you been doing with your face?" She was gazing at it.

"You may think," I said, "that you're changing the subject, but actually you're not. There's a connection. It was Rosa's husband who embroidered my face. What's your opinion of her in ten thousand words?"

"Does it hurt?"

"Come on, come on. Being sweet and womanly when you haven't even started to forget that Moore? Quit stalling."

She showed a hint of color, very faint, but the first I had seen of it. "I'm not stalling," she denied. "If you can't feel it you ought to look in a mirror and see it. What about Rosa Bendini?"

I grinned at her to show her that the muscles worked, no matter how it looked. "So you're asking me instead. Okay. She calls Moore Wally. She says that he never had any intention of marrying you, and that you went crazy—these are her words—when you found out that he was still seeing her, and that you have never recovered. I may add that I don't believe everything I hear, because if you have never recovered you must be crazy now, and on that I vote no."

The color had gone. She had held her working pose in front of her typewriter, her fingertips resting on the frame of the machine, implying that I had just dropped in to say hello and would soon drop out again, but now her torso and head came square to me to meet my eyes straight. The tone of her voice matched the expression of her eyes.

"You should have asked me to give you a list of the best ones to go to for gossip, but maybe you didn't need to, because, if you had, Rosa would have been near the top, and you've already found her yourself. When you've found the others, please don't bother repeating it to me. I have a lot of work to do." Her body pivoted back to its working position, she looked at the paper in the machine and then at her notebook, and her fingers hit the keys.

I had my choice of several remarks, among them being that Rosa had found me, not me her, but it would have had to be a loud yawp to carry over the din of the typewriter, so I saved my breath and departed.

The day was more than half gone and I hadn't made a beginning on the names I had got from Rosa. I returned to my room, got the head of the reserve pool on the phone, said I would like to have a talk with Miss Gwynne Ferris of his section, and asked if he would send her to see me. He said he was sorry, Miss Ferris was busy at the moment taking dictation from a section head whose secretary was absent for the day, and would a little later do? I told him sure, any time at his and her convenience, and as I pushed the phone back I became aware that my doorway was being darkened.

The darkener was a tall bony young man with a lot of undisciplined hair that could have used a comb or even a barber's scissors. He looked like a poet getting very deep into something, and since his eyes were unmistakably fastened on me, evidently I was what was being probed.

"May I come in, Mr. Truett?" he inquired in a rumble like low thunder from the horizon.

When I told him yes he entered, closed the door, crossed to a chair in three huge strides, sat, and informed me, "I'm Ben Frenkel. Benjamin Frenkel. I understand you're here looking for the murderer of Waldo Moore."

So if I didn't have Gwynne Ferris I had the next best thing, the intense young man who, according to Rosa, had been beckoned and promised by her until he didn't know which way was south.

Meeting his gaze, I had to concentrate to keep from being stared right out through the window behind me. "I wouldn't put it like that, Mr. Frenkel," I told him, "but I don't mind if you do."

He smiled sweetly and sadly. "That will do for my purpose," he stated. "I wouldn't expect you to commit yourself. I've been here before, several times, since I heard this morning what you are here for, but I didn't find you in. I wanted to tell you that I am under the strong impression that I killed Moore. I have had that impression ever since the night it happened—or I should say the next day."

He stopped. I nodded at him encouragingly. "It's still your turn, Mr. Frenkel. That's too vague. Is it just an impression, or can you back it up?"

"Not very satisfactorily, I'm afraid." He was frowning, a cloud on his wide brow for his thunder rumble. "I was hoping you would straighten it out and I would be rid of it. Can I tell you about it confidentially?"

"That depends. I couldn't sign up to keep a confession of murder confidential—"

"My God, I'm not confessing!"

"Then what are you doing?"

He took a deep breath, held it a couple of seconds, and let it out. "My hatred for Waldo Moore," he said, "was one of the strongest feelings I have ever had in my life. Possibly the strongest. I won't tell you why, because I have no right to drag in another person's name. I doubt if any man ever hated another one as I hated him. It went on for months, and I was frightened at it, literally frightened. I have always had a profound interest in the phenomenon of death. The two merged inside of me. There was a fusion, a synthesis, of those two reactions to stimuli. The one, the hatred, was emotional, and the other, the interest in death, was intellectual; and the two

61

came together. As a result I became preoccupied with the conception of the death of Moore, and I thought of it, over and over again, in concrete and specific terms. The conception of a car running over him and crushing the life out of him came to me many times, I don't know how many, but dozens."

"It wasn't a conception that hit him, it was a sedan."

"Certainly. I'm not suggesting anything esoteric. I live in a furnished room on Ninety-fourth Street not far from Broadway. One evening I was sitting there in my room, and those conceptions, those I have spoken of, were filling my mind. It was an extremely exhausting experience; it always was. Psychologically it might be compared to a trance resulting from a congestion of the cerebral cells brought about by prolonged and unendurable tension. My head ached and I lay on the bed."

I was getting bored. "And went to sleep and dreamed."

"No, I didn't. I went to sleep, but I didn't dream. That is, the overwhelming impression was that I had been asleep. That was a little after one in the morning, ten minutes after one. At the moment of consciousness I was opening the door of the bathroom. I thought to myself that I must have been very deep in sleep to have left the bed and got to the bathroom door at the other side of the room without being aware of it. My mind was completely empty, and rested; there were no dreams in it at all, though there often are when I get up. That was all there was to it that night; I undressed and went to bed and after a while went back to sleep; but in the morning, when I read the news of Moore's death in the paper—of course it was an electrifying experience for me—my mind was suddenly occupied, completely dominated, by the impression that I had killed him. I think one little circumstance was a major factor in the birth of the impression: the circumstance that the car that killed him had been found parked on Ninety-fifth Street, just one block from where I lived."

"Think again, Mr. Frenkel. The car wasn't found until nearly noon, so it couldn't have been in the morning paper."

"What!" He was disconcerted. "Are you sure of that?"

"Positive."

"That's strange." He shook his head. "That shows what a mind can do with itself. I clearly remember that the impression was with me that morning when I went to work, so the detail of where the car was found must have come later and only made the impression deeper and stronger. Anyhow, that was when it started, and I've had it ever since, and I want to get rid of it."

"I don't blame you," I assured him. "That first time you went to sleep, when you were exhausted with conceptions and your head ached, what time was it?"

"It was around nine o'clock. Naturally I've considered that. I can't determine it very exactly, but it couldn't have been far from nine one way or the other."

"Did you know where Moore was that evening? Or where you might expect to find him?"

"No." He hesitated. "I knew——" He left it hanging.

I nudged. "Let's have it."

"I knew where I surmised he was, or might be. No, that's not right. I knew whom I surmised he might be with, and that's all. I prefer not to mention names."

"When you woke up by the bathroom door, how were you dressed?"

"As usual. As I had been when I lay down. Suit, shoes—fully dressed."

"No hat or overcoat?"

"My God, no. That would have removed any doubt, wouldn't it?"

"Well, a couple of layers. Any other indications—dirty hands or anything?"

"No. Nothing."

"Have you ever mentioned this to anyone, your impression that you killed Moore?"

"Never. When the police were investigating, soon after it happened, a detective called on me and asked if I had been out for a walk late that night and had noticed anyone parking a car on Ninety-fifth Street. Of course that meant they were interested in me because I lived only a block away. He also asked about certain—about my relations with Moore. I told him frankly that I hated Moore."

"But you didn't tell him about your impression?"

"No, why should I?"

"You shouldn't. Why are you telling me?"

Frenkel hunched his shoulders together. His eyes were no longer probing me; now they left me entirely, going down until they reached the floor. He seemed to be getting forlorn, and I hoped he didn't have another headache coming on. I waited for him to lift his eyes again, which he eventually did.

"It's very difficult," he said in a grieved tone. "It may sound foolish, but when I learned that you are investigating Moore's murder I had a kind of vague hope that if I told you about it you might be able to check up on it—you're a detective and would know how to do it—perhaps by questioning the landlady and other people there you could establish the fact that I didn't leave my room that evening." He looked uncertain. "Or perhaps you could relieve my mind. Maybe I haven't made it plain what terrible pressure I've been under. Perhaps you could tell me whether Mr. Naylor has mentioned any names in connection with this—with that irresponsible report he sent to Mr. Pine. Specifically, has he mentioned mine?"

I was no longer bored, but if any gleam showed in my eyes it was against orders. "Well," I said offhand, "a lot of names have been mentioned of course. Have you any reason to suppose that Mr. Naylor might single you out?"

"No good reason, no. It's like this, Mr. Truett." He leaned forward, and apparently he had got his second wind, for he was probing again. "This impression that I killed a man has been the dominating element of my whole mental process for nearly four months. It is vital to me, absolutely vital, that I either validate it or destroy it with as little delay as possible. I need to know, and I have a right to know, if anyone else has the same impression, and if so for what reason and with what justification. It can't be the same reason as mine, for no one on earth, except you now that I've told you, knows what happened to me in my room that evening. So I ask if Mr. Naylor has mentioned my name. If he has, and if your telling me so is not regarded as in confidence, I would like to go to him—"

The door opened and Kerr Naylor was in the room.

In spite of Ben Frenkel's distress and SOS appeal I had sprouted no germ of brotherly feeling for him, or if I had, it had wilted fast at the suspicion that what he chiefly wanted was to pump me. But the sight of Naylor's neat little colorless face and glittery colorless eyes aroused my protective instinct, not only in behalf of Frenkel, but of the whole stock department. As Frenkel saw who the newcomer was and arose, nearly knocking his chair over in his haste, I told Naylor casually:

"Hello, I haven't seen you today. I've been discussing the personnel of his section with Mr. Frenkel. I think—"

"He isn't the head of the section," Naylor snapped.

"Yeah, but I often find in my personnel work that you get more from an assistant than you do from a head. Did you want something?"

"You can finish with Frenkel later."

"Sure," I said agreeably, "but about one point that came up, I got the impression that he wanted to ask you about it. That right, Mr. Frenkel?"

It didn't seem to be since he was edging toward the door. He had not gone wholly inarticulate, but his rumble had degenerated to a mumble, something about the outgoing mail waiting for him, and he was gone. He left the door standing open. Kerr Naylor went and closed it, came to the chair his underling had just vacated, and sat down.

"You've got them jumping through hoops," I said in admiring awe. "Even big ones like Frenkel, who could do a major operation on you with one hand."

Naylor smiled his two-cent smile. "He would like to, Frenkel would."

"Why, any particular reason?"

"No, except that he thinks I prevented his promotion in January." Naylor pulled a pamphlet from his side pocket. "I came across this in a drawer of my desk and thought you might like to read it."

I took it. The title on the cover was PROTEINS AND ENZYMES. "Did you say read it or eat it?" I inquired.

Having no sense of humor, he ignored that. It seemed that he had paid me a visit expressly to give me the pamphlet and discuss its thesis—or rather, to give me a lecture on it. It was all at the tip of his tongue, and he reeled it off as if I had paid to get in and was dying to hear about it.

I did hear a word here and there, enough to enable me to contribute an occasional grunt or a question, but mostly I was trying to decide what kept him wound up. That he really had it in his heart to sell me on the enzyme potential of foliage I did not believe for a moment. I felt helpless, and so of course I was irritated. Right there in his little head, as he sat doing his spiel, were facts and intentions that were what I needed and all I needed, and I hadn't the faintest idea how to start prying them loose. I have often felt, talking with a man in the line of duty, okay, brother, wait till Wolfe gets a crack at you, but with Kerr Naylor I wasn't at all sure that even Wolfe could get a wedge in him.

He went on and on. I glanced twice at my wristwatch, without effect. Finally I told him I was sorry, I had an appointment and was already late. He wanted to know who with. I gave him the first name that popped into my head, Sumner Hoff.

"Ah." He nodded, leaving his chair. "One of our best men —a fine engineer and a good organizer. It's regrettable—really unfortunate—that he is endangering his whole career on account of that Livsey girl. He could have gone to Brazil, taken charge there, and he wouldn't leave because of her. You know who she is—you were in her room yesterday and again today. Do you know where Hoff's office is?"

"I'll find—"

"Come along. It's near mine, I'll show you."

I followed him, thinking that his intelligence service was not only thorough but on its toes, since he already knew of my brief call on Miss Livsey. We went down the broad aisle that separated the main arena from the row of offices, and when we were nearing its end he halted in front of a closed door.

"This is Hoff's room," he announced in the thin tenor that I had had enough of for a while. "By the way, something I nearly forgot to mention. Regarding the murder of Waldo Moore, I told you yesterday that all I could furnish was the bare fact. That was not strictly true, and was therefore in the nature of a misrepresentation. I am in possession of another fact: the name of the person who killed him. I know who it was. But I can go no further. It is neither proper nor safe to accuse a person of murder without communicable evidence to support the charge. So that's all I can say." He smiled at me. "Tell Mr. Wolfe I'm sorry." He turned and went, headed for his own office at the end of the aisle.

My impulse was to go after him. I stood and considered it. He had done it in style, his style, waiting to toss it at me until we were outside, with the nearest row of desks and personnel so close that I would have had to take only two short steps to touch the rayon shoulder of a dark-haired beauty with magenta lipstick. She was looking at me, now that the big boss had departed, and so were others in that sector, enjoying a good view of the bloodhound. I made a face at them collectively, and, deciding not to go after Naylor because I wasn't sure I could keep from strangling him, I opened the door of Hoff's room and went in.

He looked up, got me at a glance, and barked at me. "Get out!"

I shut the door and surveyed. He had a nice big room. As for him, it might have been expected that the man who had plugged Waldo Moore in the jaw for romantic reasons, and was a civil engineer into the bargain, would be well designed and constructed, but no. There was heft to him, but he would be pudgy before many years passed, and also he would have two chins. He didn't get up and start for me or pick up anything to throw; he simply told me to get out.

I approached his desk, offering reasonably, "I will if you'll tell me why."

"Get out of here!" He meant every word he said. "You goddam snoop! And stay out!"

For one thing, with a man in that frame of mind the chances of having a friendly and fruitful conversation are not very good, and for another, I was there at that time only because I had told Naylor on the spur of the moment that I had an appointment with him. I hated to pass up an opportunity for a cutting remark, two or three of which were ready for my tongue simultaneously, but the look on his face indicated that he would like nothing better than for me to try to stay, so he could add some remarks of his own. Therefore I outwitted him by pivoting on my heel and getting out, just as he said.

Back in my own room, I stood at the window and examined Kerr Naylor's latest card, top and bottom. I had a notion to go down to a booth and phone Wolfe, but it was past four o'clock and he would be up in the plant rooms until six, and he never liked to be asked to use his brain when he was up there, so I rejected it. Instead, I put some paper in the typewriter and put the same head on it as on my report to Naylor-Kerr, Inc., the day before. I sat a few minutes making up my mind how to word it and then hit the keys:

Mr. Kerr Naylor came to my office at 3:25 p.m. He talked of irrelevant matters for some time, and then he told me that he knows who killed Waldo Moore. He said that was all he could say, because "it is neither proper nor safe to accuse a person of murder without communicable evidence to support the charge." He told me to tell Mr. Wolfe he was sorry. I would have tried to get him not to wait until Monday to go to see Mr. Wolfe, but he left and went to his room, and in view of his attitude and manner I thought it would be useless to go after him.

I had a couple of other items to add, regarding Ben Frenkel and Sumner Hoff, filling a page, but it seemed pretty skimpy for a full day's work. Still liking the idea that someone might be curious enough, or scared enough, to take a look at my folders, I made a second carbon, and I disposed of it as I had the day before, putting it on top of the other one inside the third folder from the top, and deploying tobacco crumbs in the same spots. By the time that was all arranged it was four-thirty. I went out and took an elevator to the thirty-sixth, and told the receptionist, Miss Abrams, that I had no appointment with Pine but would like to have one minute with him to hand him something. She said he was in a meeting and wouldn't be free for an hour or more. I thought if Pine could trust her I could too, got an envelope from her and put the report in it and sealed it, and left it with her for Pine.

On the way back to the stock department I had a bright idea. I still hadn't seen Gwynne Ferris. If a unit of personnel could waylay me on Wednesday, why couldn't I return the compliment on Thursday? Not by waylaying, but through channels. I would wait until I saw her to decide whether to invite her to Rusterman's or take her home with me and let Wolfe do some work.

But I didn't see her. Using my phone, I was told by the head of the reserve pool that he was sorry, but Miss Ferris had so much in her book that she would have to stay overtime, and he would greatly appreciate it if I could wait till morning. I told him sure.

I knocked off with the bunch, at quitting time, and going down in the elevator I couldn't complain of lack of attention. Some stared at me openly, some glanced when they thought I wasn't looking, and some used the corner-of-the-eye technique, but for each and all I was certainly it.

16.

Wolfe was reading three books at once. He had been doing that, off and on, all the years I had been with him, and it always annoyed me because it seemed ostentatious. The three current items were *The Sudden Guest* by Christopher La Farge, *Love from London* by Gilbert Gabriel, and *A Survey of Symbolic Logic* by C. I. Lewis. He would take turns with them, reading twenty or thirty pages in each at a time. In the office after dinner that evening he sat at his desk, having a wonderful time with his literary ring-around-a-rosy.

I had already, before dinner, reported to him on the day's events, and presumably he had listened, but he had not asked a single question or made a single comment. For table conversation business was of course taboo, but it might have been supposed that with digestion proceeding under control and according to plan he would have one or two suggestions to offer. Not so.

I was at my own desk, cleaning and oiling my arsenal—two revolvers and an automatic. When he finished the second heat with *A Survey of Symbolic Logic*, dogeared it, put it down, and reached for *Love from London*, I inquired respectfully, "Where's Saul?"

"Saul?" You might have thought he was trying to decide whether I meant Saul of Tarsus or Saul Soda. "Oh. It seemed pointless to waste a client's money. Did you want him for something? I believe he's working on a forgery case for Mr. Bascom."

"So I'm doing a solo. Shall I go up and start catching up on sleep, or would you care to pretend we *both* earn money?"

"Archie." He picked up the book. "I do not propose to start sorting out chaos. At present this case is merely a guggle of unintelligible babel. If Mr. Naylor killed Mr. Moore, it is quite possible that he will carry his joke too far. If he didn't, and he knows that someone else did, the same comment can be made. If neither, the corporation is spending money foolishly but we are not stockholders. We'll probably know more about it after my talk with Mr. Naylor Monday evening. Until then it would be futile to bother my head about it. Besides, you don't really want me to. You are wallowing in clover, with hundreds of young women accessible, unguarded, and utterly at your mercy."

"I do not," I said, closing the drawer where I kept the arsenal and getting to my feet, "like clover." I walked to the door to the hall, where I turned. "It is not my mercy they're at. And if I stick my foot in something down there that you have to pull it out of, don't blame me."

17.

At nine-thirty-five A.M. Friday, the next morning, I stood in front of the filing cabinet in my room in the Naylor-Kerr stock department, gazing down into the drawer I had opened with a feeling of real satisfaction. Not only were the tobacco crumbs nowhere visible, but the edge of the Thursday report was a good half inch down from the Wednesday report, and I had left them precisely even.

I enjoyed the satisfied feeling for a few seconds and then could have kicked myself. Thursday I had brought paraphernalia with me, but had taken it home again, not wanting to leave it around, and this morning I hadn't brought it. That cost me an extra forty minutes. I closed the drawer and locked it. Down on the street I had no trouble finding a taxi, since it was the time of day that the carriage trade gets to work in that part of town. At Wolfe's house I popped in and right out again, with the cab waiting, and no encounter with Wolfe since his morning hours in the plant rooms are from nine to eleven, and headed back for William Street.

I would have liked to lock my door, since the custom there was to enter without knocking, but there was no key, so I barricaded it by shoving the desk against it. With the folders from the drawer carefully and lovingly transported to the desk, I opened my kit and started to work. It was like picking peaches off a tree with all the branches loaded. Any schoolboy could have harvested that crop. Within twenty minutes I had three dozen beauts, some on the slick cardboard of the top folder, a few on the second, more on the third, and a whole flock on the coated stock of the two reports.

My feeling of satisfaction had tapered off a little. The total bulk of curiosity out in the arena, not to mention the two rows of offices, regarding me and my activities, would easily have filled a ten-ton truck, and common curiosity has led people into more complicated and perilous ventures than sneaking into a room and looking over the contents of a filing cabinet. But even at the biggest discount I was doing something, getting something you could see and show around, instead of hopping around bobbing the chin.

The next step, presumably, was to acquire additional equipment, preferably at wholesale, and proceed to take the prints of everyone on the floor. Granted that they would all be eager to co-operate, it would keep me busy for four or five eight-hour days, working alone. That had drawbacks. I went and stooped for the phone, having deposited it on the floor when I moved the desk, and told it I wished to speak to Mr. Pine.

It took a while to get him. When he was on I said, "I need an answer to a question I don't like to ask anyone else. I know some of the big corporations have adopted the custom of getting fingerprints of all their employees, and I wonder if Naylor-Kerr is one of them. Is it?"

"Yes," he said, "we started that during the war. Why?"

"I'd like to have permission to take a look at them. I mean go over them."

"What for?"

"Someone has been monkeying around my room, nosing into my papers, and it would be fun to know who."

"That seems a little farfetched, doesn't it? By the way, I got that report. It will be discussed at a meeting of some of the executives this afternoon. And Mr. Hoff insisted on seeing me; he just left a few minutes ago. He says your presence is demoralizing the whole department. Damn it, I tell you frankly, I could run a car over Mr. Naylor myself. At least you have prodded him along a little. Perhaps you should have a talk with Mr. Hoff whether he likes it or not."

"I'd love to. What about the fingerprints?"

"Certainly, if you think it's worth the trouble. See Mr. Cushing and tell him I said so."

Mr. Cushing was the assistant vice-president who had introduced me around when I started to work. I got him on the phone. It might have been expected that he would show some curiosity as to what a personnel expert expected to accomplish by inspecting fingerprints, but he didn't, so evidently the news of my real status had got beyond the stock department. He was anxious to please, even to the extent of sending me a boy with an empty carton and a supply of tissue paper for the safe transport of my specimens.

I wasn't left alone with the prints, which were filed in a locked cabinet of their own in a room on the thirty-fifth floor. A middle-aged woman with dyed brown hair and a flat chest who had apparently eaten onions for breakfast never got more than ten feet from me. She had an uncertain moment when I sent for the boy and asked him to bring me sandwiches and milk, but she fielded it nicely by phoning a pal to come and relieve her for a lunch period.

I knew what I was doing, but was by no means an expert, and I had to go slow if I didn't want to miss it and have to start all over again. I had the advantage of having an ample collection of good specimens, but even so it was a long uphill climb. A couple of times during the afternoon the onion eater offered to help, but I politely declined, with my eyes smarting and my neck developing a crick.

It was well past four o'clock when I rang the bell. Even before I put it under the magnifying glass I knew that was it, and five minutes with the glass comparing it with a dozen of the best specimens on the folders and reports, settled it good enough for any jury. Either I had let out a grunt of triumph or my manner had betrayed me, for the onion eater came to my elbow and asked:

"Found what you were after, didn't you?"

Not to waste a lie I told her yes, which was feasible since my hand was covering the name on the card. When she had backed off again I returned the card to the file, closed the drawer, repacked my stuff in the carton with the tissue paper, told her I was through for the day and was grateful for the pleasant hours I had spent with her, and went back to the thirty-fourth floor and my office with the carton under my arm. I put the carton on the floor between the window and the desk, which was back in place, got the head of the reserve pool on the phone, and asked him:

"How about Miss Gwynne Ferris? Can I see her now?"

"I'm afraid not." He was apologetic. "I'm terribly sorry, Mr. Truett, but she still has a lot—"

"Excuse me," I broke in. "I'm sorry too, but so have I got a lot. I have asked for her three times now, and of course if I have to go to Mr. Naylor or Mr. Pine—"

"Not at all! Certainly not! I didn't know it was important!"

"It may be."

"Then I'll send her right in! She'll be there right away!"

I told him I appreciated it, hung up, arose to move the visitor's chair to a better position at the end of the desk, and resumed my seat. The door was closed. I was idly considering getting up to open it, to save her the trouble, when it swung open itself and she entered, shut the door behind her, and approached.

I haven't Wolfe's stock excuse, over three hundred pounds to manipulate, for not rising to my feet when a caller enters the room, and besides, I am not a lout. But that time I was glued to my chair at least three seconds beyond the courtesy limit, until after she had asked in a sweet musical voice:

"Did you want me? I'm Gwynne Ferris."

It was the non-speller who had rested her lovely fingers on my knee before I had been in the place an hour.

18.

The psychological moment had passed for rising on the entrance of a lady, so I skipped it and told her, "There's a chair. c-h-a-i-r. Sit down. d-o-w-n."

She did so gracefully with no flutter, got one knee over the other with the nylons nearly parallel the twentieth-century classic pose, gave the ordained tug to the hem of her green woolen skirt, covering an additional sector of knee the width of a matchstick, and smiled at me both with her pretty red lips and her clear blue eyes.

"This is Friday," I stated. "So this is your fifth and last day here. Huh?"

"Well—" she looked demure.

"I am naturally magnanimous," I went on, "and how would

72

you like to spell that one? And I don't mind a little kidding, some of my best friends are kidders, including me. Besides, my suddenly sitting on the corner of your desk and firing questions at you about Waldo Moore must have given you a jolt, considering that you had been—well, I don't want to be outspoken about it—say you and he had been propinquitous. P-R-O-P-I—"

"Don't spell it," she said, with her voice a little less musical and not at all sweet. "Just tell me what it means. If it means what I think it does it's a lie and I know who told you."

"Prove it. Who?"

"Hester Livsey. And you believed her! You wouldn't stop to consider my reputation, a girl's reputation, oh no, that wouldn't matter! Not if Hester Livsey told you, because she's a section head's secretary and she wouldn't lie, oh no! What did she say? Exactly what words did she say?"

I was shaking my head. "Nope. Bad guess. Miss Livsey hasn't mentioned you, and anyhow I want no part of the idea that a section head's secretary never tells a lie." I looked at her as man to woman. "Why don't I forget that anyone has told me anything, and let you straighten me out? You did know Moore, didn't you?"

"Certainly, everybody did." Her voice was back to normal. It changed as often and as fast as the weather. "No matter what a girl's character was she stood a fat chance of not knowing him!"

"Yeh, I understand he was very sociable. Did you go out with him much?"

"No, not—" She bit that off. A tiny wrinkle appeared on her lovely smooth forehead. "Oh, he took me to a couple of shows, that was about all. Once we were out in his car, out on Long Island, and there was an accident and I got a little cut on a part of my body. Of course everyone heard about that."

"I'll bet they did. But you weren't especially intimate with him?"

"Good lord no, intimate? I should say not!"

"Then I suppose his death wasn't a particularly hard blow for you."

"No, I scarcely noticed it." She caught herself up. "Of course I don't mean—I mean, I noticed it. But more on account of my character than on account of him. What I mean about my character, I mean I don't like death. I just don't like it, no matter who it is."

I nodded. "I feel the same way about it. You mean it would have been a much harder blow if it had been, for instance, Ben Frenkel."

She jerked her chin up, and, as though it had been synchronized, her skirt simultaneously jerked itself back above the knee. She demanded, "Who the hell mentioned Ben Frenkel?"

"I did. Just now. He came to see me yesterday and we had a talk. Isn't he a friend of yours?"

"We're not intimate," she said defiantly. "Did he say we are?"

"No no, he's not that kind of guy. I was just using him as an illustration of how little you noticed the death of Moore. What's your opinion of this gossip that's going around, about Moore being murdered?"

"I think it's terrible and I won't listen to it. Gossip is so cheap!"

"But of course you've heard it?"

"Mighty little. I just won't listen!"

"Aren't you interested? Or curious? I thought intelligent women were curious about everything, even murder."

She shook her angelic head. "Not me. I guess it isn't a part of my character."

"That's funny. It really surprises me, because when I found out it was you who came in here on the sly and went through that cabinet, and looked through my folders, and read my reports about Moore, I said to myself, sure, I might have expected that, all it means is that Gwynne Ferris is a beautiful and intelligent young woman who got so curious about it that she couldn't resist the temptation. And now you say you're not curious at all. It certainly is funny."

I am no Nero Wolfe at reading faces, but I know what I see, and it was a bet that during my brief speech she had decided three times to call me a liar, and had thrice changed her mind and made a grab for some better idea. When I stopped purposely without asking a question, and sat and waited for her to bat it back, what she said was:

"It certainly is."

I nodded. "So since you're not curious I suppose you had some special reason for wanting to know how far I had got. The reason I'm speaking to you about it like this, alone with you, is because I think it's much better this way than it would be if I made a report of it and you got a bunch of nitwits barking at you—you know what police are like . . ."

I let it fade out because she had made up her mind. With

a charming impulsive movement she was out of her chair and standing in front of me, leaning over, getting my hands in hers. In the close little room with the door shut she smelled like a new name for a perfume, but there was no time to invent one then and there.

"You don't believe that," she said, not much more than a whisper, into my face. "Do you honestly think I'm that sort of girl, honestly? Do my hands feel like the kind of hands that would do mean things like that? Are you going to believe everything mean you hear about me? Just because someone says they saw me coming in your room or going out again—can you honestly look at me and tell me you believe it? Can you?"

"No," I said. "Impossible."

I was going on, but couldn't for the moment, because she thought I had earned a citation and was proceeding to bestow it when the door of the room swung open, and with my right eye, the only one that could see anything past her ear, I observed Kerr Naylor walking in.

At the sound my seducer jerked away and whirled to face the door.

"It's past quitting time, Miss Ferris," Naylor said.

I batted for her. "I sent for Miss Ferris," I told the glint in his eyes, "and we're having a talk which has at least an hour to go and maybe more. She was taking a mote out of my eye. Can I help you with something?"

Naylor smiled, stepped to the chair that was still warm from Gwynne, and sat down. "Perhaps I can help you instead," he piped. "I'll be glad to take part in the talk if you'll limit it to an hour."

I shook my head at him emphatically. "Much obliged, but it's strictly private.—No, Miss Ferris, don't leave. You stay here.—So if all you came for was to say good night, good night."

"This is my department, Mr. Truett."

"Not the part of it I'm in at any given moment. Yours is the stock department. Mine is the murder department. Good night—unless you came for something else."

He was speechless with fury. Not that it showed on his little wax face, but he was speechless, and nothing short of fury could have done that to him. He stood up, stared at Gwynne, who did not stare back, and finally transferred it to me.

"Very well. The question of your status here can be settled on Monday—if you are here Monday. I came to tell you something, and while Miss Ferris is not ideal for the purpose, it is just as well to have a witness. I am told you have reported that

75

I told you I know the name of the person who murdered Waldo Moore. Is that true?"

"Yep, that's true."

"Then you reported a lie. I have not made that statement to you, nor any statement that could possibly be so construed. I have no idea why you reported such a lie, and I don't intend to waste time trying to find out." He walked to the door, turned, and smiled at us. "You can now resume the conversation I interrupted. Good night."

He was gone, closing the door behind him. I sat still to listen, and in the silence of the depopulated arena heard his footsteps receding, fading into the silence.

Gwynne approached and began. "You see? No matter who said they saw me sneaking into your room, you wouldn't believe it, and no matter who said you had told a lie, I wouldn't believe—"

"Shut up, pet. Shut up and sit down while I sharpen a wit."

She did so. I gazed at the neighborhood of her chin, found that distracting and switched to something neuter. On a quick and concentrated survey, this latest impetuosity of Kerr Naylor looked like the beginning of his big retreat. Once started backward he would probably keep going, and by the middle of the next week would be taking the position that Moore hadn't been killed at all, maybe not even hurt.

I spoke to Gwynne. "What makes it chilly in here is the cold feet of Mr. Kerr Naylor. They are practically frozen. To go back to you, or should I say us, when Naylor came I was about to tell you that you were wasting a lot of ammunition, and damn good ammunition, because nobody told me they saw you coming in here or going out. It's fingerprints. You left about five dozen scattered all over, on the folders and the reports. I'm going to keep them to remember you by. Now what? Were you walking in your sleep? Try that."

She was wrinkling her forehead in profound concentration, as if I had been giving instructions for an intricate typing job and she was deeply anxious to get it straight. My free-for-nothing suggestion about walking in her sleep didn't appeal to her, or more probably she didn't even hear it. At length she spoke.

"Fingerprints?"

Her tone implied that it must be a Russian word and unfortunately she didn't know that language.

"That's right. Little lines on the tips of your fingers that make pretty patterns when you touch something. F-I-N-G—"

"Don't be offensive," she said in a hurt tone. "Anyway, you

said it would be impossible for you to believe I could do such a thing!"

"No you don't," I said firmly. "In the first place, I didn't say that. In the second place, one of my favorite rules is never to let a woman start an argument about what she said or what I said. You've had time now to think up something. What will it be?"

She was still hurt. "I don't have to think up something," she declared indignantly. "All I have to do is tell you the truth even if I think you don't deserve it. Yesterday you said you wanted to see me, and I couldn't come because I had a pile of work for Mr. Henderson, because his secretary is home sick, and I had to stay overtime, and when I got through I came here because I thought you might still be waiting for me, and you were gone, and I thought perhaps you had left some work for me in your cabinet, so I looked in it to see, and of course I had to look in the folders because that was where you would leave it. And now you accuse me of something underhanded just because I tried to do my duty even if it was nearly seven o'clock!"

My head was moving slowly up and down, with my eyes maintaining focus on hers. "Not bad," I conceded. "It would really be good, although loony, if you hadn't denied it at first and come clear here to my chair with your perfume and other attributes. Why did you deny it, precious?"

"Well—I guess I just can't help kidding people. I guess it's part of my character."

"And that's your story and you like it, huh?"

"Of course it is, it's the truth!"

I would have liked to use assorted tortures on her in a well-equipped underground chamber. "This room is not suitable," I admitted reluctantly, "for giving you the kind of attention merited by your character and abilities. But there are other rooms. Policemen get sore at accomplished and fantastic liars much quicker than I do. Tomorrow will be Saturday and this office will be closed, but policemen work seven days a week. It will be nice meeting you in other surroundings. Go on home."

"You're not a policeman," she stated, as if she were contradicting me. She got out of her chair. "You're too handsome and cultured."

When I had just got through saying, or at least plainly implying, that I was not a policeman!

I took the carton home with me, not caring to leave its contents there even with the cabinet locked.

19.

That evening after dinner Wolfe was going on with his three books. Since there was wide variation in the number of pages it looked to me as if he was going to run into trouble when the shortest one suddenly petered out on him, unless he had forseen the difficulty and was adjusting his installments accordingly.

After I had given him the day's report, to which he reacted the same as he had the day before, namely not at all, and after getting nothing but a grunt of indifference when I volunteered the opinion that Kerr Naylor had been read the riot act by his sister and as a result was crawling from under, I decided to take in a flat-face opera.

Ordinarily I let the movies wait when we're busy on a case, but I broke precedent that Friday evening because (a) we weren't busy—at least God knows Wolfe wasn't—and (b) I strongly doubted if it was a case. I would have been willing to settle for nothing more homicidal than a mess of dirty internal politics on the higher levels at Naylor-Kerr, Inc., and while that may have seemed important and even exciting to the Board of Directors and hostile camps of executives, I had to confess that I couldn't blame Wolfe for going aloof on it, since I was inclined to feel the same way. So I let my mind go blank and enjoyed the movie up to a certain point, staying nearly to the end. When it came to where they were preparing to wind it up right and let it out that the hero really had not put over the fake contract and cleaned up, I left in a hurry, because I had formed my own opinion of the hero from where I sat and chose to think otherwise.

Then, when I got home at half-past eleven, I found Inspector Cramer there in the office, seated in the red leather chair, talking to Wolfe. Evidently it wasn't a very amiable conversation, for Cramer's look at me as I entered was an unfriendly glare, and, since I had done nothing to earn it, it must have been the state of his feelings toward Wolfe.

"Where the hell have you been?" he demanded, as if he had me under contract or I was on the parole list.

"It was a wonderful movie," I informed them, sitting down at my desk. "Only two people in it have amnesia, this incredibly beautiful girl with—"

"Archie," Wolfe snapped. He was out of humor too. "Mr.

Cramer wants to ask you something. I suppose you have seen the piece about us in this evening's *Gazette?*"

"Sure. It's a bum picture of you, but——"

"You didn't mention it to me."

"Yeah, you were busy reading, and anyway it wasn't worth wasting breath on."

"It's an outrage!" Cramer rasped. "It's a flagrant betrayal of a client's confidence!"

"Nuts." I had to keep my eyes on the go to meet the two glares alternately. "It doesn't quote me and it doesn't even say I was interviewed. It merely says that Archie Goodwin, Nero Wolfe's brilliant lieutenant, is investigating the death of Waldo Wilmot Moore, and therefore it may be conjectured that somebody smells murder. Except for those it mentions no names. Since about a thousand people down at Naylor-Kerr know about it, and at least one of them knows who I am and probably a lot more, you can have that word betrayal back and use it somewhere else. Even so, Lon Cohen wouldn't have done it without getting my okay. It was that damn Whosis, the city editor. Whose belly aches, the client's? Have you been promoted from homicide to patting the kittens?"

Wolfe and Cramer started to speak both at once, and Wolfe won. "The piece," he said, "does indeed apply that word, brilliant, to you, and that's all I find in it to object to. But Mr. Cramer is seriously annoyed. It seems that Mr. O'Hara, the Deputy Commissioner, is also annoyed. They want us to quit the job."

"They've got a hell of a nerve," I asserted. "Will they feed us?"

Cramer started again to speak, but Wolfe pushed a palm at him.

"Nothing edible," Wolfe said with a grimace. There was no joking about food with him. "They say the piece in the *Gazette* is the opening of another campaign of criticism of the police for an unsolved murder, and that it is irresponsible because there isn't the slightest evidence that Mr. Moore's death was anything but a hit-and-run accident. They say that our undertaking an investigation is the only valid excuse the *Gazette* can have for starting such a campaign or continuing it. They say that either we have been gulled by the whimsicality of an eccentric man, Mr. Kerr Naylor, or that, not gulled, we are exploiting it in order to build up for a fee. They say that you have even gone so far as to report that Mr. Naylor said something to you—that he knows who killed Mr. Moore—which he never said, in the necessity to invent something that would justify our continued employment. Does that cover it, Mr. Cramer?"

"It'll do for an outline," Cramer rasped. "I want to ask Goodwin—"

"If you please." Wolfe was brusque. He turned to me. "Archie. If I need to tell you, I do, that I have unqualified confidence in you and am completely satisfied with your performance in this case, as I have been in all past cases and expect to be in all future ones. Of course you tell lies and so do I, even to clients when it seems advisable, but you would never lie to me nor I to you in a matter where mutual trust and respect are involved. Your lack of brilliance may be regrettable but is really a triviality, and in any event two brilliant men under one roof would be intolerable. Your senseless peccadillocs, such as your refusal to use a noiseless typewriter, are a confounded nuisance, but this idiotic accusation that you lied in that report to Mr. Pine has put me in a different frame of mind about it. Keep your typewriter, but for heaven's sake oil it."

"Good God," I protested, "I oil it every—"

Cramer exploded with a word which the printer would not approve of. "Your goddam household squabbles will keep," he said rudely. He was at me. "Do you stick to it that Naylor told you he knew who killed Moore?"

"No, I don't," I told him, "not to you. To you I don't stick to anything. This is a private investigation about a guy shooting off his mouth, and I do my reporting to Mr. Wolfe and to our client. Where do you come in? You're the head of the Homicide Squad, but you say yourself that Moore's death was an accident, so it's none of your business what I stick to and what I let go of. I don't blame you for not wanting the *Gazette* to start a howl, but if you expect any co-operation from me you're not going to get it by asking me whether I stick to it that I'm not a liar. I suppose O'Hara has been on the phone and given you a pain in the sitdown, a substitute I use out of respect for your age, but you don't need to take it out on me."

I spread out my palms. "Take it this way. Let's suppose you're a reasonable man instead of a hothead, and you come here to ask me something in that spirit, suppose you even call me Archie. And you tell me what you want in a friendly well-modulated tone. What would it be?"

"I've already told Wolfe, and he has told you." Cramer was no longer bellicose, merely firm. "I want you to quit stirring up a murder stink where there's no evidence and peddling stale rumors to the papers."

"I didn't peddle. I went to the *Gazette* boys for information, and I got it. As for stink-stirring, do you mean you want me to quit my job at Naylor-Kerr?"

"Yes. You don't need money that bad."

"I wouldn't know, I'm only the bookkeeper. That's up to Mr. Wolfe. He employs me and I follow orders."

"And I," Wolfe put in, "am in turn employed by Naylor-Kerr, Inc., through its president, Mr. Pine. I am inclined to think that in hiring me he and his fellow executives had certain special undeclared purposes in mind. Their nature is not known to me, but I have reason to suppose them to be criminal or unethical, and they may even be praiseworthy. Why don't you ask Mr. Pine about it? Have you talked to him?"

"The Deputy Commissioner has." Cramer had got out a cigar and was threatening his teeth with it. "This afternoon. I understand it was mostly about Goodwin lying about what Naylor had said to him. I don't suppose the Deputy Commissioner asked him specifically to call you off. That part of it was left to me."

"I wouldn't feel justified," Wolfe said virtuously, "in quitting the case without the approval of the client."

"Okay, then get it. Call him up now. We'll both talk to him, and me first."

Wolfe nodded at me. "Get Mr. Pine, Archie. But not you first, Mr. Cramer. You second."

I got the number from the book and dialed it. When, after a short wait, there was a voice in my ear that I recognized, I was surprised that a woman with enough money to keep pets answered the phone herself, but it was midnight and the servants probably didn't get to sleep as late in the morning as she did. I told her who I was and she reacted instantly.

"Of course, I knew your voice at once! How is your face, Archie?"

She sounded as if she had really had it on her mind and wanted to know. "Better, thanks," I told her. "I'm sorry to disturb you so late at night, but—"

"Oh, it's not late for me! I'm never in bed before three or four. The season tickets aren't available yet, but they will be next week, and yours will be sent at once."

"Much obliged. Is your husband there? Mr. Wolfe would like to speak to him."

"Yes, he's here, but he may be asleep. He goes to bed much earlier than I do. Hold the wire and I'll find out. Is it important?"

"Not important enough to wake him up if he hates it as much as I do."

"All right, hold the wire. I'll see."

It took her long enough. I sat and held it, reflecting that considering the state of their romance her husband's bed was probably not just the other side of a door. Finally she was back.

"No, I'm sorry, he's sound asleep. I thought he might be reading. Is it about what I came to see you about?"

"Yes, it's connected with that. We'll get him in the morning. Many thanks."

"Maybe I could help. What is it?"

"I don't think so, it's just a detail. Hold it a second." I covered the transmitter and announced, "He's asleep and she wants to know if she can help. She would like very much to help."

"No," Wolfe said positively.

"Wait a minute," Cramer began, but I ignored him and told the phone, "Mr. Wolfe thanks you for your offer, Mrs. Pine, but he will call your husband tomorrow."

"Then just tell me what it is, Archie, and I can discuss it with him before Mr. Wolfe calls."

It took me a good three minutes to get it concluded without being impolite.

A childish wrangle started. Cramer adopted the position that I should have persuaded her to wake Pine up, and Wolfe, who hates having his sleep interrupted even more than I do, violently disagreed. They kept at it as if it had been one of the world's major problems, like what to do with the Ruhr. Neither of them budged an inch, so they ended where they began, stalemated.

"Very well," Cramer said finally, still belligerent. "So I get nothing for losing two hours of my own sleep and coming clear over here to ask you a favor."

"Nonsense." Wolfe was belligerent too. "You haven't asked a favor. You have called Mr. Goodwin a liar and you have made preposterous demands. Besides, this is on your way home from your office."

That was the intellectual level they had descended to. I wouldn't have been surprised if Cramer had produced a map of the city, to prove that Wolfe's house was not on a direct line between his office and his home, but he skipped that and concentrated on the other point—whether he had asked a favor or not. He maintained that he had, and that if it had sounded like a demand that was only on account of his mannerisms, with which we were well acquainted and therefore had no right to misinterpret. At length, by that roundabout route, he got back to his main point: would we or would we not break off relations with Naylor-Kerr, Inc.? Apparently Deputy Commissioner O'Hara had really built a fire under him.

"It isn't as urgent as all that, is it?" Wolfe asked in his tone of fake concern, which has maddened older men than me, or even than Cramer. "For a long time Mr. Kerr Naylor—"

The phone rang. I gave it a glance of distaste before reaching for it, thinking it was certainly Mrs. Pine, with nothing special to do for another two hours till bedtime, calling to ask about my face. But no. A gruff male voice asked to speak to Inspector Cramer, and I moved out of my chair to let Cramer take the call at my desk.

It was a one-sided conversation, with Cramer contributing only a few grunts and, at the end, three or four questions. He told someone he would be there in five minutes, hung up, and swiveled to us.

"Kerr Naylor has been found dead on Thirty-ninth Street near Eleventh Avenue. Four blocks from here. Apparently run over by a car, with his head smashed." Cramer was on his feet. "They got his name from papers in his pocket." He growled at me, "Want to come and identify him?"

"Indeed," Wolfe muttered. "Remarkable coincidence. Mr. Moore died there too. It must be a dangerous street."

"And now," I complained, "I'll never be able to make him take back calling me a liar. Sure, glad to help. Come along, Inspector."

20.

Since so far as I knew I was still on the Naylor-Kerr payroll, it was a good thing they didn't work Saturdays, because Saturday morning I didn't get out of bed until noon was in plain sight. At that I had been there something short of six hours, having got home just as the sun was taking its first slanting look at Thirty-fifth Street.

Coincidence was right. On Thirty-ninth Street between

Tenth and Eleventh Avenues, not thirty feet from the spot where the body of Waldo Wilmot Moore had been found nearly four months before, a car had run over Kerr Naylor flattening his head and breaking his bones. I had appreciated better than I had when he had told me about it, the difficultie Kerr Naylor had encountered when he had gone to the morgue to identify the remains of Waldo Moore, but there had been no doubt about it. It was unquestionably Naylor, when you had made the mental adjustment required by the transformation of a sphere into a disk.

To go on with the coincidence, the body, which had been discovered by a taxi driver at twelve-forty A.M., had been there unnoticed for some time, anyway over half an hour, if the guess of the Medical Examiner on the time of death was any good. Not only that—and this was really stretching it too far —the car that had run over him had been found parked on Ninety-fifth Street just west of Broadway, in front of a branch laundry, in the identical spot where the car that had finished Moore had been found. On that one I had to hand it to Inspector Cramer. One of his first barks on arriving at the scene had been at a squad dick, telling him to beat it to Ninety-fifth Street and go over the cars parked in that block. Showing that an inspector knows a coincidence when he sees one. Already, before I had left to go home for a nap, the owner of the car had been brought in from Bedford Hills and thoroughly processed. The processing was mostly unnecessary, since it was easily established that he had reported to the police at eleven-eighteen that his car had been stolen from where he had parked it on Forty-eighth Street, having driven to town to go to the theater; and having, as lots of boobs do every day, forgotten to lock the car or even take the key.

It had taken two laboratory men, working with spotlights on the tires of the car where it stood on Ninety-fifth Street, to get the proof that it was the one that had rolled over Naylor, and that was one more detail of the coincidence.

Part of the time I had been a kibitzer, but had been made to feel welcome throughout because Inspector Cramer wanted me handy to answer some more questions when he got a chance to work them in, between other chores. During all the hours he made no reference to Wolfe's objectionable behavior, and mine, in trying to stir up a murder stink when there had been no murder, and I, knowing he was busy and it would aggravate him, brought it up only eight or nine times. Even then he didn't have me bounced because he wanted me around. The first session with him I stalled a little on the ground that it would be outrageous for me to betray the confidence of a client, but when he got to the point of a certain tone I gave him everything that I knew he would soon be getting elsewhere anyway. I told him all, or nearly all, about the folks I had been meeting down at Naylor-Kerr, including, of course, such details as the impression Ben Frenkel had been carrying around since December. When I had tried to loosen Gwynne Ferris up by threatening to tell the cops all and let them take a crack at her I hadn't dreamed I would actually be doing so within ten hours.

Cramer shifted headquarters three times, taking me along. For half an hour or so he worked outdoors there on Thirty-ninth Street and then moved inside, to the 18th Precinct Station House on Fifty-fourth Street. Around three o'clock he moved again, to his own hangout, the office of the squad on Twentieth Street, and an hour later made another transfer, this time to the office of Deputy Commissioner O'Hara at Centre Street. O'Hara himself was there and things had really started to hum. I was right in the middle of it and was even given the pleasure of an interview with the Deputy Commissioner himself. From the way he started in on me it was a fair inference that he not only regarded me as a damn liar but also had inside dope to the effect that I had done it all myself, and that when I had got home and joined Wolfe and Cramer in the office at 11:30 I had just come, not from a movie, but from parking the murder car on Ninety-fifth Street. Since I had already given Cramer all the information I had that could help any, I though I might as well let O'Hara keep his illusions and fed him a peck or more of miscellaneous lies, such as I didn't know how to drive a car and in strict confidence I had not been at a movie, but in a hotel room with the wife of a prominent politician whom I would rather die than name. Eventually O'Hara caught on and there was quite a scene.

Kerr Naylor's sister had of course been notified, not on the phone, but by dispatching Lieutenant Rowcliff to her house on Sixty-seventh Street. When Rowcliff returned—we were then at the 18th Precinct Station House—Jasper Pine was with him, having had his sleep broken into after all. Pine had been taken by Rowcliff, on their way, to identify the body, and since I knew from having done it myself how jolly that was, I didn't blame him for looking a little pale. He didn't have the appearance of a man overcome by grief, but neither did he look like a top executive with everything under control. Cramer, having learned that both he and his wife disclaimed any knowledge of Kerr Naylor's whereabouts Friday evening and had no idea of what he might have been doing on Thirty-ninth Street, spent only a short time on him and then gave him back to Rowcliff for more talk. I spoke just sixteen words to him. As he started away with Rowcliff he confronted me and demanded, "Did Naylor tell you what you reported to me? That he knew who had killed Moore?"

"Yes," I said. "If I had wanted to make something up I could have done better than that."

Before the night shift was through I met other acquaintances, after we got down to Centre Street. Not Hester Livsey. The dick who was sent for her came back with a report that her mother, with whom she lived in Brooklyn, had stated that her daughter was not there and had not been home that evening because she had gone straight from work to Grand Central to catch a train, to spend the week-end with friends in Westport, Connecticut. She had furnished the name of the friends, and they had been phoned to. No answer. But Cramer and his boys were moving fast and in all directions. They had phoned the Westport police, who had made a call on the friends and reported back that Hester Livsey was there, snug in bed, having arrived on a train that had reached Westport at one-nine A.M. Since it takes around seventy minutes, not eight hours, for a train to go from Grand Central to Westport, the caller had insisted on speaking to Miss Livsey and had done so. She had stated that she had decided to take a later train and that how she had spent the evening in New York was her own business. Told of the death of Kerr Naylor, she repeated her statement, and said that she knew nothing about Mr. Naylor and that her association with him was extremely remote, since he was head of a large department and she was merely a stenographer. Asked if she would return to New York in the morning so the police could talk with her, she refused, saying that she couldn't possibly tell them anything helpful.

There was a report from a sergeant who had had a chat with Sumner Hoff in his apartment in the East Fifties. Hoff had been able to contribute nothing, but was quite willing, as a responsible citizen, to co-operate with the police in the investigation of a crime—which sounded to me like a distinct and encouraging improvement in his manners.

Bell ringing and door knocking had produced no results at the Greenwich Village room-and-bath tenanted by Rosa Bendini. In her case there was no mother around to get information from, and no one else in the building knew where Rosa was. I had a healthy conviction, knowing as I do what a liking for companionship can lead to, that when Rosa showed up her mind would be a blank as to where she had spent Friday night, but that was one of the things I didn't communicate to Cramer, not wanting to lower his opinion of American womanhood. They thought they might find her with her husband, where he lived with his folks on Washington Heights, but no. Harold Anthony, hauled out of bed, dressed and came down to Centre Street without being asked. His story was that he hadn't seen Rosa since Wednesday evening, when she had left him and me to fight it out on the sidewalk in front of Wolfe's house; and as for him, he didn't know Kerr Naylor from Adam, and had spent Friday evening at a basketball game at the Garden, where he had gone by his lonesome, and had then walked all the way home—some six miles—to use up energy.

I asked him, "So you got some energy back in the short space of forty-eight hours? After what I took out of you?"

"What the hell," he bragged, "I'd forgotten about that the next day. What do they want Rosa for? Are they fools enough to think she would kill a man? What have they got?"

He had actually come clear down to Centre Street at that time of night through anxiety for his wife! Loyalty is a very fine thing, but it shouldn't be allowed to get the bit between its teeth. I told him not to worry, the cops were just shaking it all through a sieve. Regarding his energy, I didn't believe him. Three of my kidney punches do not kill a man, but neither do they fade utterly from recollection the next day.

But that was along toward the end. Before that we had had a session with Ben Frenkel, one of the first things after our arrival at O'Hara's office. At the moment Cramer was seated at the big desk and I was standing behind him, looking over his shoulder at the carbon copy of my reports to Naylor-Kerr, which I had stopped off at Wolfe's office to get. A dick towed Frenkel in and planted him in a chair at the end of the desk. I had thought his hair was undisciplined when he came to see me on Thursday, but now no two hairs were parallel. He was trying to look nowhere and at no one, which really cannot be done unless you go at it with all your might and shut your eyes.

"Hello there," I said.

He returned no sign of recognition.

Cramer growled at him, "You're Benjamin Frenkel?"

"Yes, that's my name."

"Are you under the impression that you killed Kerr Naylor?"

Frenkel gawked at him, then made another try at looking at nothing, and did not speak.

"Well, are you?"

Frenkel looked straight at me and cried, "You rat! I told you that in confidence!"

"You did not," I denied. "I told you I couldn't keep a confession of murder confidential."

"I didn't confess to a murder!"

"Then do it now," Cramer urged. "Confess now. Come on, let's have it, get it off your chest, you'll feel better."

That didn't work at all. Put straight that way, an invitation to confess to murder seemed to be just what he had wanted for his birthday. He quit trying to look at nothing, his big bony shoulders went to the back of the chair for normal support, and his voice, though still intense, had no note of panic at all as he said:

"I was told I had to come here to answer questions. What are the questions?" He smiled sweetly and sadly.

Cramer asked the questions and he replied. He had last seen Kerr Naylor around three o'clock Friday afternoon, at the office, and knew nothing of him since that hour. After work he had gone to his room on Ninety-fourth Street, bathed and changed his clothes, eaten dinner alone in a restaurant around the corner on Broadway, and taken the subway downtown to call for a young woman who lived on Twenty-first Street with whom he had an engagement for the evening. He preferred not to mention her name. They had gone to Moonlight, on Fiftieth Street, and stayed there, dancing, until after twelve. He had taken the young woman home and then gone home himself, arriving about one o'clock. He would not give the young woman's name because there was no reason why he should. If for any good reason it became necessary the name would be forthcoming.

What about his impression that he had killed Waldo Moore?

That, he had decided, was one of the mental vagaries to which high-strung men like him were subject. He had often been bothered by them. Once he had become obsessed with the idea that he was secretly a Nazi, and had gone to a Bund meeting at Yorkville to get rid of it. He did not state categorically, but strongly implied, that his coming to me had been the same thing as his going to a Bund meeting, which did not increase my affection for him.

Hadn't he come to me only for one purpose, to find out if

Naylor had mentioned his name in connection with Moore's death?

No, that wasn't true. He hadn't even thought of that until it occurred to him during the conversation.

Did he know Gwynne Ferris?

Yes, she was one of the stenographers in the stock department.

Had he spoken with her on Friday?

Possibly; he didn't remember.

Hadn't she told him that Naylor had stated that he knew who had killed Waldo Moore?

No, not that he remembered. But of course, he added, he had known that Mr. Naylor had made that statement. Everybody did. It was being discussed all over the department.

That was news to me. I goggled at him. I took it away from Cramer and demanded, "When?"

"Why, today. Yesterday. Friday."

"Who did Naylor make the statement to?"

"I don't know—that is, I only know what I heard. The way I got it, he made it to you and you reported it to the president's office."

"Who did you get it from?"

"I don't remember." Frenkel had reverted to form. His rumble was low from deep in his throat and his eyes were probing me again. "It is not a quality of my mind to cling to factual details like that. Whereas matters which have an intellectual content—"

"Nuts," Cramer said in bitter disgust. He had thought for one shining moment that he had a confession coming, and now this blah. He aimed a half-chewed cigar at Frenkel's face, brandished it, and asserted:

"Gwynne Ferris told you. Didn't she?"

"I said she didn't."

"And I say she did! I happen to know—What do you want?"

The question was for a city employee who had approached the desk. He answered it. "Sergeant Gottlieb is here, sir, with the Ferris woman."

Cramer scowled at him. "Keep her until I get through—no. Wait." He looked at Frenkel and then at me. "Why not?"

"Sure, why not?" I agreed.

Cramer told the dick, "Bring her in here."

21.

Gwynne Ferris entered, not aware or not caring that a detective sergeant was right behind her elbow, halted a moment to survey the big room, and then approached us at the desk.

"Hello, Ben," she said in her sweet musical voice. "Of all the terrible things, but what are you here for?" Not waiting for a reply, her glance darted to Cramer and then to me. "Oh, then you are a policeman!"

She was, I admitted, equal to any situation, and that applied not only to her nerves but also to her appearance. Routed out by a cop at four in the morning, getting dressed while he waited, and brought down to headquarters in a police car, she looked as fresh and pure and beautiful as she had when she had raised her clear blue eyes to mine and told me she couldn't spell.

"Sit down, Miss Ferris," Cramer told her.

"Thank you," she said sarcastically, and sat, on a chair a couple of paces from Frenkel's. "You look terrible, Ben. Have you had any sleep at all?"

"Yes," Frenkel rumbled from a mile down.

Gwynne spoke to Cramer and me. "The reason I asked him that, I saw him only a few hours ago. We were dancing. But I suppose he's told you that already. It's a good thing tomorrow isn't a workday. Are you an inspector, Mr. Truett, or what?"

"This is unspeakable, utterly unspeakable," Ben Frenkel declared with deep intensity. "I didn't tell them who I went dancing with because I thought they'd be after you to verify it, and they did it anyway, for no reason on earth. Were they decent about it? Were they rough with you?"

Harry Anthony had been anxious about Rosa, and here was Frenkel, being anxious about Gwynne. I made a note to quit trying to understand women and start trying to understand men.

"No, he was really very courteous about it," Gwynne testified generously.

Cramer had been glancing from one to the other. He opened up. "So you two were together all evening. Is that right, Frenkel?"

"Yes. Since Miss Ferris has told you so."

"Not just since she has told me so. Were you?"

"Yes."

"Did Mr. Frenkel take you home, Miss Ferris?"

"Certainly he did!"

"What time did you get home?"

"When was it, Ben, about—"

"I asked you."

"Well, it was a quarter to one when I got upstairs to my room. I went up alone of course. We talked a while downstairs."

Cramer surprised me. He was seldom plain nasty, leaving that to the boys, but now he barked at her, "When Waldo Moore took you home you didn't go upstairs alone, did you?"

Ben Frenkel sprang from his chair with his fists doubled up and his eyes blazing. A dick standing in the rear moved forward. I tightened up a little myself, not knowing how far Frenkel's impulses might go. But evidently Gwynne did, for she was on her feet and in front of him, with her hands up to grasp his coat lapels.

"Now, Ben, honey." When she put appeal in her voice it could have been used for a welding torch. "You know that isn't so, haven't I told you? He's just being malicious." She put pressure on him. "Sit down and don't even hear things like that." His knees started to give, she maintained the pressure, and he was back in his chair.

She returned to hers and told Cramer, "There was a lot of malicious talk about me and Waldo Moore, and this is what I get for it. I know better than to lose my temper over those kind of things any more. I just ignore it."

So Cramer's nastiness had paid no dividend. He shifted his ground and asked, "Why were you so anxious to know what Goodwin was reporting about Moore's death?"

"Goodwin? What Goodwin?"

"Truett," I explained. "Me. My name's Goodwin."

"Oh! I'm glad you told me. Then you were sailing under false—"

"I asked you," Cramer rasped, "why you were so anxious to know what he had found out about Moore's death."

"I wasn't anxious. Not at all."

"Then why did you sneak into his room and go through his papers?"

"I didn't!" She looked at me reproachfully. "Did you tell him that? After I explained that I thought you might still be waiting for me, and you were gone, and I thought perhaps you had left some work—"

"Yeah," Cramer cut her off, "I've heard that before. You're sticking to that, are you?"

"Why, it's the truth!" She was marvelous when she was showing forbearance in the face of injustice being done her. So marvelous that I would have liked to cut her into thin slices and broil her.

Cramer gazed at her. "Listen to me, Miss Ferris," he said in a different and calmer tone. "That sort of thing was okay as long as it was just a matter of investigating a death that might have been an accident that took place months ago. As long as that was all it amounted to there was nothing wrong especially about your not telling the truth when Goodwin asked why you looked at his papers. But now it's different, now we know it was murder, and that's what I'm telling you, it was murder. That changes the whole thing, doesn't it? Don't you want to help? If you're not involved in it yourself, and I don't think you are, shouldn't you help out by telling us why you did that?"

"What is all this," Frenkel demanded, evidently on speaking terms again, "about her looking at papers? What papers?"

He got no reply.

Gwynne appealed to Cramer, "I have to tell the truth, don't I? It wouldn't help for me to tell a lie, would it?"

Cramer gave up and exploded at her, "Who did you tell about it?"

"About what?"

"What you saw in that report! About Naylor saying he knew who killed Moore! Who did you tell?"

"Let me see." The frown appeared on her forehead. She had to think hard. "One of the girls, which one was it, and I mentioned it to one of the men too—it was—no, it wasn't Mr. Henderson—" She looked at Cramer apologetically. "I guess I can't remember."

Deputy Commissioner O'Hara strode into the room. It was his office.

Cramer arose and said grimly, "We'll go into another room to finish our talk, Miss Ferris. We're through with you for now, Mr. Frenkel, but we may need you at any time. Keep us informed where you are."

O'Hara said, "You're Archie Goodwin? I want to talk with you."

I've already told about that.

22.

As I said, I didn't get out of bed Saturday until nearly noon. My face was no longer in a condition to cause boys on the street to make comments, but it took me longer than usual to shave, and also my movements under the shower were a little cautious and deliberate. So by the time I got downstairs Fritz was about ready to dish up lunch. Because I didn't feel like breaking my fast with Rognons aux Montagnes, which is lamb kidneys cooked with broth and red wine, not to mention assorted spices, and because Wolfe would not permit talk of business during a meal, and because I wanted to look at the morning papers and couldn't if I sat at the table with him, I ate in the kitchen. Fritz, who understands me, had fresh hot oatmeal ready, the chill off my bottle of cream, the eggs waiting in the pan, the ham sliced thin for the broiler, the pancake batter mixed, the griddle hot, and the coffee steaming. I made a pass as if to kiss him on the cheek, he kept me off with a twenty-inch pointed knife, and I sat down and started the campaign against starvation with the Times propped up in front of me.

After lunch, or breakfast, depending on which room you ate in, I went to the office and before long Wolfe joined me. From the expression on his face I gathered that coolness was absent from our relationship until the next one, now that he had surrendered on the typewriter, but if he thought I was going to reciprocate by surrendering on the new car he should have known me better. However, I decided not to bring it up immediately after his lunch. He got adjusted in his made-to-order chair behind his desk and asked:

"What have they decided about Mr. Naylor? Death by misadventure?"

"No, sir. They think someone tried to hurt him. At that, Cramer shows signs of having a noodle. He can discover nothing on Thirty-ninth Street, or in that neighborhood, that would account for Naylor being there. Also he refuses to believe that Naylor obligingly lay on the pavement, and lay still, so the driver of the car could make the wheels hit exactly the same spots, his head and legs, that had been hit on Moore. He concludes that Naylor was killed somewhere else, probably by a blow or blows on the head, that the body was taken to Thirty-ninth Street in the car and deposited on the pavement and the car driven over it, and that the car wheels smashing the head obliterated the mark or marks of the blow or blows that killed him. The scientists are going over the inside of the car with microscopes for evidence that the body was carried in it. Cramer doesn't say so out loud, but he's wishing to God he had done likewise with the car that killed Moore."

"Has anyone been arrested?"

"Not up to six o'clock, when I left. Deputy Commissioner O'Hara wanted to arrest me, but Cramer needed me. I was very helpful."

"Does Mr. Cramer still think you lied in your report to Mr. Pine?"

"No, but O'Hara does. I admit I lied to him. I told him that you're just a front here and the real brains of this business is a skinny old woman with asthma that we keep locked in the basement."

Wolfe sighed and leaned back. "I suppose you'd better tell me all about it."

I did so. Assuming that he wanted everything, I gave it to him, including not only facts but also a few interpretations and some personal analysis. It was obvious, I explained, that Cramer was now taking my word for gospel, since he had concentrated on the units of personnel I had told him about, though he had also used the police file on the death of Waldo Moore as a reference work, and doubtless they were all in that. I interpreted Gwynne Ferris by remarking that her broadcasting of the news she got from my filing cabinet might have been a highly intelligent cover for intentions and plans of her own, or it might have been merely promiscuous chin pumping, and I refused to commit myself until I had known her much longer—a minimum of five years. Whichever it was, the result was the same: assuming that Naylor had been finished off because of his announcement that he knew who had killed Moore, everyone was eligible. Up to six o'clock, when I had left, neither elimination nor spotlighting had even got a start, although Cramer had his whole army going through the routine—collecting alibis, tracing the movements of people, including Naylor, trying to find witnesses of events on Thirty-ninth Street, Ninety-fifth Street, Forty-eighth Street, and other vital spots, and all the rest of it. They had found no one who would admit seeing Kerr Naylor after he left the building on William Street Friday afternoon, or any knowledge of him. That was interesting, because it left it that Gwynne Ferris and I were the last people who had seen him alive. It had been around half-past five when he had walked in on us in my room at Naylor-Kerr to tell me I was a liar. Everybody else had left for the day, and none of the elevator boys remembered taking him down. One of O'Hara's strongest convictions had been that Naylor and I had left the building together, and I had merely shrugged it off. It's a waste of time trying to extract a conviction from an Irishman.

When I was empty, both of facts and of annotations, I observed, "One thing to consider, you know what we were hired for, to establish the manner of Moore's death. Remember your letter to Pine? Well, that seems to be established, anyhow as far as the cops are concerned. So have we still got a client? If we go on wearing out your muscles and my brains, do we get paid?"

Wolfe nodded. "That occurred to me, naturally. I telephoned Mr. Pine this morning, and he seems a little uncertain about it. He says there will be a directors' meeting Monday morning and he'll let us know. By the way, his wife came to see me this morning."

"What! Cecily? Up and around before noon? What did she want?"

"I haven't the slightest idea. Possibly she knows, but I don't. I suspect she's hysterical but manages somehow to conceal it. Her ostensible purpose was to learn exactly what her brother said to you his last three days. She wanted it verbatim, and she wanted to pay for it. How the devil that woman has any money left, with her passion for getting rid of it, is a mystery. She asked me to tell you that the baseball tickets will reach you Thursday or Friday. She also wanted to know if you are taking care of your face." He wiggled a finger at me. "Archie. That woman is a wanton maniac. It would be foolhardy to accept baseball tickets—"

The doorbell rang.

"If it's her again," Wolfe commanded me in quick panic, "don't let her in!"

It wasn't. I went to the hall, to the front door, and opened up, and was confronted by one of the faces I like best, Saul Panzer's.

"What the hell," I asked as he entered and hung his cap on the rack, "did you trip up on Bascom's forgery and have to solicit?"

Saul is always businesslike, never frolicsome, but now he was absolutely glum. He didn't even return my grin.

"Mr. Wolfe?" he asked.

"In the office. What bit you?"

He went ahead and I followed. Saul never sits in the red

leather chair, not on account of any false modesty that he doesn't rate it, but because he doesn't like to face a window. Having the best pair of eyes I know of, not even excepting Wolfe, he likes to give them every advantage. He picked his usual perch, a straight-backed yellow chair not far from mine, and spoke to Wolfe in a gloomy tone.

"I believe this is about the worst I've ever done for you. Or for anybody."

"That could still be true," Wolfe said handsomely, "even if you had done well. You said on the phone that you lost him. Did he know he was being followed? What happened?"

"It wasn't that bad," Saul asserted. "It isn't often that a man spots me on his tail, and I'm sure he didn't. Of course he might have; but we can't ask him now. Anyhow, he was walking west on Fifty-third Street, uptown side, between First and Second Avenues—"

"Excuse me," I put in. "Shall I go upstairs and take a nap or would you care to invite me to join you?"

"He was following Mr. Naylor," Wolfe informed me.

It was nothing new for Wolfe to take steps, either on his own or with one or more of the operatives we used, without burdening my mind with it. His stated reason was that I worked better if I thought it all depended on me. His actual reason was that he loved to have a curtain go up revealing him balancing a live seal on his nose. I had long ago abandoned any notion of complaining about it, so I merely asked:

"When?"

"Yesterday. Last evening. Go ahead, Saul."

Saul resumed. "I was across the street and thirty paces behind. He had been walking, off and on, for two hours, and there was nothing to indicate he was ready to quit. There was no warning, such as keeping an eye to the rear for a taxi coming. He did it as if he got the idea all of a sudden. A taxi rolled past me, and just as it got even with him he yelled at it, and the driver made a quick stop, and he ducked across to it and hopped in, and off it went. I was caught flatfooted. I ran after it to the corner, Second Avenue, but the light was green and it went on through. There was no taxi for me in sight, so I kept on running, but either he had told his driver to step on it or the driver liked to get places."

Saul shook his head. "I admit it looks as if he was on to me, but I don't believe it. I think he took a sudden notion. I don't especially mind losing one, we all lose them sometimes, but just three hours before he was murdered! That's what gets me. Even say it was bad luck, if my luck's gone I might as well quit. At the time, of course, not knowing he would be dead before midnight, I wasn't much upset. I tried some leads I had, his chess club and a couple of other places, but didn't get a smell. I went home and went to bed, thinking to try him again this morning. As soon as I saw the morning paper I phoned you, and you told me—"

"Never mind what I told you," Wolfe said crisply. So he was getting up another charade, I thought. He asked Saul, "What time was it?"

"It was eight-thirty-four when I quite running, so it was eight-thirty, maybe one minute one way or the other, when he got his taxi."

"Get Mr. Cramer, Archie."

I tried to fill the order but couldn't, because Cramer was not to be had. He was probably home asleep after a hard night and morning, though no one was indelicate enough to tell me so. I was offered a captain and my choice of lieutenants, but turned them down and got Sergeant Purley Stebbins. Wolfe took it.

"Mr. Stebbins? How are you? I have some information for Mr. Cramer. At half-past eight last evening, Friday, Mr. Kerr Naylor stopped a taxicab on Fifty-third Street between First and Second Avenues. He got in the cab and it proceeded westward, through Second Avenue and beyond. He was alone. —If you please, let me finish." He consulted a slip of paper that Saul had handed him. "It was a Sealect cab, somewhat dilapidated, and its number was WX one-nine-seven-four-four-naught. That's right. How the devil would I know the driver's name? Isn't that enough for you?—If you please. This information can be depended on, I guarantee it, but I have not, and shall not have, anything to add to it. Nonsense. If the driver denies it, bring him to me."

I was thinking that at least I was no longer the last one to see Naylor alive, though it was no great improvement since the honor had been transferred to Saul. It would be nice when they hauled in the taxi driver and took it entirely out of the family.

"What happened," Wolfe asked Saul, "before you lost him? You got him at William Street?"

Saul nodded. "Yes, sir. He left the building at five-thirty-eight, walked to City Hall Park, bought an evening paper, and sat on a bench in the park and read it until a quarter past six. Then he went to Brooklyn Bridge, took the Third Avenue El, and got off at Fifty-third Street. He seemed now to be in a hurry, he walked faster. At First Avenue and Fifty-second

Street he met a girl who was apparently expecting him. A young woman. They walked together west on Fifty-second Street, talking. At Second Avenue they turned right, and turned right again on Fifty-third Street, and walked back to First Avenue. There they turned left, and again left on Fifty-fourth Street, and back to Second Avenue. They were talking all the time. They kept that up for a solid hour, walking back and forth on different streets, talking. I couldn't tell whether they were arguing or what. If they were, they never raised their voices enough for me to hear any words."

"You heard no words at all?"

"No, sir. If I had got close enough I would have been spotted."

"Were they friends? Lovers? Enemies? Did they embrace or shake hands?"

"No, sir. I don't think they liked each other, from their manner, and that's all I can say. They met at six-thirty-eight and parted at seven-forty-one, at the corner of Fifty-seventh Street and Second Avenue. The woman started downtown on Second Avenue. Naylor walked east on Fifty-seventh Street, stopped at a fruitstand around the corner on First Avenue and bought a bag of bananas, walked east to the Drive and sat on a bench, and ate nine bananas, one right after the other."

Wolfe shuddered. "Enough to kill a man."

"Yes, sir. He took his time at it, and then started walking again. He didn't hurry, not much more than a stroll, and at Fifty-fifth Street he started the crosstown promenade again, over to Second Avenue, back on Fifty-fourth to First Avenue, and west again on Fifty-third. By that time I was expecting him to keep it up until he hit the Battery, and maybe I got careless. Anyhow, it was on Fifty-third that he suddenly flagged a taxi and I lost him."

Saul shook his head. "And he was on his way to get killed. Goddam the luck."

Saul never swore.

Wolfe heaved a sigh. "Not your fault. Satisfactory. The woman?"

"Yes, sir. She was twenty-three or four, five-feet-five, hundred and eighteen pounds, wearing a light brown woolen coat over a tan woolen skirt or maybe dress, a dark brown hat with a white cloth flower, and brown pumps without open toes. Brown hair and I think brown eyes, but I'm not sure. Good figure and good posture and walks with a swing but not exaggerated. Hair soft and fine. Face more long than round, with oval chin. Features regular, nothing to fasten on, light complexion, attractive. Her back was to me nearly all the time, so that's as good as I can do with the face. What I could see of her legs curved down well to narrow ankles."

Wolfe turned to me. "Well, Archie?"

Anywhere else, with anyone else, I would have stalled to get a little time for consideration, and would have had no difficulty. But this was Nero Wolfe and Saul Panzer.

"Yeah," I said. "Her name is Hester Livsey."

"Good. Week-ending in Connecticut? Told the Westport police that she knows nothing of Mr. Naylor and her association with him was remote?"

"Yes, sir."

"Get Mr. Cramer—or Mr. Stebbins."

23.

It is a simple thing to make a swivel-chair swivel a half-turn and to pick up a phone, but sometimes the simple things are the hardest. I did not perform that maneuver. Instead, I wet my upper lip with my tongue, then my lower lip, and then got the tip of the tongue between my teeth and experimented to see how hard I had to bite to produce pain.

"Well?" Wolfe demanded. "What's the matter?"

I gave the tongue its freedom. "I am reminded," I said, "of the famous remark of Ferdinand Bowen up at Sing Sing when they told him to walk to the chair they had got ready for him. He muttered at them, 'The idea is repugnant to me.' Not that I regard the fix I'm in as identical, but I am strongly disinclined—"

"What's repugnant about it?"

"I like the way the sun shines through Miss Livsey's hair."

"Pfui. Phone Mr. Stebbins."

"Also, while it is true I pronounced her name, all I had was a description and I think it should be verified by having Saul look at her before we toss her into the fire."

"We're not engaged to catch the murderer of Mr. Naylor. I'm not going to pay transportation to Westport for Saul and you."

"You don't have to. He can see her Monday down at the office."

"It would be improper to withhold information—"

"Listen to you! Will you please listen to you?" My voice

was up without needing any instructions. "One of the main reasons you love to get information is so you can keep it from the cops, and you know it! You're just being pig-headed, and if you phone Stebbins yourself, which you won't because exercise is bad for you, I'll withdraw my identification. From Saul's description I would guess that it was the Duchess of Brimstone, who is in this country—"

"Archie." Wolfe was glaring. "Has that girl enravished you? Has she cajoled you into frenzy?"

"Yes, sir."

That took the edge off him instantly. He leaned back, nodded to himself, made a circle with his lips, and exhaled with a sort of hiss that was the closest he ever got to a whistle.

"Monday will do," he declared, as if no one but a fool could think otherwise. "I was impetuous." He looked at the clock on the wall, which said two minutes to four, time for his afternoon session with the orchids. He engineered himself out of his chair and was erect. "You can come here Monday morning, Saul, and go downtown with Archie. For the present —come up to the plant rooms with me. I have one or two suggestions for you."

They left, Saul for the stairs and Wolfe for his elevator. Their destination reminded me that I had got behind on the germination and blooming records, and I opened a desk drawer to get the accumulation of memos from Theodore.

24.

I had got behind on sleep too, and I caught up that night, Saturday. But not quite to the extent that Wolfe thought I did. Soon after he had gone up to the roof with Saul my mind had informed me that it was too restless to concentrate on germination records, at least of plants, and I had gone and got the car and driven to Twentieth Street to see what was stirring. Sergeant Purley Stebbins had not thought it necessary, just because for some hours I had enjoyed the important role of last man to see the victim alive, to open all the books for me, but I was allowed to hang around long enough to get an impression that nothing startling had developed. Of course a couple of them took a stab at trying to filter out of me the dope on how Wolfe had learned about Naylor taking a taxi on Fifty-third Street, but I had insisted that I had had nothing whatever to do with it, which was perfectly true. The taxi driver had not yet been collected, though the number of his cab had of course led them straight to where he should have been. He had gone to Connecticut to fish for shad, and a courier had been sent to get him, and I only hoped to God he wouldn't find him walking back and forth on a river bank with Hester Livsey.

It was because of her that Wolfe thought I got more sleep Saturday night than I really did. Saturday nights I usually take some person of an interesting sex to a hockey or basketball game, or maybe a fight at the Garden, but that one I worked in the office a while after dinner and then announced that I was sleepy. Taking some doughnuts, blackberry jam, and a pitcher of milk upstairs with me, I sat in the chair I had selected and paid for myself and went over matters. On account of Saul's description of her clothes, particularly the dark brown hat with a white cloth flower, I knew darned well it had been Hester Livsey he had seen with Naylor. I deny I was in a frenzy, but when a garl has patted a man's head he should be willing to go to a little trouble to see that she gets a break. Besides, it isn't often that at first sight, in the very first minute, a girl gives you the feeling that no one on earth but you knows how beautiful she is, and that too seemed to me to be worthy of consideration.

I thought she should have a chance to wipe off the smudge, in case it hadn't made a stain that wouldn't come out, and I well knew what the wiping process would be like if we turned her over to Cramer and his bozos. It could be that her walkie-talkie with Naylor had concerned a private matter not connected with what was about to happen to him, and if it had, and if she chose to keep it to herself, she was as likely a prospect as I had ever seen for an all-day and all-night conference with men, coming at her in shifts, who think nothing of taking their coats off in front of ladies. What I had come to my room to consider was whether to go get the car and drive to Westport and have some conversation with her. I decided against it finally, and undressed and went to bed, because if it turned out wrong in the end it would be Wolfe who would have to save the pieces, not me.

Next morning, Sunday, I was in the kitchen finishing breakfast, enjoying the last two swallows of my second cup of coffee and reading the paper, when the doorbell rang. Fritz went to answer it, and when, a moment later, I heard a female voice in the hall I tossed the paper down and went to see.

"A lady, Archie," Fritz told me.

"Yeah, that's what you always think. Hello there."

It was Rosa Bendini, Mrs. Harold Anthony, and she was good and scared if I know what emotions look like.

She came down the hall to me and practically demanded, "For God's sake put your arms around me!"

I didn't regard the request as offensive per se, but Fritz was there, on his way back to the kitchen, and in his Swiss-French way he can be a very tenacious kidder. So I tried to hold her off and spoke sharply, but she kept uttering sounds, possibly even words, and was determined to crawl inside of me. Fritz was staying as an impartial observer. She wasn't keeping her voice down, we were at the foot of the stairs, and Wolfe was in his room one flight up, eating his breakfast. I picked her up, carried her into the office, deposited her in the red leather chair, and told her roughly:

"You look like you just escaped from night court and the chase is hot. Is your husband out front?"

"My husband?" She slid forward to the edge of the chair. "Is he here?"

"I don't know, I was asking you, and stay in that chair. After you ran out on me the other night I knocked him flat and made him tame." I thought it might give her some perspective and steady her to refer to the past. "Have you seen him since?"

She didn't answer that. Apparently her husband was the least of her troubles. But she slid back again until enough of her fanny was on the chair so she could sit instead of squat, and said so the words could be heard:

"The police are after me!"

"I'll shoot the first six and then start throwing rocks. How far back are they?"

She bounced out of the chair and was on my lap before I could even brace myself, requesting me for the second time to put my arms around her, and it seemed less trouble to comply than to argue with her. I gathered her in and held her, and she encircled my neck, twisting her body around so as to make the contact more comprehensive. There have been occasions on which I have held a creature like that and as time passed she has begun to tremble, but this time it was the other way around. She was trembling at first, but gradually it tapered off, and after a while she was warm and quiet against me, with her face burrowing into the side of my neck, which I kept relaxed for her.

Finally she lifted the face an inch to murmur at my ear, "I was so scared I was going to jump off a pier. I always have been scared of the cops, ever since I can remember, I guess because they came and arrested my brother when I was a little kid." She kept close against me. "When I got home and the janitor and Isabel—she's the girl that lives across the hall—when they told me the police had been there three times and they might come back any minute—no, hold me tight, I don't mind if it's hard to breathe—I didn't even go in my room, I just scooted. I ran towards the subway, I don't know where I thought I was going, and after I got on an uptown express I remembered about Nero Wolfe, so I got off at Thirty-third Street and came here to see him. And you were here! How did that happen? Now you ought to kiss me."

I held her firm enough to keep her from changing position. "I never kiss people before noon except the one I had breakfast with. Then you just got home?"

"Yes. Then let's eat breakfast. Oh, I know how you happened to be here! That piece in the paper! Your name's Archie Goodwin and you're Nero Wolfe's brilliant lieutenant!"

"Right. Here you are in the house you didn't want to come to with me, and look at you. Where were you Friday night and Saturday and Saturday night?"

She bit me on the neck.

"Ouch," I said. "That's where your husband hit me before I got him. Where were you?"

She kissed where she had bit.

"Come on, girlie," I said realistically. "You're going to tell the cops or else, so you might as well practice on me."

That was a mistake. She actually started to tremble. I squeezed all the breath out of her to make her stop and told her with authority, "I go through cops like the wind through Wall Street, and it's quite possible I can arrange to be with you when they are. If so, I ought to know what the score is. Where were you?"

She was scared again, and I had to quiet her down and then drag it out of her. The way she told it, she had gone home early Friday evening to her room-and-bath in Greenwich Village, around nine o'clock, because the man who had taken her out to dinner had got a completely false idea of their program for the evening. She had been asleep for hours when the bell-ringing and door-knocking started, hadn't answered at first because she was too startled and had suspected it was her dinner host, and later, having crept to the door and heard the caller questioning the girl across the hall, had crawled back into bed and shivered, awake, until morning, afraid of cops. Between six and seven she had got up, dressed, packed a bag, sneaked out, taken the subway to Washington Heights, and gone to the apartment where her husband lived with his parents. The parents had advised her to let the police know where she was so they could come and ask their questions and have it over with, but they hadn't insisted on it, and it looked as if she had picked a good hole until late Saturday night, or Sunday morning rather, when the husband had got the notion of doing some insisting on a purely personal matter and had gone to her bedroom with that in mind. That situation had developed to a point where the whole household was up and around, and she would have been ordered out into a snowstorm if it had been snowing. She had dressed and packed her bag and got out, and after a spell of random subway riding had collected enough spunk to go to her own address for a reconnaissance. The news that it had indeed been the cops, and they had been there three times, had finished the spunk, and here she was.

It took a while to tell it. When she got to the end we were no longer glued together, but she was still perched on my lap.

I was irritated. "Damn it," I said, "you haven't got a thing for the very hours they're after, from ten to twelve Friday night. In bed alone, when you could easily have had a witness. Virtue never pays. Did your husband tell you he had been down to headquarters?"

"Yes, he told me all about it."

"Did he admit I lammed him?"

"Yes, I wish I had stayed."

"At present you have more important wishes to wish. You're in for it, girlie, but I'll see what I can do. What do you like for breakfast? Juice, oatmeal, eggs, ham—"

"I like everything except fish. But could I have a bath first? My bag's in the hall."

That meant that by the time she was through eating it would probably be eleven o'clock and Wolfe would be finished with the plants and downstairs, so when I took her up to the spare room, the south one on the same floor as mine, I first saw that towels and others luxuries were in place and then gave her the kiss to which I had morally committed myself, just to have that out of the way. This time the trembling came where it belonged. I returned to the office, got Wolfe on the house phone and told him about our guest, and then went to the kitchen and arranged with Fritz for her breakfast.

In spite of the companionship record Rosa and I were building up, and in spite of her dimples and her wholehearted way of making me feel at home, I had not adopted the idea that there was nothing much to her character but truth and innocence. It was not yet settled that our professional connection with the death of Moore was ended, and the death of Naylor certainly went with it; therefore I saw no reason why Wolfe shouldn't do a little work for a change and spend his two hours between plant time and lunch time on one of his thorough exploring jobs with Rosa as the jungle. I sold the idea, stated somewhat differently, to her as she ate breakfast.

It started off nicely, shortly after eleven, with Wolfe behind his desk in the office and Rosa in the red leather chair. She was wearing a very informal cherry-colored rayon something.

"That's a frightful combination," Wolfe growled. "That garment and that chair."

"Oh, I'm sorry!" She moved to a yellow one, the one Saul Panzer liked.

That put them on a basis of mutual understanding, and the prospect for an interesting conversation looked bright, but it didn't get very far. Wolfe had covered nothing but some preliminary details, such as precisely the kind of work an assistant chief filer does, when the doorbell rang. Formerly on occasions calling for discretion, as for instance a fugitive from justice sitting in the office, I had had to finger the curtain back enough to make a slit to see through, but recently we had had a one-way glass panel installed. I still had to persuade myself each time, looking through, that I could see him but he couldn't see me. Having done so, I returned to the office and told Wolfe:

"It's Mr. Cross. Do you want to see him?"

"No. Tell him I'm busy."

"He might have an orchid for you." I was displeased and allowed my voice to show it.

"Confound it." Wolfe compressed his lips. "Very well. If you don't mind, Miss Bendini? Please go up to your—to that room? This shouldn't take long."

She was up and out like a flash. Going to the hall, I waited until she had mounted the two flights and the door to the south room had been opened and closed. Meanwhile the bell had rung again.

I went and pulled the front door open and protested, "My God, you might give a man time to untwist his ankles."

Inspector Cramer, with Sergeant Purley Stebbins at his heels, wasn't even polite enough to give me a nod, after all the help I had been to him Friday night. They marched down the hall and into the office, with me in their rear.

"Good morning," Wolfe said curtly.

"God almighty," Cramer yawped, "so you're at it again!"

"Am I? At what?"

"This," Cramer yawped. "can take one minute or it can take hours! It's up to you which! What did Kerr Naylor come here for Friday night, what time did he leave, and where did he go?"

"That won't take even a minute, Mr. Cramer. Mr. Naylor wasn't here Friday night. I don't like your manner. I seldom do. Good day, sir."

"Are you saying—" For a moment Cramer was speechless. "Naylor didn't come to see you at twenty minutes to nine Friday, the night he was killed?"

"No, sir. That's twice, and that's enough. You may—"

"By God, you're crazy!" Cramer whirled. "He's off his nut, Stebbins!"

"Yes, sir."

"Bring that man in here."

Purley strode out. Cramer strode to the red leather chair and sat down. I kept my eye on Wolfe, not to miss a signal to take steps to keep Purley and that man, whoever he was, on the outside, but got none. Wolfe had evidently decided that the most exasperating thing he could do was look bored, and was doing so. The only sound was Cramer breathing, enough for all three of us, until footsteps came from the hall. A man entered with Purley behind him. The man was middle-aged and starting to go bald and had shoulders as broad as a barn. He was absolutely out of humor. Purley moved a chair up for him and he plumped himself down.

"This," Cramer said distinctly and impressively, "is Carl Darst. Friday evening he was hacking with Sealect cab number nine-forty-three, license number WX one-nine-seven-four-four-zero. Darst, who did you pick up on Fifty-third Street between First and Second Avenue?"

"The guy you showed me a picture of." Darst's voice was husky and not affable. "He yelled at me. I wish to God he hadn't. My one Sunday—"

"And the man whose body you saw at the morgue?"

"Yeah, I guess so. It was hard—sure, it was him."

"That was Kerr Naylor. So was the photograph I showed you. Where did you take him to?"

"He told me Nine-fourteen West Thirty-fifth Street and that's where I took him."

"That's this address where we are now?"

"Yes."

"What happened when you got here?"

"When he paid me he said he wasn't sure there would be anybody home, so would I wait till he found out, and I waited until he went up the steps and rang the bell, and the door opened and he started talking to someone, and then I shoved off. I didn't wait until he went inside because he didn't ask me to."

"But the door opened for him and he spoke with someone?"

"Yeah, I can say that much."

"All right, go out to the car and stay there. I may want you in here again. Do you want to ask him any questions, Wolfe?"

Wolfe, still bored, shook his head indifferently. Darst got up and left, but Sergeant Stebbins stayed put. Cramer waited until the sound of the front door closing behind Darst came to us and then spoke with the calm assurance of a man who has cards to spare.

"So I say you're crazy. This is completely cockeyed and if you can brush this one off I want to hear it. Try telling me that the fact that Naylor came and rang your bell and the door was opened doesn't prove that he came on in, and then I ask you please to tell me, in that case, how did you happen to know that he got in a cab on Fifty-third Street at half-past eight? Wait a minute, I'm not through. That sounds like good reasoning, don't it? But if it is, why in the name of God did you phone my office to tell about his taking a taxi, and even give us the number of the cab? Knowing it would be pie to find it. I say you're crazy. Usually when you're staging a runaround at least I have a general idea which direction you're going, but this time you'll have to spell it out. I would love to hear you."

"Pfui," Wolfe muttered.

"Okay, phooey. Go on from there."

"Archie," Wolfe asked me casually, "you went to a movie Friday evening?"

"Yes, sir."

"What time did you leave here?"

"Right around eight-thirty."

"Then you couldn't have opened the door for Mr. Naylor." Wolfe pushed a button on his desk, and in a moment the door to the hall opened and Fritz appeared.

Wolfe addressed him, "Fritz, do you remember that Friday evening after dinner Archie went out? To the movies?"

"Yes, sir."

"And that somewhat later, around a quarter to eleven I think, Mr. Cramer called?"

"Yes, sir."

"That should identify the evening sufficiently. Did the doorbell ring soon after Archie left?"

"Yes, sir."

"You answered it?"

"Yes, sir."

"Who was it?"

"He didn't tell me his name. It was a man."

"What did he want?"

"He asked for Mr. Goodwin."

"Go on, finish it."

"I told him Mr. Goodwin was out. He asked if Mr. Wolfe was in and I told him yes. After thinking to himself a brief period he asked when Mr. Goodwin would be back and I said probably some time after eleven. I asked him if he wished to leave his name and he said no. He had turned and was going down the steps when I closed the door."

Cramer made a sound which Wolfe ignored. "What time was this?"

"It was eight-forty-five when I got back to the kitchen. I made a note, as always—God in heaven!"

"What's the matter?"

"I forgot to tell Archie about it! When he returned Inspector Cramer was here, and then he was gone all night and slept late Saturday—this is extremely bad, sir—"

"Not at all. It wouldn't have mattered. Did you tell me about it?"

"No, sir. You were reading those three books, and he hadn't left his name—"

"Describe the man."

"He was short, shorter than me, and he wore a coat and hat. He had a small face and looked pinched and worried, as if he wasn't a good eater."

"All right, Fritz, that's all, thank you." Fritz went, closing the door to the hall behind him. Wolfe turned to Cramer. "Well, sir?"

Cramer shook his head. "No," he said emphatically. "Even with Fritz coached like that I still say you're crazy. How did you know about Naylor taking a cab and why did you phone—"

Wolfe cut him off. "Don't start shouting at me again. You'll never learn, I suppose, how to detect when I'm lying and when I'm not. Saturday afternoon a man came to this office and told me he had seen Mr. Naylor taking that taxicab. I questioned him and was satisfied that the facts he gave me were authentic, and I immediately phoned your office and gave those facts to Mr. Stebbins. What the devil is obreptitious about that?"

"Who was the man that came to your office?"

"No, sir. You don't need that."

"Excuse me, Inspector," Purley Stebbins put in.

Cramer glared at him. "What is it?"

"Why, if we want any part of this that item won't worry us. If we buy this it wasn't Goodwin, so it was one of the boys that do jobs for Wolfe—Gore, Cather, Durkin, Panzer, or Keems. It stands to reason he was tailing Naylor. So either you can bear down on that, or if he's too damn stubborn we can send out and collect 'em—"

The phone rang. I whirled my chair and got it. It was Saul Panzer, desiring, he said, to speak to Wolfe.

"Sure," I said, in a tone you would use to a client you expected to send a nice bill too, "he's right here, Mr. Platt. By the way, while I'm on the wire, that big downtown law firm that says all it wants is justice, not to mention names, you know, they're going to try to serve a summons on you and it would be good policy for you to duck it, anyhow for a day or two. There are lots of places you can go besides home. Don't you agree?"

"Nothing simpler," Saul said, "if I understand you. Who's there, Cramer?"

"Yes, I suppose they're going to be quite insistent about it. Here's Mr. Wolfe."

Wolfe got on. He followed me on the Mr. Platt. Since he signaled me to hang up, meaning that his arrangements with Saul were still none of my business, I got as little out of the conversation as Cramer and Purley did, which was nothing at all. Wolfe's end was mostly grunts. Purley sneezed. The three of us sat and waited for him, looking at him, until an event occurred which caused us to move our eyes elsewhere.

The door to the hall came open and Rosa Bendini was there among us.

It was a fairly embarrassing situation, with Wolfe still busy on the phone and the two public servants and me sitting staring at her as she stood just inside the door in that cherry-colored thing which, whatever its name might be, was certainly not intended for street wear. I thought of saying something like, "Mabel dear, we're discussing business with these

109

gentlemen so go back to your room and wait for me," or something like, "We're engaged at present, Miss Carmichael, but we'll see you shortly," but the first seemed indecent and the second illogical, and no satisfactory substitute got to my tongue in time.

Wolfe, finished, dropped the phone back in its cradle and snapped at her, "What do you mean, coming in here dressed like that? Go back upstairs until I'm ready for you!"

His effort, it seemed to me, was no improvement on the ones I had rejected. But no effort would have been good enough. She hadn't merely blundered in. She came forward, on past Cramer and Purley, clear to me. She might easily have had it in mind to resume her former seat on my lap, so by the time she reached me I was standing up.

"You promised you'd be with me when they are," she said. That was not strictly true, but close enough for a woman, especially for one who was scared to death of cops. "There's a police car out in front, so I came to the hall and listened, and that's who they are, and I knew I'd never get a better chance, with you here and Mr. Wolfe too."

She turned and told Cramer and Purley right to their faces, "My name is Rosa Bendini, or it's Mrs. Harold Anthony, either one will do, and I live at Four-eighteen Bank Street, second floor, and when a cop came for me Friday night I was there in bed all the time. Now what do you want to ask me?"

One thing I approved of, she didn't hook onto my arm or try to climb into my pocket. She just wanted to say it with me there.

"This," Cramer declared in as gloaty a tone as I had ever heard from him, "is really rich. How long have you had her hid here, Wolfe? Wasn't there time enough to train her?"

"Mr. Cramer, you're an imbecile," Wolfe told him for his information.

I broke in, thinking the best thing now was to mess it up good. "I bolixed it up," I said regretfully. "Like a damn fool, I told her to bust in when I sneezed, and then Purley sneezed." I glared at Purley. "How the hell could I know you had a cold?"

"Okay." Cramer rose, still gloating. "I suppose you have some things here, Miss Bendini? Some clothes?"

"Yes, but I—"

"You have three minutes to change, unless you want to travel around like that. Go and change."

"No," Wolfe said. His forefinger was tapping on the desk, which meant he was ready to pick up tigers and knock their heads together. "Stay here, Miss Bendini." His eyes darted to Cramer. "Have you a warrant? Or are you charging her?"

"Nuts. Murder. Material witness."

"Witness to what?"

"I'll tell her, not you."

"Bah. Miss Bendini, I advise you not to leave here unless you are taken by force. Make them carry you."

I intervened for several reasons. First, Wolfe was not following a program but was simply so mad he couldn't see. Second, Rosa had gone so white and rigid that I doubted if she could walk, especially accompanied by a cop, and I didn't regard it as desirable to let her be carried out of our house in the costume she had on. Third, while I hadn't promised her, I had unquestionably given her an inducement.

"Look," I said to Cramer, "why all the war paint? If you do carry her out, and if she proves to be no more material than I am, with Mr. Wolfe as sore as he is you'll get blisters. If you don't like conversing with her here I'll make an offer, take it or leave it. She changes her clothes, and Purley and I drive her downtown in Mr. Wolfe's car, and I am present, not too talkative, during your talk with her. I'll stay as long as she does. When the time comes, unless you are prepared to charge her, she leaves with me. What the hell, I was with you all Friday night, wasn't I? Well?"

"You might," Wolfe said testily, "ask my permission, Archie."

"This is Sunday." I told Cramer, "It's no deal unless you say yes out loud so everybody can hear you. I would prefer to see you carry her and let Mr. Wolfe see what the law can do, but Miss Bendini is like a sister to me. Yes?"

"Yes," Cramer snarled.

I was thinking, as I went for the car, that one of the leading roles had bounced back to us again—the last to see Naylor alive. For a while it had been me. Then Saul Panzer, who had passed it on to the taxi driver. Now it was once more back in the family, with Fritz ticketed for it. Who next?

25.

I missed Sunday dinner but not supper.

It was no wonder that under the circumstances Cramer thought he had hooked a real fish and had also made a monkey out of Wolfe. But after half an hour with Rosa and me in his office, beginning to suspect that he had merely got caught on a snag, he left us to Lieutenant Rowcliff and beat it for Centre Street. Rowcliff didn't care much for the assignment, since his opinion of me is a perfect match for mine of him. He shot questions at Rosa for an hour or so in his correspondence-school grammar, meanwhile trying to keep me from contributing any kind of sound, let alone a word, and halted only when he was interrupted by the return of a squad man who had been sent to Washington Heights to check with the in-laws.

Not only had father-in-law and mother-in-law verified Rosa's story, but husband-in-law came back with the squad man to try to raise some hell. He wasn't going to let his wife be abused and would see to it personally that she wasn't. Knowing what had led up to his wife's departure from his parental apartment in the Sunday dawn, I regarded him with awe. I had noticed on the Naylor-Kerr stationery that the motto of the firm was ANYTHING IN THE WORLD, ANYWHERE IN THE WORLD. It struck me that the motto of the male personnel of the stock department appeared to be PROTECT THE WOMAN. Or if they wanted it to have eight words like the firm's it could be PROTECT YOUR WOMAN NO MATTER WHOSE SHE IS.

That left Rowcliff with nothing to discuss with Rosa except the time she had spent in bed Friday night, especially the hours from ten to twelve, which gave him limited space to turn around in. He sent a man down to Bank Street to see the janitor and the other tenants, but all they could say was that they hadn't happened to see Miss Bendini come home Friday evening. Finally, around seven o'clock, he adjourned sine die, and I drove Rosa, with her luggage, to her home address, having phoned Wolfe and been told that there was no reason to suppose she had saved anything for him. The husband went with us and then came with me, and I let him out at a subway station. Knowing by now that his wife's relations with me were purely on a business basis, he even wanted to buy me a drink.

I spent Sunday evening in the office with my typewriter. Wolfe was there too, but sight was the only one of my five senses that knew about it. When Saul Panzer phoned to make another classified report to Wolfe I arranged for him to meet me downtown in the morning instead of coming to Wolfe's place. The authorities, looking for him, had phoned his home a few times, and he was going to spend the night at a friend's apartment. It was just possible that they were eager enough about it to keep an eye on our address, and I still thought it would be polite to give Hester Livsey a chance to do some explaining in a congenial atmosphere.

I fully expected Saul's check on her to be nothing more than a formality, and so it was. Monday morning I met him and took him with me to the lobby of the building on William Street, and chose a strategic point for overlooking the arriving throng and the stampede for the elevators. I recognized a few of the faces as the feet trotted, walked, marched, and click-clicked on the way to another week's paycheck. At two minutes to nine I was thinking we had missed her and would have to proceed upstairs, where it would be more awkward and would require arranging, when Saul suddenly pinched me and muttered at me:

"To the right, thirty feet, turning now, same hat and coat, behind the tall man with glasses, going on the elevator—"

"Okay," I said as she was swallowed up in the elevator and its door started to close. "How many coats do you think she has? She's an honest working girl."

"It's none of my business," Saul said.

"Meaning, not her honesty, but her name. Yes, you have heard the name. If you happen to be phoning Wolfe and he happens to ask, you can tell him yes, and also tell him I'll bring her to see him but I don't know when. I have to find out whether I'm still working here or not. There's to be a directors' meeting—you're not listening."

"I'm looking. Do you know that man"—his eyes were pointing—"gray coat and hat, big and broad, fleshy face, now his back is to us—he's stepping on the elevator—"

"Yeah, I know him. Why?"

"I've seen him."

"I wouldn't doubt it." The combination of Saul's eyes and the filing equipment in his skull is the equal of any card system yet invented. "You probably saw him August seventeenth, nineteen hundred and thirty-eight, crossing Madison Avenue against a light—"

"No. I saw him Friday, twice. When Naylor met the woman at First Avenue and Fifty-second Street that man was standing across the street in a doorway looking at them. An hour later, when they parted at Second Avenue and Fifty-seventh Street, he was standing forty feet away, again in a doorway, and when the woman walked downtown on Second Avenue he started after her. That's all I saw because Naylor was on his way and I was tailing him."

"Is this certified?"

"For me it is."

"Then me too. In case this head-flattener is going on with his career and picks me next, the man's name is Sumner Hoff. He works for Naylor-Kerr and his office is in the stock department. File it."

"I will. Is that all here?"

I said it was, and Saul went.

I took an elevator to the thirty-fourth floor, not knowing what to expect. It was quite possible that a delegation of executives would be waiting for me, to tell me to get the hell out and stay out. But nobody at all was waiting for me. It is true that when I got to the arena, skirted it, and started down the long aisle, I was on the receiving end of plenty of assorted glances, but that was only more of the same as last week. I left my coat and hat in my room, emerged immediately, crossed to the other side of the arena, opened the door of Hester Livsey's room, entered, and shut the door behind me.

"What do you want?" she demanded.

She had straightened up from dusting off her desk. She looked nervous, unhappy, and annoyed. Fritz would have said that she did not have the appearance of a good eater. I did not entirely lose the impression that she was in some kind of trouble that no one but me could understand and no one but me could help her out of, but the most vulgar eye could have seen at a glance that she was in trouble. That much of it I would have to share.

"My name," I said, "is Archie Goodwin and I work for Nero Wolfe."

"I know that. What do you want?"

Evidently everybody in the stock department knew everything. "I'm afraid," I told her, "that I can't make my answer quite as direct and to the point as your question. I can tell you what I want, but I'll have to leave it more or less blank why I want it. I want to date you up—to meet me at five o'clock this afternoon and go to Nero Wolfe's office with me. He wants to have a talk with you—"

"What about?"

"You're so damn gruff," I complained. "I can't tell you what about except that it's connected with the murder of Kerr Naylor, and you could guess that with both eyes shut. Let me try it that way first, just ask you, will you do it?"

"Certainly not. Why should I?"

"In that case that comes next, why you should. I would have liked it much better without that, but I can't have everything. Mr. Wolfe has learned a certain fact which has to do with you and Kerr Naylor, and he wants to ask you about it. The nature of the fact is such—"

"What is it?"

I shook my head. "Its nature is such that if you don't go and let him ask you about it he will be obliged to give the fact to the police and then there will be no question of letting. You won't go, you'll be taken, and the asking atmosphere will be different."

"My God," she said in a tone with no expression at all, as if she were too stunned to feel anything.

It irritated me. "It's a good thing for you I'm not a policeman," I declared. "You'd better think up a better entrance than that for them if it goes that far. Your chin's sagging."

She came to me, abruptly and swiftly, put her hands on me, her open palms flat against my chest so I had to brace myself, raised her face to me, and half commanded, half implored, "What—is—the—fact?"

She nearly got the desired result at that. But I stopped it before it reached my tongue and shook my head firmly. "Nope. You'll get it from Mr. Wolfe."

"You won't tell me?"

"No."

"There isn't any. I don't believe it. There isn't any fact."

"The hell there isn't." I was disgusted with her for not doing better. "You're just like glass to look through. You have just told me that there's not one fact, but two and maybe more, and you've got to know which one Wolfe has."

She had certainly uncovered herself, but she was not floored, and she now showed that she could grab a nettle. She went to the rack in the corner and got her coat and stuck an arm in it.

"I'll go now," she said.

"You can't." I went to relieve her of the coat. "The one appointment Mr. Wolfe wouldn't break is the one with the orchids from nine to eleven in the morning." I glanced at my wrist. "We can leave in an hour and a quarter. I'll meet you in the lobby at a quarter to eleven."

But she knew what she wanted. "I'm not going to just sit here," she said, "and if I tried to take dictation—I couldn't. We can go now and wait for him. Wait here a minute while I tell Mr. Rosenbaum."

Having her coat, I hung it up, and explained that anyway I had an errand in the building that had to be attended to before I could leave. She gave in, but only because she couldn't

115

help it. I got out of there, not being absolutely sure how I would react if she snapped out of it and started to work on me in earnest. She agreed to meet me in the lobby at 10:45, and I returned to my room, picked up the phone, and called Wolfe and told him to expect us at eleven. I also told him of Saul's recognition of Sumner Hoff. Then I got the Naylor-Kerr switchboard and gave the extension number of the office of the president.

I had to fight for him that time. He was in an important meeting and couldn't be disturbed, but I finally persuaded his secretary that no meeting was more important than me that morning and was told to hold the wire. It was a long hold. After five minutes I wondered who was kissing her now, and after three more I suspected I had been left to starve. I had my finger poised ready to start jiggling when the secretary's voice came.

"Mr. Goodwin."

"Still here and still hoping."

"Please come up to the Board Room on the thirty-sixth floor. You will be admitted."

Her tone implied that that was a break in a thousand, so I thanked her warmly.

On the thirty-sixth floor the executive receptionist told me where the Board Room was, and when I reached it an executive sentinel, outside the door, made sure my name was mine and then opened for me. I walked in looking dignified.

It was up to snuff. The room was big, high-ceilinged, well lighted, and impressive to a rank-and-filer like me, who had only been on the payroll three-fifths of a week. An enormous rug nearly covered the floor. The table, of bleached walnut, was about the size of my bedroom though not the same shape. All around it were roomy armchairs, upholstered in brown leather, twenty or more, with all but four or five of them occupied. There were two chairs at each end of the table and the others were along the sides.

In one of the chairs at the far end sat Jasper Pine. In the other one was a man of whose bulk there was so little left that most of the chair was being wasted. Age had certainly withered him. At the first glance I recognized him, from a portrait of him on the wall of the president's office, as old George Naylor, one of the founders of the firm and the father of Mrs. Jasper Pine, Cecily to me, and of Kerr Naylor, deceased.

Pine said, not getting up, "Gentlemen, this is Mr. Archie Goodwin. Goodwin, this is a joint meeting of the Board of Directors and some of the executive staff. It is a special meeting, called to consider the matter of the death of Mr. Kerr Naylor. We have discussed it at some length in all its aspects. The suggestion has been made that we instruct Nero Wolfe, your employer, to continue the investigation and extend it to include Mr. Naylor's death. Some of those present think that before deciding that point we should—"

He stopped because old George Naylor uttered an emphatic word. It was a word often heard among engineers doing field work, truck drivers, and detectives when working under strain, but I wouldn't have expected it to be used at a directors' meeting.

The founder added to it, "It's already decided! Certainly Wolfe continues!" It wasn't from him, I noted, that his son had got a tenor voice. His was baritone and still had volume and force, though his age was in it too.

There were murmurs. Pine told him with courteous deference but with not quite all the impatience filtered out, "It was agreed, I thought, Mr. Naylor, that we should hear from Goodwin first. Goodwin, tell us what you have done since you came here last Wednesday."

Nothing was said about sitting down, in spite of five empty chairs, so, seeing that one there at my end was vacant, I got into it and adjusted myself comfortably.

"Do you want the high spots," I asked, "or all the trimmings?"

Pine said to go ahead and they would stop me if it was too detailed. I did so. I gave them what I thought should be enough to satisfy, but nothing to compare with one of my all-out performances with Wolfe, and skipping a few items entirely, as for instance my first encounter with Gwynne Ferris when she put on her non-spelling act. They interrupted me whenever they felt like it, to ask questions or make critical comments, and when I got to the scene at the door of Sumner Hoff's office, where Kerr Naylor told me he knew who killed Waldo Moore, they came at me in pairs and threes. Evidently there were two schools of thought and maybe more.

One bird told me to my teeth, "I knew Kerr Naylor twenty years, Goodwin, and I never knew him to tell a lie. I don't know you at all!"

That specimen had been riding me from the start and I was developing an attitude toward him. His age was about halfway between mine and the founders, he was by far the best-dressed man in the room, he had a wide mouth with full lips, and he loved to interrupt people. I had a retort on its way to the tongue, but old George Naylor got in ahead.

"Nonsense! Kerr was an inveterate liar from the time he was a baby!"

That didn't set the best-dressed man back any. "Of course," he told me, "Kerr Naylor is dead. But you're not!" His tone implied that that was regrettable.

"I keep a list," I said, "of the people who call me a liar. What's your name?"

He smiled at me condescendingly with his wide mouth.

"You're too old to hit," I conceded, standing up. "But I know a trick that's supposed to make dumb animals talk, and it would be fun to try—"

"His name's Ferguson," a wiry little guy with a mustache tossed in. He had a dry look and a dry voice and was as crisp as Melba toast. "Sit down, Goodwin. Emmet Ferguson. He's a lawyer and owns most of a bank and has been trying for ten years to have Kerr Naylor made president of this company. The last time the vote went against him nine to five, and—"

"Is this proper?" an indignant voice demanded. "With an outsider—"

"If you had made Kerr president," old George Naylor declared, "I would have come down here and kicked him out myself! He was my son, but he couldn't have run this business!"

"He wanted to bad enough," the wiry little guy muttered.

I had sunk back into my chair and was trying to convey the impression that I wasn't present, hoping they would go on with the family quarrel, which seemed interesting. They did, long enough for me to infer that the reason Kerr Naylor had refused to be an officer of the company was because he was holding out for top billing, namely president. Apparently the Board, which of course had the say formally, had been a solid two to one for Pine, but at that Kerr Naylor had had five votes. I wondered which side Cecily had been on and how much weight old George Naylor had been able to pull. About all I got was the general idea, for Pine, presiding, stopped it before long and told me to proceed.

With the question of who was a liar, Kerr Naylor or me, out of the way, or anyhow tabled, I was permitted to continue without many interruptions. I covered the ground adequately, right up to the end, but still omitting details which I thought they could get along without, such as the recent developments concerning Hester Livsey. When I was through they asked questions, with the best-dressed man furnishing more than his share, until Pine put in:

"We've been at this over two hours, gentlemen, and it's

time we reached some decisions. The first question is what to do about Nero Wolfe. Goodwin, if we instruct Wolfe to continue this investigation, and extend it to include the death of Mr. Naylor, what could he do?"

Half of them started to talk. Pine tapped with his gavel and asserted the authority of the chair:

"Let Goodwin tell us."

I looked around at them, giving an extra half a second to Emmet Ferguson. "Mr. Wolfe could catch the murderer," I stated, "if that's what you want. He—"

"Why not the police?" Ferguson asked offensively. "That's their job."

"I am not," I told the table, "going to argue with Babble-mouth Ferguson. Shall I go on?"

The wiry little guy threw back his head and laughed. Someone said, "Shut up, Emmet, or we'll be here all day."

"It all depends," I said. "If you think something about it is hotter than you like it, call Mr. Wolfe off immediately. If you would just as soon have the murderer caught but don't really give a damn, let the cops do it, you would be wasting your money on Mr. Wolfe and he comes high. If you feel that you owe it to yourselves or to anyone else to make sure that the job isn't muffed, and if you suspect that it may require something more than good standard detective work, you need Mr. Wolfe no matter what it costs. As to—"

"You weren't asked for a sales talk," Ferguson sneered. "You were asked—"

I merely lifted my voice. "As to what Mr. Wolfe could do, I don't know. Nobody ever knows what Mr. Wolfe can do on a case until after he has done it. I could tell you what he has done, but it would take a week, and anyhow most of you have probably already heard some of it."

"I move," the wiry little guy said, "that we authorize the president to engage Nero Wolfe—"

The gavel sounded. "Wait a minute." Pine addressed me, "Goodwin, will you step out to the reception room and wait there?"

I glanced at my wrist. "I'm late for an appointment."

"We all are," someone growled.

Pine said it wouldn't take long, and I left.

Judging from the customers distributed around on the chairs in the reception room, some of them looking as if they were running short on patience, the appointments were piling up. One of them I recognized, an Assistant District Attorney, and I wondered which one of the gang in the Board Room he was waiting for. I fully expected to be kept there on my fundament for half an hour or more, and was debating whether to drop down to the lobby and tell Hester Livsey I was held up, when the executive sentinel arrived with word that I was wanted. Evidently they had agreed with Pine that it was time to can the talk and make some decisions. Unless what they had decided was to ask me more questions.

But no, they had executed. As I approached the table Pine spoke to me.

"Goodwin, we wish to instruct Nero Wolfe to extend his investigation to include the death of Mr. Kerr Naylor. Do you need a letter?"

"No, not with all these witnesses. Then it's a straight murder job, and you might as well take me off the company payroll, with the understanding that I can come and go in the stock department. I assume we get co-operation?"

"Certainly."

"Okay. Mr. Ferguson, Mr. Wolfe will be expecting you at his office at six o'clock today."

The best-dressed man goggled at me and his mouth came open. He was speechless. The wiry little guy threw his head back and laughed.

"What for?" Pine asked.

"Skip it," I said graciously. "Mr. Wolfe can get in touch with him. How did the vote go?"

"The vote?"

"On hiring Mr. Wolfe."

"That's an improper question, Goodwin, and you know it. I've told—"

"Excuse me, Mr. Pine, it's far from improper." I sent my eyes around the table. "In a murder investigation, gentlemen, nothing is improper, and that's the hell of it for everybody concerned. I told you that I don't know what Mr. Wolfe will do, but I know what he'll ask me, and one of his first questions will be who voted not to hire him. If you had let me stay in the room—"

"The vote," the wiry little guy said, "was eleven to four. Those voting no were Ferguson, Wyatt, Volk, and Thomas. The chair of course did not vote, but his remarks indicated that he was for it. My name is Armstrong."

"Much obliged. Now I'll keep that appointment."

26

At the far side of the executive reception room were a couple of phone booths, and I dived into one of them on my way through and dialed a number. Ordinarily when I'm not there Fritz answers, but that time it was Wolfe himself.

"Where the devil are you?" he demanded. "It's eight minutes past eleven!"

I didn't resent it because I knew he wasn't being critical. He regards going from one place to another place in New York City as being one of the most hazardous feats a man can undertake, and he was worried about me.

"I have," I declared importantly, "just left a directors' meeting. You were hired to investigate Naylor's death by a vote of eleven to four, and I would greatly appreciate it as a personal favor if you will manage to frame a heel named Emmet Ferguson for it. When you see him you'll agree with me. I'll be there with Miss Livsey in fifteen minutes."

Late as I was, I had no fear that Hester would have got tired waiting for me. She wanted that fact. And I was right. She was standing, looking uneasy, patient, and beautiful, by the mailbox on the William Street side of the lobby. But as I approached she turned her head to say something to a man there at her elbow, and I was thrown off my stride for an instant as I recognized the man. It was Sumner Hoff, with his hat and coat on.

I stopped in front of them and spoke to her. "I'm sorry to be so late, but I was detained upstairs. This way's best for a taxi—"

"You know Mr. Hoff," she said. "He's going with us."

I had expected that on account of his hat and coat. I looked down my nose at him. "Come ahead. If Mr. Wolfe decides you're not welcome I'll know how to handle it since you showed me last week."

"I'll do the handling," he snapped.

"Well, don't be rough with me," I said plaintively.

When we found a taxi, which was easy at that time of day, he helped Hester in and then followed her, planting himself in the middle and leaving me the near corner, so he would be between us. That's the right idea, brother, I thought, don't forget the good old stock department motto, protect your woman. It was gratifying to see that although he was a civil engineer and therefore an aristocrat he didn't set himself up above the others but stuck to the code. Frankly, considering his imminent double chin, it seemed to me that Hester was running low on knights, but it was quite possible he had some good points I hadn't noticed.

At our destination he kept it plain that he was doing the handling—out of the taxi, up the stoop, through the door, and down the hall to the office. I hoped he wouldn't mind that I took the initiative to do the introducing.

"You may remember," I told Wolfe, "that last Thursday a person named Sumner Hoff, when I entered his office in a friendly manner, told me to get out and called me a goddam snoop. This is him. It might be thought he came to apologize, but no. He came along, he says, to do the handling."

"Indeed." Wolfe reached to pour beer. "Sit down, Miss Livsey. Sit down, Mr. Hoff. Will you have some beer?"

They accepted the chairs but not the beer. Wolfe, who thinks foam is fine for the upper lip, was drinking, so I filled in, as I lowered myself into my chair.

"I might add that if you prefer to speak with Miss Livsey privately I would have no objection to performing an engineering operation on Hoff and removing him."

"No, thank you." Wolfe put his glass down, wiped his mouth with his handkerchief, and leaned back. "Perhaps later." He looked at Hoff and told him, "Handle it."

"I will," Hoff said aggressively, "when I know what it is."

"Ah. You must have extraordinary resources, to be prepared for all conceivable phenomena. I have been engaged by the firm you work for to investigate the death of Mr. Naylor. I tell you that so you'll know what I'm doing." Wolfe's eyes went to Hester. "Miss Livsey, I believe you told a policeman at Westport that you knew nothing about Mr. Naylor and that your association with him was restricted to your role as an obscure employee in his department. Is that correct?"

"Don't answer him," Hoff snapped, starting to handle it.

"Certainly I'll answer," Hester said. She was in the red leather chair, facing the window. "I'll answer that. Those weren't my words, but it amounted to that, yes. Mr. Goodwin told me that you had learned a certain fact about Mr. Naylor and me, and that if I came here you would tell me what it was. What—"

"There is no such fact," Hoff snapped, "and we want to know what you're talking about!"

Wolfe pointed a finger. "That door," he said, "leads to

what we call the front room. The wall and door are sound-proofed. I suppose, Mr. Hoff, you'd better go in there."

"Oh, no. I'm staying here."

Protect your woman.

"Nonsense. Even if you weren't flabby Mr. Goodwin could put you anywhere I told him to. Archie. If Mr. Hoff interrupts again remove him, I don't care where."

"Yes, sir."

"Without ceremony."

"Yes, sir."

"You keep still, Sumner," Hester admonished him. "All I want is what Mr. Goodwin asked me to come for," she told Wolfe. "There can't be any fact about Mr. Naylor and me. What is it?"

"When was the last time you saw Mr. Naylor, Miss Livsey?"

"Don't ans—" Hoff began. I had started for him before he finished the first syllable. He didn't bite it off, the words just stopped coming, and I saw to my regret that I would never have the pleasure of plugging him. He wasn't up to it. There might be occasion for shoving him or bundling him, but he would never rate a real sock. I sat down again.

Anyhow, Hester didn't obey. "I don't know," she said. "I suppose I saw him at the office some time Friday, but I didn't notice and I don't remember."

Wolfe shook his head. "Not at the office. At six-thirty-eight Friday afternoon you met him at the corner of First Avenue and Fifty-second Street, walked back and forth with him over an hour, and parted from him at seven-forty-one at Second Avenue and Fifty-seventh Street. What were you talking about?"

Hester was wide-eyed. "That isn't so," she asserted in a loud voice, unnecessarily loud.

"No? What did I get wrong?"

"All of it's wrong. It isn't so."

"You didn't see Mr. Naylor after office hours on Friday?"

"No. I didn't."

So far so good. Obviously her talk with Naylor had been about something she didn't want to broadcast, and naturally she would deny it as long as that seemed feasible. I had not yet reported to Wolfe on her awful fumble that morning in her office, and I saw no need for it now, since he had the high card and all he had to do was play it.

"It's no good, Miss Livsey," Wolfe said. "Abandon it. I have a witness."

"You can't have," she declared. "You can't have a witness to my being with Mr. Naylor where you said, because I couldn't have been there, because I was somewhere else. Friday afternoon I left the office at five o'clock and went to Grand Central Station and went to the soda fountain on the lower level and had a sundae. I had intended to catch a train to Westport, but at the office that day Mr. Hoff had said he wanted to talk with me about something and we had made an appointment. We met there at the soda fountain at six o'clock. We talked there a while and then went upstairs to the waiting-room and talked some more. He persuaded me to go to the theater with him and take a later train to Westport. By that time it was too late to eat in a restaurant and make it to the theater, so we ate in that big cafeteria near the station on Forty-second Street. Then we had bad luck and couldn't get seats for the show we wanted to see and we went to a movie instead—*The Best Years of Our Lives*. Then I caught the eleven-fifty-six to Westport. Then the next day, Saturday, Mr. Hoff—he knew where I was—he came to Westport and said it was my duty to co-operate with the authorities, so I came to New York and went to the District Attorney's office and told them what I have told you and answered their questions. So when you say you have a witness—well, I'd like to know who the witness is."

I was thinking to myself savagely, you will, my beautiful little liar, you'll know all right. But I only felt it; I didn't look it. I kept my face deadpan.

Wolfe didn't. He looked concerned and apologetic. "It seems," he said, "that you had facts for me, not me for you. I do have a witness, Miss Livsey, but manifestly a mistaken one. Of course you certify all this, Mr. Hoff?"

"I do," Hoff said emphatically.

"Then that settles it. I owe you an apology, Miss Livsey, which is a rare debt for me to incur. As for my witness—I wonder if you'll do me a favor. Will you send me a photograph of yourself—a good one, as recent as possible?"

"Why—" Hester hesitated.

"Certainly," Hoff agreed for her. "I don't know what for, but certainly she will."

"Good. I'll appreciate it. Today, if possible, by messenger collect. The witness may have an idea of going to the police, and there's no use getting them more confused than they are already." Wolfe was out of his chair. "Good day, Miss Livsey. Good day, Mr. Hoff. Thank you for coming."

I went to the hall with them. At the door Hester told

me, offering a hand, "I'm sorry if I was impolite this morning, Mr. Goodwin. I guess I was upset."

"Don't mention it," I told her eyes. "You were nervous. Everybody in the neighborhood of a murder gets nervous, sometimes even the murderer himself."

I returned to the office, resumed my chair, and sat and glared at Wolfe as he opened a fresh bottle, poured, waited until the foam was exactly a quarter of an inch below the rim of the glass, and drank. He put the glass down empty and used his tongue on his upper lip first and then his handkerchief. When company was present he omitted the tongue part.

"Superficially neat," he muttered at me, "but they're a pair of idiots."

"Enravished," I said, "is no word for it. I'm absolutely nuts about her. Did you notice that she even named the movie they went to? She left out the kind of sundae she had. That was an oversight. One thing you didn't know about, but I doubt it would have mattered, all I told her was that you had a fact you wanted to ask her about, and she was so anxious to know which fact that she nearly lost her pants. There was a time when the mere thought of her pants would have made my heart beat. Anyhow, our fact isn't the only one, I'll guarantee that. What do we do now, feed her to the animals?"

"No." Wolfe was grim. "I doubt if Mr. Cramer could shake them. Even if he could, she sat there and told me that preposterous lie and I will not tolerate it. What about Saul? Did he look twice?"

"No. Not a chance. He spotted her himself and said yes, and with Saul you know how good that is. Even if she has a twin, it was her. Also, as I told you, he spotted Sumner Hoff." I snorted. "Protect your woman."

"What?"

"Nothing. It's a motto. The corny performance we have just witnessed has got me voting for the stock department again. When I left the directors' meeting I was voting for the thirty-sixth floor, murder on the highest executive level, but not now. What I would really like is to combine the two. I hate to leave Emmet Ferguson out of it."

"Tell me about the directors' meeting."

I did so, and hoped he was listening. That was open to question because he kept his eyes open. When he doesn't close his eyes while I am making a report it usually means that part of his mind is on something else, and I never know how big a part. On that occasion I suspected it was more than half, knowing as I did what he was doing with it. He was peeling strips of hide off of Hester Livsey and sprinkling salt on the exposed tissue. She had diddled him good. He had counted on getting from her, at a minimum, a hint as to where the path either entered the thicket or left it, and all he had got was a barefaced lie with Sumner Hoff to back it up.

When I finished the report, instead of asking questions or making comments, he muttered that he wished to speak to Mr. Cramer, and when the connection was made he told Cramer that in checking alibis and tracing movements of people for Friday evening a special effort should be made in the case of Sumner Hoff for the two hours from six to eight. Cramer naturally wanted to know why, since the hours they were concentrating on were from ten to midnight, and Wolfe's refusal to explain naturally got growls. Wolfe hung up, sighed deeply, and leaned back, and then in a matter of seconds had to straighten up again when a call came from Saul Panzer.

Saul made a report, a brief one, with me off the wire. Wolfe took it with no remarks but grunts, told Saul to come to the office at six that afternoon, and added:

"That confounded woman is a nincompoop. Has Mr. Cramer reached you? Of course not. Now you may let him. Let him find you. Tell him about Mr. Naylor but make no reference to Miss Livsey or Mr. Hoff. Leave them out. They have concocted a story that can't be disproven except by your word. It would be two to one, and Mr. Cramer would keep you for hours and perhaps days, accomplishing nothing. You'd better go to see him and finish with him so you can be here at six o'clock."

Wolfe hung up and glowered at me.

"Archie. At least we've been hired to do a job and we know what the job is. After lunch go back down there and use your eyes, ears, and tongue as the occasion suggests and your capacities permit." He glanced at the wall clock. "Get Durkin, Gore, Cather, and Keems. I want them all here at six o'clock. If they're working and need an inducement give them one. That woman is going to regret this."

27.

A week went by. Seven days and seven nights. They brought us to another Monday, the last day of March, and they brought us nowhere else at all.

It was the longest dry spell we have ever had on a murder

126

case. When I finished breakfast that second Monday morning and put on my coat and hat to go downtown for the start of another week at the office of Naylor-Kerr, Inc., if Wolfe had intercepted me to tell me to type for him a summary of the headway made during the week, it wouldn't have delayed me more than ten seconds. I could merely have stepped into the office for a blank sheet of paper and handed it to him— or, if he wanted it in triplicate, three sheets. That would have covered the accomplishments not only of me, but of everybody—Wolfe himself, Saul Panzer, Bill Gore, Orrie Cather, Fred Durkin, Johnny Keems, and Inspector Cramer with his entire army.

The cops had done everything they were supposed to do and then some. Their scientists, with microscopes and chemicals, had demonstrated that Naylor's body had been carried in the tonneau, on the floor, of the car that had run over him, proving that he had been either killed or stunned somewhere else and transported to Thirty-ninth Street for the last act. The theory was that the body had been where the murderer didn't want it to be, so he had needed to take it somewhere else, and why not Thirty-ninth Street again if it was as suitably deserted as it had been before? He could choose a moment when no one was in sight for dumping it out of the car, and if someone appeared before he could back the car up and run over it he could merely decide not to add that touch, and step on the gas.

Naturally the curiosity of the cops was aroused by the fact that the murderer had thought it undesirable for people to know where Naylor was killed and what with, so a few platoons worked on that. In their effort to find out where the car had been the scientists used the microscope on every particle of dust and dirt from the tires, and even from underneath the chassis. Purley told me that one of them had sold himself on the notion that the car had been in Passaic, New Jersey, but had found no other buyers. Otherwise no results.

Something over two hundred units of personnel of the stock department were conversed with, anywhere from one to five times. Rosa Bendini and her husband, Gwynne Ferris, Sumner Hoff, Hester Livsey, and Ben Frenkel were among the most popular but were by no means the only ones. The assumption was that the murderer of Naylor had also killed Waldo Moore, but it was not allowed to exclude other possibilities, and since at least half of the people on the thirty-fourth floor might conceivably have felt murderous about either one or the other, there was plenty of territory to move around in. It would have been a good training school, Purley told me, for any rookie wanting to learn how to trace movements and check alibis, there were so many different kinds.

That operation was not confined to the thirty-fourth floor. Up on the thirty-sixth, on the executive and directorial level, the approach was of course somewhat different, since vice-presidents and directors are more sensitive and bleed easier than typists or heads of sections, but the job was actually just as thorough, especially when the days and nights stretched into a week without even one measly little lead. The police elite who worked on it found the normal tangle of jealousies and rivalries, and inclinations to trip and shove, but it all added up to nothing really helpful, including the movement-tracing and alibi-checking. The most promising angle, on the face of it, was Kerr Naylor's attempt to have Jasper Pine booted out and himself made president, but that too produced no bacon because, first, Naylor had been after the president's job for years and was getting nowhere, and second, Pine had been in bed asleep the night Naylor was killed, as Wolfe and Cramer and I had learned from Cecily.

Not satisfied with all the wonderful raw material at Naylor-Kerr, the cops had tried other places too. They had broadened out to include everybody either Moore or Naylor had been known to associate with, getting the same amount of nothing that they got on William Street. On Wolfe's hint that there might be something phony about Sumner Hoff's account of his movements from six to eight o'clock, they had questioned both Hoff and Hester several times, and had also tried other lines of inquiry, with no result. By Saturday afternoon, eight days after Naylor's death, they had got so desperate that Lieutenant Rowcliff himself invited me to go along for their third examination of Naylor's papers and effects, but I found them just as uninteresting as the cops had, except for a document of forty-six hand-written pages in which Naylor had set down his program for the firm of Naylor-Kerr, Inc., if and when he became president. His list of executives and directors that he intended to get rid of might have been helpful if the list hadn't been so damn long.

Meanwhile all Wolfe was doing was getting upset. True, he was paying five operatives besides me—Panzer, Gore, Durkin, Keems, and Cather—but that wasn't costing him anything since it would all go on the client's bill. And what do you suppose the last four were doing? It might be supposed, naturally, that they were developing some subtle and intricate plan which Wolfe had cooked up with his celebrated finesse and imagination. Haha. They were tailing Hester and Sumner, which was exactly what they would have been doing if Naylor-Kerr, wanting to hire an investigator, had picked an agency at random from the Red Book. That was how far Wolfe's genius had got him on this case. As for Saul Panzer, I had not heard his instructions, but I knew he had the photograph which Hester Livsey had sent us at Wolfe's request, and I suspected he was going around town asking people to guess who it was.

The reports covering Hester's and Sumner's movements from Gore, Durkin, Keems, and Cather weren't even worth filing. But our four men were having fun, because the subjects were also being tailed by the cops and that made it more sociable.

I am not being snooty. I can't afford it, because during that long dry spell I was being as futile as everybody else. I performed occasional and miscellaneous errands which aren't worth telling about, but most of the time I was at William Street, in the stock department, trying to kid somebody. The only meal I ate at home was breakfast because I worked overtime. Monday evening I took Rosa to dine and dance. Tuesday I took Gwynne Ferris. Wednesday I made a try for Hester. First she said she would go and then a couple of hours later reneged, stating that she had tried to cancel another engagement and couldn't. My guess was that Sumner Hoff was handling things and that if I tried for the next evening or the next I would only get humiliated and perhaps a start on an inferiority complex, so I passed it up and made a stab at a possible fresh source of gossip which weighed around a hundred and fifty and went by the name of Elise Grimes. She proved to be unprofitable no matter what I was after, and Thursday I repeated with Rosa, and Friday with Gwynne. I won't go so far as to say the time and effort were wasted, but I had to be stern with myself to persuade me that it was entirely proper, nothing but routine really, to put it on the client's expense account.

Wolfe and I, during that week, had three hot arguments about Hester Livsey and Sumner Hoff. I lost the first one, when I took the stand that we should let the cops have a try at them. Wolfe was dead against it. He said, first, that Cramer would be sore and suspicious because we had held it back so long; second, that Cramer wouldn't do a real job on them because he wouldn't be sure we weren't trying to put something over and Saul was lying; and third, that even if he took Saul for gospel, it would be two against one and Hester and

Hoff would probably hold fast. I hated to agree with him but had to.

The other two arguments ended in a tie. I insisted that Hester and Hoff should be got to the office one at a time, offering to do the getting myself no matter how they felt about it, and Wolfe should give them the works. He maintained it was hopeless. He would have nothing to go on, he said, but one little fact regarding which they had agreed to lie, and they knew we knew they were lying. It was stalemate, and he would have nowhere to start from. I said it was the only crack we had found anywhere and he ought to try to get a wedge in it anyhow. He flatly refused. I thought at the time he was just being contrary, but it may be that he was already considering the experiment that he finally decided to try on Sunday evening and didn't want to run any risk of spoiling it.

At least it wasn't laziness. He was really working. With a minimum of pestering from me he agreed that the executives and directors required some attention, and even took my advice where to begin, so I had the satisfaction, Thursday morning, of putting the bee on Emmet Ferguson. At first he was going to sneer me right off the phone, but a few well-chosen dirty insinuations put him where he belonged, and at two o'clock he came tearing into Wolfe's office with his ten-dollar Sulka tie off center, full of words and ready for war. Wolfe spent two hours on him, and when he finally tore out again two things were perfectly plain: one, Ferguson would always vote against hiring Wolfe or me by anyone for anything at any time, and two, if Wolfe and I should run short on morals and resort to a frame for the murders, we would heartily agree on who to pick for the victim.

I would say that probably nobody engaged with the investigation of Naylor's death got a single thing out of the whole week, except me. Not only were there those opportunities to study women, which any detective under eighty should be glad to have, at the client's expense, but also I got season tickets for both the Giants and the Yankees. And not by mail or messenger; Cecily brought them herself. When I got home Thursday after midnight I found Wolfe still up, reading apparently only one book, at his desk in the office.

He grunted at me. "Where have you been?"

"I told you where I was going. With Rosa. At one time, months ago it seems, I thought she thought her husband killed Moore, but I'm beginning to think she did it herself. She has a great deal of vitality."

He shuddered. "The plant records are getting badly behind and Theodore needs them."

"They sure are," I agreed. "I can't help it if this case is so tough that I have to work days and nights both." I yawned. "You got me that job down there. You told me to use my organs as the occasion suggests and my capacities permit." I yawned. "I guess I'll go to bed."

"No. Mrs. Pine is coming. She telephoned that she wants to give you your baseball tickets and I told her you would be home shortly."

"My God. Shouldn't you—let us be alone?"

"No. I want to see her. Anyhow, that's what she really wants. Why the devil should she want to give you baseball tickets?"

That, it seemed to me, called for an argument, and I sat down to give it my attention, but before I got a word out I had to get up again because the doorbell rang. I went down the hall, glanced through the one-way panel, opened the door, and invited her in.

She put out a hand and exchanged a firm friendly clasp with me, gave me a warm wholesome smile, looked searchingly at my face and nodded—to herself, not to me—and said cheerfully:

"I could see you would be like that even when you were all red and bruised. Is that fat man in there? I'd like to see him."

Without waiting for clearance she was on her way, and I followed her down the hall and into the office. She offered no hand to Wolfe, only a polite nod with a good evening, and took the straight-backed chair she had used before, after I had moved it up for her.

"I surmised, madam," Wolfe said peevishly, "that you wished to see me as well as Mr. Goodwin."

"Not particularly," she declared. "Except that it is always a satisfaction to remind a man—especially a conceited one like you—that I was right. If you had done what I asked you to my brother would not have been killed."

"Pah. He wouldn't?"

"Certainly not." Mrs. Pine looked at me. "You know perfectly well, Archie, that you are responsible, spreading it around that he told you he knew who killed Waldo Moore. If you had stayed away from there as I wanted you to it wouldn't have happened. Not that you're to blame, since you work for this Mr. Wolfe and have to do what he tells you to." She smiled at me. "Oh, here are those tickets." She opened her bag, a medium-sized embroidered thing with a gold frame, fingered in it, and produced an envelope. I crossed to get it, and thanked her, trying to speak like a pet. She asked if I would dispose of her wrap, and I took it—this time it was chinchilla—and put it on the couch. Apparently she was in mourning, as her gray and black dress covered a lot of pink skin that had been visible the other time.

"I doubt," Wolfe muttered, "if that conclusion is sound. Your brother had adopted a policy of jaunty indiscretion long before Mr. Goodwin got there. Besides, you said last week that Mr. Moore's death was accidental. Now you're assuming that he was murdered and that the murderer killed your brother to anticipate disclosure. You can't have it both ways, madam."

He was wasting logic on her again.

She completely ignored it. "My brother jaunty? Good lord!" She added, "The funeral was yesterday."

Whether she was merely stating a deplorable fact, or whether she meant to imply that it was up to us to have the funeral repealed or nullified, there was no way of telling. Evidently it was the former, for she didn't follow through on it, but sent me an unsmiling glance.

"You see, Archie, this wouldn't have happened if you had taken my suggestion and quit working for him and started your own business. How much will it cost?"

"Eleven thousand, four hundred and sixty-five dollars," I told her.

"That much?"

"Yeah, inflation."

"It seems high, but we'll see." She switched back to Wolfe. "What are you going to do now?"

"I have been engaged," he said, "to catch the murderer of your brother."

"I know you have, but what are you going to do?"

"Catch him. Or her." Wolfe wiggled a finger at her. "Now, madam, wouldn't you like to help?"

"No," she said decisively. "I am not vindictive." She glanced over her shoulder. "Will you close that door, Archie? Or bring me my wrap?"

Preferring the door idea, I went and closed it.

Meanwhile she was going on, "The police have been asking about the relationship between my brother and me, which is impertinent and ridiculous. One of them, a vulgar little bald man, openly resented it because I am not prostrated with grief! Actually I was extremely fond of my brother, but my feeling about him and about his death are my private affair

132

and concern no one else. The wish that was dearest to him, the wish to become the active directing head of the firm our father founded, was utterly hopeless because he wasn't fitted for it. He should have been either a policeman or a fireman—that was what he wanted when he was a little boy. You can't make him a policeman or a fireman by finding out who killed him. Anyway, I don't think he was killed—not deliberately. I think it was an accident. What do you think, Archie?"

"I think what you do, Mrs. Pine." I gave here a personalized grin. "I mean what you think, not what you say you think. If you're leading up to a cash offer for proof that it was an accident, forget it, no one could deliver, not even us. Is that what you came for?"

"No." She smiled at me. "Those tickets came today and I wanted to get them to you, and I wanted to see how your face looks." She was leaning forward to see me better. "You must have extremely good blood, to heal so rapidly. How old are you?"

"Thirty-three."

"Wonderful! Men in their twenties are so raw. Have you got a list of that eleven thousand, four hundred and sixty-five dollars?"

Wolfe made an emphatic sound without words, arose, told the visitor good evening, and left the room. In a moment we heard the opening and closing of the door of his elevator.

"There is no list," I said in a hurt tone. "If your trust in me is so shaky that you have to see lists . . . And speaking of my blood, it ought to be good, since I'm half gypsy." I crossed to her and put a hand on her shoulder. "That's why I can understand things, without knowing exactly how, that even Mr. Wolfe can't understand. About these two deaths, Waldo Moore and your brother—"

She began to laugh, a real laugh, from her throat and on out. "You certainly don't understand me!" she declared, and laughed some more. "Your father's name is James Arner Goodwin, and you were born in Canton, Ohio, in nineteen-fourteen. Your mother's maiden name was Leslie. You have two brothers and two sisters. No, no gypsy. I'm a very cautious woman, Archie, cautious and dependable." She stood up, abruptly, and I must admit not clumsily. "The reason I want to see a list is to make sure you're including everything. Let's sit on the couch and talk about it."

We were alone, with the whole floor to ourselves. Fritz had gone to his bed in the basement. I had been up and around all of eighteen hours, Cecily probably not more than twelve. It was not a situation that could be handled with half-measures.

"This," I said, "is dangerous. Mr. Wolfe already suspects me. You'll have to go, for my sake. If I stay here alone with you he'll think I'm double-crossing him on this case and he'll have my license revoked, and then I couldn't go into business for myself even if you wanted me to. When this case is finished we'll talk . . . and talk . . . and talk . . . but you'll have to go now, Mrs. Pine."

I thought I might as well clinch it, and added, "Cecily."

28.

The next day, Friday, I got home from Naylor-Kerr around five-thirty and went up to my room to bathe and change. Gwynne Ferris had maneuvered me into an agreement to try the food and music at the Silver Room at the Churchill that evening, and that called for black and white. I had to step on it because Wolfe expected me in the office at six o'clock, when he would descend from the plant rooms, to report on the day. The report, God knows, would be totally without nourishment, but by that time Wolfe would have welcomed an underfed straw to grab at, and he would want all details.

He didn't get them, not then, for when I got down to the office at five past six Inspector Cramer was there with him and was already off to a good start.

It was obvious from the first growls I heard that Cramer had come to try something that he had often tried before, and never with any profit. He had come to take the lid off of Wolfe and look inside. That meant he was all out of everything. It had come to snafu and he was helpless.

"So you were having Naylor tailed," he was barking. "So, by God, you knew something was going to happen to him! I'll tell you what I think! That Saul Panzer is the best tailer in New York. I don't for a minute believe he lost Naylor! He don't lose 'em! Even if he did, when Naylor came here, wouldn't you have had him tailed when he left, since you were interested in him? Of course you would! I think Panzer was right up with Naylor all that evening, right up to the time he was killed and then some, right up to the car running over him on Thirty-ninth Street!"

"Pfui," Wolfe muttered.

"Look at this." Cramer put up a finger. "One. You were hired to smoke Naylor out in connection with the death of

Moore." Another finger. "Two. Goodwin pressured him into a deadly threat against someone." A third finger. "Three. You had your best man on his tail." A finger. "Four. You kept Panzer away from me for two days." Thumb. "Five. You tried to sick us on that Hoff and it's a phony." The fingers made a fist. "And six, you keep Goodwin down there to sit on it, not doing a damn thing but play with the girls! Look at him, dressed for a party!"

"I didn't know you had noticed me," I murmured politely. "Thanks."

But Cramer was beyond minding me. "Look at it!" he bellowed.

"I am," Wolfe said dryly. "Is that all there is?"

Cramer settled back, then suddenly jerked forward again and laid the fist on Wolfe's desk. "I'm going to come out with it," he said slowly and emphatically. "I've had occasion many times, Wolfe, to ride you—or to try to. But actually, and you know it, I have never accused you of covering for a murderer, and I have never considered you capable of that." He lifted the fist and brought it down again. "I do now. I think you're capable of it, and I think you're doing it. I think you know who killed Moore and Naylor, and I think you intend to keep me from getting him. Is that plain enough?"

"You know what you're saying, Mr. Cramer."

"You're damn right I do."

"Archie." Wolfe's eyes came to me. "Get him out of my house. By force if necessary."

That did not appeal to me. He was a police inspector, he was probably armed, and I had on my best clothes.

I stayed in my chair. "Gentlemen," I said sneeringly, "I had supposed you could take it, both of you, but I see I was wrong. You're both licked, that's all there is to it, and you're trying to take it out on each other by acting childish. Inspector Cramer, you know damn well how tricky Mr. Wolfe is, and you know he's at least ten times too tricky ever to go around—or rather sit around—with a murderer in his pocket with the idea of guarding his health. You're just mad and kicking the furniture. Mr. Wolfe, you are fully aware that he is merely shooting off his mouth, and if you were yourself you would be only bland and offensive to him instead of ordering me to make an ass of myself. You're just sore and savage because you've finally run into one too slick for you."

I arose, crossed to the hall door, and turned. "You'll have to excuse me, gentlemen, I've got a date with a suspect. I'm a detective and I'm working on a murder case."

I have never learned how that conversation ended. Wolfe never mentioned it, and when, somewhat later, I tried a question or two about it, all I got was a grunt.

Saturday and Sunday it was really pitiful. Saturday morning Wolfe buzzed me to come to his room while he was eating breakfast, and when I went, he, having remembered his taboo on talk of business during meals, let me sit and watch him gloomily dispose of four pieces of toast and a dish of eggs au beurre noir. When he had finished he had instructions for me, and they were a knockout. He was sure going to wade into it. I was to spend my week-end getting Ben Frenkel, Harold Anthony, Rosa Bendini, and Gwynne Ferris, one at a time, and bringing them to him! And he was to spend his week-end getting things out of them!

So it was. That's how we spent Saturday and Sunday, with one or two other items worked in, such as my going with Lieutenant Rowcliff to look over Naylor's papers and effects. Nor was Wolfe merely making motions and trying to pass the time. Saturday he spent three hours on Harold Anthony and four hours on Gwynne Ferris. Sunday he spent five hours on Rosa Bendini and six on Ben Frenkel. He was really digging and sweating. Late Sunday evening, after Frenkel had gone, he stayed motionless in his chair a long while and then remarked in a low rumble that indicated he had caught it from Frenkel:

"I suppose I'll have to see those other people. The directors and executives. Can you have them here tomorrow morning at eleven?"

I was busy at the typewriter, catching up on the germination records. Without bothering to turn my head I declared firmly, "I cannot. They're busy supplying engineers. They think we're a false alarm as it is. Even Armstrong—you know, the wiry little guy—even he is beginning to suspect they're wasting corporation funds."

He didn't even grunt, let alone argue. I resumed on the typewriter. I finished with the Miltonias and started on the Phalaenopsis. The minutes collected enough for an hour and started on another one. It was midnight, bedtime, but I stayed on because Wolfe was leaning back with his eyes closed and with his lips working—pushing out, then back in, then out and in again—and I was curious to learn if anything would come of it.

He stirred in his chair, sighed clear to his solar plexus, and opened his eyes to a slit.

"Archie."

"Yes, sir."

"You were correct."

"Yes, sir."

"I have, as you put it, run up against one too slick for me. Either too slick or too lucky. Mr. Moore has been dead nearly four months, and Mr. Naylor nine days, and what have we got?"

"An expense account."

"Yes. It is wholly unprecedented. We have one fact only that might be helpful—Miss Livsey's promenade with Mr. Naylor—but we don't know whether it is significant or not, and no way of finding out. We can't sort out the real clues and the false ones because we have no clues at all. Literally none. Neither has Mr. Cramer. Has that ever happened to us before?"

"No, sir."

"No. It hasn't. I find it interesting and stimulating. What do we do when we have no clues? Do you know?"

"No, sir."

"We make one. We may have to make more, but we'll start with one. Experimentally. Cover that confounded machine and turn your chair around and listen to me."

"Yes, sir."

It took him nearly an hour to complete the diagram, with me making notes. At the end he asked sharply, "Well?"

I nodded uncertainly. "If it's the best you can do we'll have to try it—or rather I will. The least we can get is another murder."

29.

The best evidence of where we stood and how we were doing on that case was the changed attitude toward me, when I appeared in the Naylor-Kerr stock department that Monday morning, on the part of the personnel. The time had been when my progress down an aisle had been followed by hundreds of pairs of eyes. No more. I got about the same attention as one of the messenger boys toting mail around.

The first item of the build-up was a visit, not too brief, with Hester Livsey, and, wanting to be sure of getting it in before she got called by Rosenbaum for the morning dictation, I crossed the arena to her office as soon as I had deposited my hat and coat in my own room, which I was still being allowed to occupy. Her door was standing open, but I closed it behind me when I entered.

She had finished dusting and was sorting papers on her desk. She sent me a sidewise glance, then jerked her head around and demanded, "What do you want?"

I sat down and grinned at her. "That's a bad habit you're forming, that what do you want. It's nerves."

"What do you want?"

She looked older and somewhat more used, and I didn't try to kid myself that to me she had become merely a collection of assorted cells and was around ninety per cent water. I could still look at her and not be repulsed by the notion that she needed me, and the hell of it was that I was committed to an operation that was likely to make her need me a lot more.

"Sit down and relax," I told her.

"No." She stood with papers in her hand. "I could tell Mr. Rosenbaum that you're annoying me."

"Indeed you could," I agreed. "And I wouldn't deny it. I'm annoying lots of people, and so are you. That's the way it goes under circumstances like this. I doubt if Rosenbaum would try to bounce me, it would make such a commotion, with me yelling and hanging onto the doorjamb, and maybe breaking loose and dodging around the desks out there. However, you can try it—or you can just ignore me and go on with your work. I won't pounce on you from behind."

She was sorting papers, with her face looking distorted because of the way her jaw was set, with tight muscles.

"Speaking of your work," I went on, "do you remember that you told me once that you like it here and have to have a job? I shouldn't think you'd like it here much now, with all the annoyance. But I can understand your having to have a job because I do too. I can understand your not wanting to do anything that would get you fired. So don't get fired. Quit. Mr. Wolfe knows a lot of people, and one of them is a senior partner in one of the best and biggest law firms in New York. You can have a job with them, secretary to a member of the firm, seventy a week to start, nine-thirty to five and closed Saturdays, haven't skipped a Christmas bonus for eighteen years. Your room will be three times as big as this one, two windows, two rugs, any kind of typewriter you want, good view of the harbor and the Statue of Liberty. What do you say?"

She sorted papers, with no glance at me. I warmed up to it and proceeded to analyze her chances for a glowing future in the law business. To get the effect I was after it was desir-

138

able to spend at least a quarter of an hour with her, and twenty minutes would be better. So I went into the matter thoroughly and considered it from every angle. I found as I went on that what appealed strongest to my fancy was the possibility of her becoming a court stenographer, with all the dramatic opportunities and financial advantages which that offered. On that I really went to town. I had been with her twenty-three minutes, and saw no reason why it shouldn't go on until lunchtime, when I heard the door opening behind me. Twisting my head, I saw Sumner Hoff.

He shut the door, circled around to confront me, and told me in a low threatening tone, "Get out of here."

I couldn't have asked for anything better. This would be a real help. I looked up at him and matched his tone. "Get out yourself, you goddam snooping son of a bitch."

He reacted as might have been expected from the cavalier who had plugged Waldo Moore in full view of the whole arena. He made me aware, in fact, that I might have done him an injustice that day in Wolfe's office; he was capable of rating a sock when his emotions were fully aroused. But it would have been bad tactics to smash him at that point, and anyway his ideas of combat were so ill advised that it would have been a shame. As I left my chair he came for me with his right as if it was the only fist in the world and nothing else was worth considering. I jerked my head aside out of the way, and while he was recovering his balance I stepped to the door and opened it, saying in a loud voice:

"You're too late to stop her, Hoff! You're too late!"

Then I ran. I ran across the middle of the arena, glancing over my shoulder, in flight, to see that Hoff had started after me, got as far as the fourth desk, and stopped. I kept going, getting, now, the attention I deserved from all eyes. When I reached the other side I darted into my room, grabbed my hat and coat, emerged, left by the main entrance, took a down elevator, flagged a taxi on William Street, and gave the driver Wolfe's address.

I found Wolfe up in the potting room with Theodore, inspecting a newly arrived shipment of osmundine. It was humid and warm in there, so I perched on a stool, got out my handkerchief, and wiped my brow.

"Well?" he inquired.

"Yes, sir. I was with her over twenty minutes. Hoff busted in and ordered me out, and I called him names and let him chase me. He must have spies."

"Excellent. Proceed."

"Yes, sir. I'll stay here a while, to show that I had to consult you on an exciting development, and then go back. But there's one thing I still don't like. Each and every day I have been typing my report in the afternoon and taking it upstairs around four-thirty. If I change that routine and turn in a report before noon someone may suspect it's a phony."

"You said that last night."

"I say it again today."

"The substance of the report justifies it."

"It did with Naylor too, but I followed routine."

He shrugged. "Very well. It doesn't matter. Make it this afternoon as usual."

I left, went downstairs to the office, dialed the Naylor-Kerr number, asked for the extension of the head of the reserve pool in the stock department, and said I wanted to speak to Gwynne Ferris. I was told she was busy. So, I said, was I. In a couple of minutes I heard her voice.

"Listen, darling," I beseeched her. "I'm up at Thirty-fifth Street, had to come to see Mr. Wolfe. But I'll be through here in about an hour, and there's something I want to ask you about, and I'll even go so far as to buy you a lunch. Meet me at the corner of William and Wall at twelve-thirty?"

"You bum," she said resentfully. "Letting that Hoff chase you clear off the floor and me not getting to see it because I was in Mr. Henderson's office working. What do you want to ask me about?"

"Something special. The next to last step in that rumba. Twelve-thirty?"

She said all right.

I was sitting with my legs extended and my hands pushed into my pants pockets, frowning at the knob of the combination on the safe, when Wolfe came down from the plant rooms. After he got in his chair and had his center of gravity adjusted I transferred the frown to him and asked:

"Did the boys come?"

He nodded.

"All four of them?"

He nodded.

"You gave them the set-up?"

He nodded.

I shook my head. "Okay. If this thing really works, which I admit is one chance in a hundred and so do you, I only hope to God they don't lose her and I have to do some more identifying."

"Nonsense." Wolfe pushed the button for beer. "As I told

you, I expect nothing as conclusive as that. But there may be some word, some gesture, some cautious countermove, and you, I trust, will not miss it."

"Yeah." My frown remained. "Some trust. I have dated Gwynne for lunch and have reserved a booth at Frisbie's, where shad roe is three bucks. Have you any further suggestions?"

He said no, and Fritz entered with the beer.

30.

"Yes, turtledove," I said, "you may have another Martini if it's okay with Emily Post in the middle of a meal, and further if you don't get dizzy. I need your head clear."

I had been with Gwynne enough to know that with the third or fourth drink her lovely eyes had a slight tendency to protrude and also to acquire a film of excess moisture. Also she was inclined to start cussing. I preferred her pure and angelic and had told her so frankly.

We were eating shad roe and avocado salad in a corner booth at Frisbie's.

"I don't get dizzy," she pouted. "A girl like me can't afford to. My head is always clear, and what do you want it clear for? Some more crap about that awful night, that Friday night I'll never forget? Out of bed to police headquarters! I never thought I'd come to that, I can tell you!"

"Neither did I," I said earnestly. "No, it's not about that awful night, or at least not about your part of it." I took time out to tell the waiter to bring the Martini, and, to be sociable, more bourbon for me.

"The reason I've been hesitating," I said, "is that it's extremely confidential. On the other hand, I badly need your advice. I have a fair idea of what your opinion of Hester Livsey is, but—well, is she actually a little batty? What do you think?"

Gwynne snorted. I had told her she should give up snorting. "That girl batty? I should say not! What's she trying to put over on you?"

"That's just it," I said in a puzzled tone. "I can't figure it that she's trying to put anything over. I can't figure it at all."

"I bet she is. What's she done?"

I hesitated. I gazed seriously at the lovely blue eyes. "This is very confidential, Gwynne darling."

"Sure."

"You've got to promise to keep it that way."

"Sure."

"I've told Mr. Wolfe, and he has given me permission to consult you."

"For God's sake go on and spill it!"

"Well—I suppose—Hester Livsey told me this morning that she knows who killed Waldo Moore. She said she has known for a long time."

Gwynne's fork, with a hunk of avocado, stopped halfway to her mouth. "She told you she *knows*?"

"Yep."

"No!"

"So she told me."

"Jesus!"

The fork with the avocado slowly descended to the plate and rested there.

"I don't wonder you're impressed, darling," I said sympathetically. "So am I. She was telling me when Hoff butted in and chased me. I went to tell Mr. Wolfe about it, and we're up a stump because we don't know her well enough. He thought I should consult someone who is well informed and trustworthy and who knows all about her. Obviously that meant you. Is she batty or what?"

The waiter came with the drinks. Gwynne looked at her Martini as if it were a complication she was not prepared for, then picked it up and downed it in two gulps.

"Is she batty?" I persisted.

"She is certainly not." Gwynne used her napkin. "My God, how awfully audacious! Did she say who it was?"

"No. She might have, I don't know, if Hoff hadn't interrupted us. What do you—"

"Did she say the—the same one killed Naylor too?"

"Not in so many words, but it amounted to that."

"Did she say how she knows?"

"No, but I think she will. That's what I want to ask you about, how to handle her. If she's not merely off her nut she must have—"

"I'm late," Gwynne declared. She pushed her plate away, upsetting the salt shaker. "I only have an hour and I've got to get—"

"No you don't," I said firmly. "I need help. I need advice, and I'm depending on you." I glanced at my wrist. "You've got a good ten minutes. What about her? Would she say a thing like that just to get even with someone? What's she like?"

"She's a snooty conceited bitch."

I kept her there the full ten minutes, but got no further useful information regarding Hester Livsey or anyone or anything else. Gwynne didn't really put her mind on it. She was too anxious to get back to her work.

31.

It wasn't essential to the build-up, I thought, for me to be seen upstairs returning from lunch with Gwynne, so I parted from her down in the lobby of the building. After the elevator door had closed on her I walked past the cigar stand, gave a sign en route to a broad-shouldered man who was standing near by, and continued on out to the sidewalk and around the corner. The broad-shouldered man caught up with me and I greeted him.

"How's it going, Orrie?"

"Tedious as hell," he grumbled. "She had lunch in an orangeade tavern and then back to work. Trade jobs with me?"

"Next week maybe. It may not be so tedious starting at five o'clock. You're not sleepy?"

"I could follow her with my eyes shut. Anything new?"

"Nothing, except that tonight's the night, or maybe tomorrow. If you trip and hurt a finger—"

"I know, I know. The name is Cather. Orrie."

"Okay, my brave fellow."

I returned to the building lobby, went to a phone booth, called Wolfe, and told him that the ball was rolling. He had no new suggestions, nothing in fact but a grunt. I took an elevator to the thirty-fourth floor, went to my little room—noting that the units of personnel had decided I was worth looking at again—sat at my desk, and inserted paper and carbons in the typewriter.

The headings were of course routine. I got them down, then considered how to word it. That might or might not be important, depending on whether the hoped-for reaction would come from the thirty-fourth floor or the thirty-sixth. It should, I thought, be purely factual, without any suggestion of fireworks, to conform to the style of my other reports, but that could be overdone. Finally I tapped the keys:

143

There is a development that looks promising. At 9:40 this morning I called on Hester Livsey in her room. As explained previously, she had refused to go and see Mr. Wolfe again, and he wished to talk with her at length, as he has with others. That has been reported. Miss Livsey was extremely nervous. At first she refused to speak with me, and when I persisted she suddenly blurted out that she didn't dare to go to talk with Wolfe again because she knows who murdered Waldo Moore. She assumed, I believe, that she was telling me that in confidence, but there was no stated arrangement to that effect. The implication was that she also knows that the same person murdered Naylor. I think I would have got more from her, perhaps much more, if Mr. Summer Hoff had not suddenly entered the room and ordered me out. There is no reason to think that he knew what she was saying to me, as our voices were not raised and the door was closed.

I went immediately to Mr. Wolfe's office to report the incident to him. It is his opinion that for the time being this matter should be left entirely to me, but that it would be improper to withhold the information from the client. Any further developments will be reported without delay.

That was the way it finally came out. There were a couple of things about the first draft I didn't like, so I did some editing and then typed it over. I was still setting my trap in the cabinet with a second carbon of my reports, wiping the folder covers and deploying the tobacco crumbs, not with any strong hope of making a catch but to maintain the tradition. After attending to that and putting the original and first carbon in my pocket, I opened my door wide, placed a chair so as to have a view of the door of Hester's room across the arena, and sat.

Her door was closed.

Within a minute the several dozen females inhabiting the segment of the arena overlooked from my post were aware of my open door and of me sitting there. Eyes were coming at me, all the way from hasty quickly averted glances to marathon stares. It was an interesting experience, or would have been if I had been in a frame of mind to explore all the possibilities. Under the circumstances nothing came of it. I did not actually expect someone to come rolling down the aisle in a stolen sedan, swerve and head for Hester's room, and run the sedan over her. I would have been surprised if anything at all had happened, but even so, during all the time that I sat there I did not yawn once, and there was no interval of more than three seconds when Hester's door could have opened without me seeing it.

It did in fact open, seven times. At 2:35 she emerged, went

to Rosenbaum's room, and returned to her own at 2:48. At 3:02 she emerged again, went to the end of the arena where the women's room was, and returned at 3:19. At 3:41 Sumner Hoff came marching down the far aisle and opened her door and went in, closing it behind him. At 3:55 he came out again and headed straight for me—more about that later. At 4:12 Hester came out—more about that later too. That made the seven.

The first proof that I had used good judgment in picking Gwynne as a repository of confidential information came around three o'clock, when my view of the arena was suddenly obstructed by an object appearing in my door. The object was Rosa Bendini. Her black eyes were shining with excitement, but as she entered and approached all she said was:

"This is Monday, Archie."

I nodded. "March thirty-first. Six days till Easter."

"Do you remember last Monday?"

"I'll never forget it. I remember Thursday even better."

"So do I. What are you doing, sitting here?"

"Remembering Monday and Thursday. Excuse me. Down in front." I stretched my neck to see. Hester had emerged from her room. When I was satisfied that she was bound for the restroom I came back to my caller. "What are the eyes all lit up for? Not just for me."

"Shall I shut the door?"

"No, ma'am. Not during office hours."

She came a step closer. "Hester's lying to you," she said with sudden startling intensity. Her head jerked around for a look at the door and then back to me. "Didn't I tell you about her? She may know who killed Wally, that part's all right, but she's trying to play a trick on you. I told you about her, didn't I?"

"You did. Keep your voice down. What makes you think she knows who killed Wally?"

"She told you so." Rosa put a hand on my arm, saw my glance at the open door, and took the hand away. "Don't let her fool you, Archie. Next she'll be telling you who it was."

"If she does that will be more than you did. You said you knew who killed him but you wouldn't get down to a name. Then you said you didn't know. Is that what you call a trick?"

"I—I—" She looked around again. "I'm going to shut the door."

"Why, are you ready to name a name?"

"I don't know any names, Archie. I want you to put your arm around me. I'll shut—"

145

I got her elbow, stopping her. "No, Rosa, not now, we'll save it for next time. Who told you—"

She jerked free, her eyes flashing. "There may not be any next time," she said, and went.

It was satisfactory to know that Gwynne had not failed me, but beyond that it was doubtful what I had got, if anything. Wolfe was expecting some word or gesture or countermove, and my instructions were to keep him posted, but I couldn't for the life of me see anything helpful in Rosa's wanting me to embrace her. Why shouldn't she? It had been four days since Thursday. I was making up my mind whether to go to a phone booth and tell him about it, and had decided to wait at least until Hester had returned from the restroom, when my door was darkened again.

It was Ben Frenkel. He advanced two long strides from the door, stopped, gazed down at me with his probe working, and rumbled his thunder:

"Am I intruding?"

"Sure." I grinned up at him. "What for?"

"You had lunch with Miss Ferris today."

I nodded. "Nothing personal. There was something I wanted to discuss with her."

"I don't believe it." He was keeping his thunder low.

"Then I'm a liar again. Ask her."

"I don't have to ask her. She told me. You said you wanted to ask her advice, which is preposterous. You have talked with her several times now at great length, both you and Mr. Wolfe, and it is impossible to believe that you would want to ask her advice. You must be aware that she is completely devoid of intellect, and therefore that her opinion on any subject whatever is without value. She is not a moron, but the quality of her brain is distinctly inferior."

"What's this?" I was gaping at him. "I thought you liked her!"

He waved that aside with a wide sweep of his long bony arm. "I don't like her. I am passionately in love with her and you know it. Another thing, you told her something in confidence, which is even more preposterous. She is utterly incapable of keeping her mouth shut. You know that. That is your best assurance that I did not kill Waldo Moore—nor Naylor either. If I had I couldn't have kept it from her—I can keep nothing from her. And if she knew it she would have blabbed it long ago, not just to you, to everybody. That's how you know I'm innocent."

"It's a point," I conceded.

"Certainly it is. Then how do you account for the fact that you told her something which you said was highly confidential, pledging her to tell no one?"

"I don't see why—excuse me." I stretched my neck again to gawk. Hester was returning from the restroom. As she entered her office I glanced at my wrist and registered the 3:19. I returned to Frenkel.

"You may be wrong about Miss Ferris. You can't take it for granted that everybody's opinion of her brain power agrees with yours. You may be blinded by love."

His arm swept that away too, describing an arc with its full radius. "You're just talking," he rumbled. "You are trying to obscure an extremely serious matter by degrading it to a triviality. Also you are making use of Miss Ferris, using her as a tool, in a manner that may be dangerous to her. That is a vicious thing to do. Vicious is not too strong a word." His eyes were boring into me. "She is incapable of seeing the danger or of guarding against it, and I have a right to ask, I have a right to demand, that you tell me exactly what Miss Livsey said to you. The exact words. Since you chose Miss Ferris as your puppet, I assume that Miss Livsey mentioned my name. Did she?"

"Not yet." I tilted my head to see him better. "That's sort of funny, how you're repeating yourself. It was the same about Naylor, remember? You came to ask me if he had mentioned your name. Funny, huh?"

"Not at all." Frenkel whirled, took a step, grabbed the chair at the desk, planted it facing me, and sat. I had the impression that his eyes hadn't left me at all. "I'm an introvert," he declared as if that explained everything. "You could even say that I am egocentric. That's why my infatuation for Miss Ferris has so deeply disturbed my personality. It has created an inner conflict . . ."

He was off. There were, of course, various ways of stopping him, but I saw no point in hurting his feelings since I could stick to my observation post as well with him there, though he could have only my ears since my eyes were engaged in another direction. So I listened to him attentively on the slim chance that the word or gesture or countermove might come from him, and I even tossed in an occasional question or comment. I was listening to him at 3:41, when I saw, across the arena, Sumner Hoff marching down the aisle and entering Hester's room, and I was still listening at 3:55, when Hoff emerged and started in my direction.

Hoff came straight to my door and on in. I was on my feet

by the time he arrived because there wasn't room in that cubbyhole for any fancy acrobatics. Ben Frenkel stopped in the middle of a sentence and stood up too.

Hoff looked at him. "I want to speak with Goodwin. When you're through?"

"I'm never through," Frenkel declared. He strode to the door, told us over his shoulder, "I never will be through," and was gone.

Hoff started to close the door. I moved, put out a hand, and swung the door open again.

"I like to see out," I said. "All the pretty girls. If it's a private talk just keep your voice down."

For a second I thought he was going to insist on having the door shut, then he changed his mind. He went to the chair Frenkel had vacated and sat down. I would hardly have recognized him for the Hoff I knew. He looked neither belligerent nor indignant; it was even doubtful if he regarded himself as adequately prepared to handle things.

"I underestimated you," he said. "Either you or Wolfe or both."

"Don't mention it," I said amiably. "As Eve said to Adam, we all make mistakes."

"Are you going to report upstairs and to the police that Miss Livsey told you that she knows who killed Moore and Naylor?"

So it was improving with age, probably started that way by Gwynne herself. "I'm not employed by the city," I asserted. "Of course it's usual and proper to report to our client all important developments." I patted my breast pocket. "Yes."

"She denies that she told you that. She denies that she told you anything whatever."

I nodded regretfully. "I expected that, though I hoped she wouldn't. She also denied that she took a walk with Naylor for an hour and three minutes the evening he was killed. She's quite a denier."

Hoff wet his lips with his tongue. He swallowed. "You've got the report ready. There in your pocket."

"Yes, sir." I took my lapels, one in each hand, and pulled my coat open wide. "On the right, the pocket with the report in it. On the left, the armpit holster with my Wembly automatic. Everything in place."

He didn't seem impressed by the holster; it was the pocket he was interested in. Then he came back to my eyes. His were not as penetrating and intense as Ben Frenkel's, but they were steadier. "What," he asked, "are you trying to force Miss Livsey to do?"

I shook my head. "That's up to her. Maybe we're just trying to teach her a lesson, how immoral it is to deny things."

"She"—he wet his lips again—"she has told the truth."

"Okay, brother. You ought to know."

"I do know. I'm not a rich man, Goodwin. When it comes to money I can't talk big, I have to stick to realities. I'll give you five thousand dollars cash, I can get it by tomorrow, if you'll just think it over and decide that you misunderstood her. That wouldn't be difficult, you won't have to revoke, you can just say you misunderstood her."

"Not for five grand I can't."

"But I—" He stopped to think. "How much?"

"Not for money. I don't like money. It curls up at the corners. I could listen to reason if Miss Livsey came in here now, or came with me to see Mr. Wolfe, and delivered a dime's worth of the truth. Provided we were satisfied it was a full dime's worth."

"She has told you the truth."

"You ought to know."

He was silent. Slowly his fingers and thumbs closed to make fists, but obviously not with intent to attack or destroy. They stayed fists for a while, then opened up and were claws, then went loose.

"For God's sake," he implored, "don't you realize what you're doing? Don't you realize the danger you're putting her in?" He was coming close to whimpering. "You know what happened to Naylor—don't you know her life isn't safe, not for a minute? What kind of a coldhearted bastard are you anyhow?"

I leaned forward to tap him on the knee. "Lookit, my friend," I said slowly and distinctly, "the score is exactly what you think it is. It's tied up. Like it or lump it."

He jerked his knee aside as if my fingertip might be rubbing germs on him, went sidewise out of his chair and up, and trotted out of the room.

I had enough now, it seemed to me, to justify blowing a nickel, so after watching Hoff recross the arena to Hester's room I went out and down the aisle to the corner where the phone booths were.

I told Wolfe, briefly, what had happened, and asked if he wanted me to fill in on the phone. He said no, that could wait until I got home, and then proceeded to ask questions that amounted to contradicting himself. He was counting on getting something all right, a good deal more than I was. Finally he let me go. As I returned down the aisle three hundred typewriters stopped their clatter, and all the eyes were mine. It was enough to make Dana Andrews feel self-conscious.

When I reached the door of my room I stopped and stood, but not to prolong the treat for my audience. The door was closed, and I was sure I had left it wide. I opened it and went in, and then closed the door behind me when I saw that Hester Livsey was standing there.

I took a step, and she took two, and her right hand took hold of my left arm.

"Please!" she said, her face lifted to me.

I asked her stiffly, "Please what?"

"Please don't do this to me!" Her other hand got my other arm. "Don't! Please!"

I stood still, neither inviting her hands to stay, nor, by any motion, implying that I didn't want them there. The nearness, with her face so close that I could see how black her pupils were, was her doing, and if it suited her it suited me.

"I'm not doing anything to you," I said. "I think you're wonderful—"

"You are! You're lying about me! You're telling a deliberate malicious lie!"

I nodded. "Sure I am." Her breath was sweet. "You've never met Saul Panzer, have you?"

"What—who—you're just—"

"Saul Panzer. A friend of mine and the best leg-and-eye detective on earth. He saw you that evening with Naylor. So you lied. I admire you so much that I want to do everything you do, I can't bear it not to. So I lied."

She took her hands away and backed up a step.

"It makes me feel better all over," I said.

"You admit it's a lie," she said.

"To you, sure. Not to anyone else. It's our first secret, just you and me. If you don't love me enough to have secrets with me, we can fix it. We can go to Nero Wolfe and confess we both lied, and tell him the truth. Shall we?"

She was breathing hard, as sweet as ever presumably, but I was no longer close enough to get it.

"You mean it, don't you," she said, not a question.

"I mean everything I say. Let's go to see Mr. Wolfe and get it over with."

"I thought—I thought you—" She stopped. Her voice

wanted to quiver but her chin didn't. "You're terrible. I thought—you're terrible!"

She moved to the door, not hurrying, just walking, pulled it open, and went.

32.

At a quarter past eleven that evening, in Nero Wolfe's office, the phone rang. I answered it, and Fred Durkin's voice told me:

"The lights are all out and so she's safe in bed. For Christ's sake, Archie, you don't want me—"

"I do," I said firmly, "and so does Mr. Wolfe. You've got your instructions, and what do you do for a living anyway? You stick and stick good."

I hung up and told Wolfe, "Fred says the lights are out. I'm relieved and I admit it. I was going to marry her if she hadn't gone partners with Hoff on that damn lie, and I don't care for my share of this at all. I suppose I'll have a nightmare tonight."

Wolfe didn't bother to grunt.

Although I know Wolfe as well as anybody does and a good deal better, I hadn't been able to tell whether my report for the day had given him anything that would pass for the word or gesture or countermove he wanted. He had received it all, complete, with the attention it deserved, leaning back motionless, with his eyes closed, and had had plenty of questions. He even wanted to know exactly what Miss Abrams, the receptionist on the thirty-sixth floor, had said when I gave her the report to be taken in to Jasper Pine. I had performed that errand at four-thirty, as usual, and she had told me that Pine was engaged at the moment but she would be sure he got it before he left for the day.

That night I had no nightmare, but if there had been a wife in bed with me she would probably have asked me in the morning why all the tossing and turning. It was by no means the first time I had been responsible for putting someone's pursuit of happiness in jeopardy, but this was something special. Things had somehow got reversed. At first sight of Hester Livsey I had instantly got the feeling that she was in some trouble that no one but me could get her out of, and here I was poking her head through the bull's-eye of a target

151

for a killer who had made two perfect hits, which was certainly a peculiar way to go about it.

When I left the house Tuesday morning, April Fool's Day, I was fidgety because there had been no phone call, though there was no good reason to expect one. Fred certainly wouldn't call until Hester showed herself, and after that happened there would be no opportunity. I got to the William Street building a quarter of an hour ahead of time, at nine-fifteen, and lurked in the lobby at the spot Saul and I had chosen eight days earlier. The incoming throng had already started. Five minutes before the deadline here she came. As she entered the elevator I caught sight of Fred Durkin, who had followed her into the lobby and stopped ten paces away. As I glimpsed him Bill Gore appeared from the other direction, exchanged signals with Fred, and strolled on. Fred went to the newsstand and bought a paper and then beat it.

I took an elevator to the thirty-fourth floor, went to my room, left the door open, and sat at my observation post. I was having a letdown. Our fire hadn't smoked Hester out and didn't seem likely to, and it was hard on my temperament just to sit there and wait for someone to make a peep. However, I hadn't been sitting long when the phone rang, I dived for it as if I was expecting word that it was an eight-pound baby boy, but all I got was a summons from Jasper Pine to come to see him. I obeyed it.

On the thirty-sixth floor I was shooed into Pine's office without any wait. He was there alone, standing in the middle of the big room, looking as if he had a grievance, with a sheet of paper in his hand. As I approached he shook the paper at me.

"This report," he said in his strong deep voice, as deep as Ben Frenkel's, but not a rumble. "What is this?"

"Have you read it?" I asked him.

"Yes."

"Well, that's what it is, Mr. Pine."

"This—" He glanced at the paper. "This Hester Livsey, what did she say?"

"What it says there. That she didn't dare to go to Mr. Wolfe and let him have another session with her because she knows who murdered Moore. You may remember, she's the one who was engaged to marry Moore. That's all, unless you want me to try to give you her exact words. I understand that she is now denying that she said that to me. So did Naylor, but you know what happened. I'm going to work on her, and I'm going to take her to see Wolfe if I can manage it."

"No name? She didn't say who it was?"

"No. Not yet."

"Have you reported this to the police?"

"Again not yet. We don't think the tactics they would use are likely to work, not with her."

There was a buzz from Pine's desk. He walked to it and picked up a phone, talked for a few minutes about something not connected with death, and then circled the desk and dropped into his chair.

"Damn it," he said, "always too many things to do at once." He was scowling at me. "Mr. Naylor said he never told you that. He insisted that you lied. Now this woman does the same."

I nodded. "Yeah. I'm building up a hell of a reputation. You didn't believe Naylor. This time you can believe her if you want to even up."

"I hope you realize what you're doing—what might happen to her."

I nodded again. "We're keeping an eye on her."

"All right." He picked up one of his phones. "Keep me informed. Let me know if she agrees to go to see Wolfe."

I said I would and left. On the way out of the reception room I used a phone booth to tell Wolfe that we were now getting words and gestures from the executive level.

The remainder of the morning I played solitaire, without any deck. I stayed glued to my chair, facing my open door, and not a soul entered to pass the time of day. It was monotonous and extremely unsatisfactory. Hester kept her door closed. She emerged once, at ten-fifteen, for a trip to Rosenbaum's room, where she remained over an hour, presumably for the morning dictation. The only other time I saw her was at one o'clock, her lunch hour, when she showed with her hat and coat on. I descended in the same elevator, with no exchange of greetings, saw Bill Gore pick her up in the lobby, and went myself to a joint down the street and consumed sandwiches and milk.

Back again in my room, deciding that I had been lonely long enough, I called the reserve pool and said I wanted a stenographer and only Miss Ferris would do. By that time I had them trained, and in no time at all Gwynne entered with her notebook in her hand. I moved a chair so she would be facing me, with her back to the open door, without obstructing my view of the arena.

"This is the first time I've taken from you," she said, sitting. "You'd better go a little slow."

"Sure," I agreed, "we've got all afternoon. Take a letter to the Police Commissioner. p-o-l-i-c-e——c-o-m——"

"You think you're smart, don't you?"

"You bet I'm smart. Dear Mr. Commissioner. I wish to make a complaint. The most beautiful girl on earth has betrayed my confidence. She said she wouldn't tell and she did. She told a hundred people in a hundred minutes. Her name is Gwynne Ferris and she—"

"I won't write that! That isn't so!"

"Don't talk so loud, the door's open." I grinned at her charmingly. "I know, Gwynne darling, you only told five or six and they promised not to breathe a word. Remember the first day I was here, how helpful you were?" I reached and got her notebook, tore out the page she had used for me, and handed her the book closed. "Forget it. All I wanted was to look at you. But we'd better talk to keep up appearances, people are looking at us. Is there any news?"

"There certainly is." She put one knee over the other and performed the skirt rite. "They're fighting like cats and dogs about who's lying, you or Hester."

"I hope I'm winning."

"Oh, yes, I'm sure you are, but some of them seem to like her, the dopes. That little fool Ann Murphy—do you know her?"

"Not intimately."

"She says she's going to put a complaint in the complaint box that you're putting Hester in peril! What do you know about that? And oh, yes—my God, I should have told you— Mr. Pine, the president—he had his secretary phone Hester to come to see him, and she said she wouldn't go, and then Mr. Pine phoned her himself and she still said she wouldn't go! What do you know about that? Telling the president she wouldn't go to his office when he told her to. Isn't that just like her? I hope to God she gets fired."

"Don't talk so loud. Where do you get all this? How do you know she wouldn't go? I don't believe it."

"You don't *believe* it?"

"No."

"All right, then don't. The girls at the switchboard ought to know, I would imagine. I ate lunch with one of them. Of course they're not supposed to listen in, but you know how it is, they have to see if they're through talking, don't they? You don't believe it?"

"Maybe I do. I'll let you know." I reached to pat her on the knee, a knee that was fully worthy of being patted. "You're

154

my favorite broadcaster, sweetheart. When did all this happen, this phoning and refusing?"

"This morning, before lunch, I don't know exactly what time. I think it shows she has guilty knowledge, don't you?"

"Well, at least knowledge. Any other news?"

"Lord yes, I should say so. Mr. Hoff didn't answer his mail all day yesterday, just let it lay there, he probably didn't even read it, and old man Birch, you know, the correspondence checker with the wart on his nose—"

She stopped because I suddenly stood up. "Excuse me," I apologized, "I forgot something, I have to make a phone call. I forgot all about it."

"I'll wait here."

I told her not to bother, I was through with dictation for the day, went out and down the aisle to the phone booths, and dialed Wolfe's number. Fritz answered and switched me to Wolfe.

"You said," I told him, "that you wanted them as they left the griddle. You may consider this garbage, but it's the first one for hours and I was afraid you might starve. This morning Pine had his secretary phone Miss Livsey to come to see him—to see Pine— and she refused. Then Pine phoned her himself to come to his office to see him and still she refused. That's all. Apparently she's upset and is not accepting invitations, no matter what. What seems strange, she says she has to have a job, and she likes it here, or she did."

"Have you seen her? Talked with her?"

"No. If I had you would have heard of it."

Silence. It kept on being silence, through a minute and a second and a third, until I asked:

"Hello, you there?"

"Yes. How did you learn this?"

"One of my girl friends, Gwynne Ferris, who got it from a girl on the switchboard. It wouldn't be invented. I'd pay for it myself."

"Where are you phoning from?"

"A booth."

"Good. Here are your instructions."

He gave them to me. It wasn't hard to see what was in his mind, and since the three or four lies I would have to tell wouldn't make it any riskier than it already was, I offered no objections. It was fairly complicated, with several contingencies involved, and I had him repeat it to be sure I had it straight.

Leaving the booth, thinking I might as well have one of

the contingencies provided for, I went first to my room for my hat and coat, and then crossed the arena to Hester's room. Her door was closed. I went in, shut the door behind me, sat on a chair, and kept my hat and coat on my lap.

Hester stopped banging the typewriter and looked at me. She was not the same woman I had met there two weeks previously. Then she had been a thousand miles away. Now she was right there with me, all of her. I meant something to her, I did indeed, and she was searching my face to see what it was I meant, coming to her. She didn't ask what I wanted. She didn't ask anything.

"I'm in a difficult position," I said in a matter-of-fact tone. "There are people that want to know who's lying, you or me. That's all right, I have no kick coming on that, but they have a nerve to ask me to act as a messenger boy. However—" I shrugged. "I understand Mr. Pine, the president of the company, sent for you this morning and you refused to go to see him."

She didn't move a muscle.

"That's correct, isn't it?" I inquired.

She spoke. "Yes. I—yes."

"Will you go to see him now? With me or without me?"

She didn't hesitate. "No."

I frowned at her. "One thing I'm not completely satisfied about. Has anyone tried to put any pressure on you? Since you refused to go to see Pine?"

"No."

"Then they gave me that straight. Okay. Their position is this, and you must admit they've got a point. I have told them that you told me that you know who killed Waldo Moore. They have been informed that you deny you told me that. They have had a talk with me, and they want to have a talk with you. That seems reasonable. I don't see how you can escape it. If you prefer not to talk with Pine, it can be some-one else. When I say 'they,' I don't mean they want to gang up on you. Just one of them—any of the three vice-presidents will do. Will you go to see one of the vice-presidents?"

I suppose she was blinking now and then, since it is sup-posed to be impossible not to, but I could have sworn she wasn't.

"I don't want to," she said, her voice so thin that it was nearly a squeak.

"Of course you don't. I can understand that, but will you?"

"Yes."

"Now?"

"Yes."

"Which one? Who?"

"Any—I don't care."

"But you just refused to go to see Pine."

"I mean—any other."

"Okay. Now it's like this. Their idea is that you should be willing to discuss this with a representative of the Board of Directors, and they would prefer to have you do it with the man they have hired to work for them and represent them regarding these murders. That man is Nero Wolfe. Will you come with me to see him?"

She didn't reply.

"I'm not urging you," I declared. "Yesterday I asked you to come and tell him the truth. Now you can tell him anything you want to. They would prefer to have you see Mr. Wolfe, but if you don't like the idea, take a vice-president. Suit yourself. Why don't you go ask Hoff about it?"

She flushed, and I was glad to see that her blood was still on the job. "I don't have to ask him," she said in a voice not so thin. "I don't have to ask anybody." Abruptly she pushed her chair back and was on her feet. "All right, I'll go. Wait till I tell Mr. Rosenbaum."

She left the room, in a minute returned and put on her hat and coat, and we departed. If I had known then that that was the last I would ever see of the Naylor-Kerr stock department I would have given it some kind of parting gesture, but even so I was leaving in a blaze of glory, with Hester Livsey just in front of my elbow and not an eye in the place anywhere except on us.

In the lobby downstairs, as we passed Bill Gore, I gave him a sign to stay put. It was quite possible that Hester would be back before long, and it was far from certain, anything but, that Wolfe was set for a clean-up.

In the taxi we were strangers. Not a word.

Our welcome from Nero Wolfe was not, I must admit, calculated to make us glow with pleasure. When I escorted her into the office and we approached his desk he growled at me:

"What the devil did you bring her here for?"

She goggled at him and then at me.

"That," I told him, "was my own idea. Everything went according to plan. She was willing to talk with anybody except Pine, which was what you wanted to know, and it occurred to me why not you? So I brought her where I'd know where she was. I told the lie that put the bee on her, and I didn't intend to spend the rest of the day and night wondering whether she was alive or dead. It's the humanitarian in me."

Wolfe looked at her. "I have work to do, Miss Livsey," he said in a fairly decent tone, "and I don't need you. But Mr. Goodwin is correct. Your life is in danger, or it may be. You may know more about that than I do, but in any case you ought to stay here. In the south room, Archie?"

Hester looked as if she thought we had a screw loose, and I didn't blame her. She took it up with me.

"You said they wanted me to talk to him!"

I took hold of her arm without either of us realizing that I was doing so. "Just another lie," I said. "You and I are doing swell on lies. Mr. Wolfe is ready to close in, or thinks he is, and you heard him say he doesn't need you. Unless you're ready to start from scratch and tell us all about it?"

"No!"

"I thought not. You're very tough, dearie. I also think you'll be a damn fool if you go back downtown or anywhere else."

"I have decided," Wolfe said curtly, "that she is not to leave here under any circumstances, now that she knows I am ready to act."

I still had her arm. "See? I don't want to stuff you in a closet. Upstairs is a nice sunny guest room—"

I stopped because she pulled her arm free. She walked across to the corner where the big globe was, with one of the yellow chairs beside it, and sat down in the chair.

"I'll stay here," she said.

I told Wolfe, "She's as stubborn as you are. The only way would be to carry her, and she'd scream and try to kick."

"Let her alone," he said. "Get Mrs. Pine on the phone."

I went to my desk and dialed the number.

33.

I didn't like it. I thought he was dead wrong and I still think so, in spite of the fact that he got away with it. He had got the giveaway gesture he was after, no doubt of that, but the thing to do now, since at last he had found the trail, was to deploy forces on all sides and make the main advance slow and careful but sure. No, not for him. He was going to bull it through with only one shot in his gun, and that one possibly a blank. If Hester hadn't been sitting there I would have put up an argument, and a hot one, but she had already heard more than was good for her. So I dialed the number.

I have since wondered what he would have done if Mrs. Pine had been out shopping or looking over the pet situation on Fifth Avenue, but that was a contingency he did not have to meet. An impersonal male voice answered the phone. I told it that Mr. Wolfe wished to speak with Mrs. Pine, and in a moment she was on and I signaled to Wolfe.

"Good afternoon, Mrs. Pine." Wolfe was making it bland. "I find myself in a disagreeable position. Certain information has come to me, and the proper thing for me to do would be to communicate with Mr. Cramer—you know, the Police Inspector—and suggest that he should send immediately for your personal staff of servants, and also for all members of the staff of the apartment building where you live who were on duty Friday evening, March twenty-first—the evening your brother was killed.—Please let me finish. I realize that would be a frightful annoyance for you. So there is this alternative. Why don't you bring them, yourself, to me? At my office. Your own servants, all of them, and also those of the apartment."

Her voice, incisive, pushed in. "What for? What on earth are you talking about?"

"Don't you know?"

"No!"

"Nonsense. Certainly you know. Unless I've underrated you, and I don't think I have. Doesn't my request make it plain that I have everything I need but a few details? I intend to get them without delay, and I'm giving you this chance to furnish them." Wolfe's voice suddenly went sharp and started to cut. "Either that or Mr. Cramer gets them, and that will be a different matter. You know what that would mean. Your husband lost his head. He sent for Miss Livsey, twice, and she refused to go. She came here instead. She is sitting here now under my eyes. Mr. Cramer's first step, of course, would be to get your husband, after I turned Miss Livsey over to him. I prefer to be more direct about it. I come straight to you."

"Where is my husband?"

"At his office. He hasn't been disturbed yet."

"And Miss Livsey is there with you?"

"Yes."

"I don't believe it."

"Very well, madam. Good-by. I thought it fair to give you this opportunity, since you own a large share of the corporation I'm working for—"

"Wait. Will you wait?"

"Not long. If you want a minute to decide, take it."

She took more than a minute, at least three. Wolfe and I sat with the receivers to our ears. I had my chair turned so as to have an eye on Hester, in case she took a notion to bounce over and do some yelling loud enough for the transmitter to pick it up. I still thought Wolfe was wrong, and I was pressing the receiver against my ear so hard it was a wonder I didn't crush a cartilage. Finally Cecily's voice came:

"I'll be there in half an hour."

Wolfe, having her, pressed, "With the others? The servants?"

"No. You won't need them."

"It shouldn't take you half an hour."

"I have to dress. I'll get there as soon as I can. You won't do anything?"

"Not until you get here, no."

Wolfe hung up and turned to Hester. "Mrs. Pine is going to come and tell me all about it. Do you want to go upstairs?"

Hester didn't speak. Nor did she move, not even her eyes. She was inspecting a rug. She was sitting straight, her coat still on, her hands grasping the ends of her leather bag, and the rug was evidently the most enthralling object she had ever gazed at in her life.

What I wanted to say to Wolfe would not have been fitting with a guest present, so I didn't say it.

I still hadn't said it thirty minutes later, when Mrs. Pine arrived.

34.

She sat in the red leather chair. That day her coat was mink and her dress was tightly woven brown wool with an elegant black check. She had never met Miss Livsey, she had said, and had offered a hand which Hester had not taken. That had not disconcerted her. Nothing, as far as could be told from her appearance, had disconcerted her, though her mind was sufficiently occupied to keep her from making any personal remarks to me. She sat in the red leather chair and told Wolfe:

"This would not have happened if you had done what I asked you to. My brother would not have been killed. He would have stopped his foolishness. Everything would have been all right."

"No," Wolfe said, "it wouldn't. It seem clear that your brother would never have abandoned his determination to become president of the firm. Nor would the death of Mr. Moore have been cleared up, but that didn't interest you. I wish you would start with that Friday evening. Why did you tell me your husband was home in bed when he wasn't?"

"Because I saw no—what are you doing there, Archie?"

"Shorthand," I told her. "I'm good at it."

"Then stop it. I won't have any record of this."

"I will," Wolfe said curtly. He wiggled a finger at her. "I intend, madam, to be in a position to satisfy your Board of Directors that I have done the job they hired me for. As far as I'm concerned that's all the record will be used for, but I'm going to have it. And I don't need to make any pretenses to you. At this moment I know barely what I need to know and that's all. For example, I had nothing but a surmise, a mere assumption, that your husband was not in bed asleep when you said he was, until you reacted as you did to my request to speak with your servants. That of course made the surmise a certainty. Why did you lie about it?"

"I didn't."

"Pah. You didn't?"

"I didn't intend to." Cecily kept glancing in my direction, but at the notebook, not at me. "When you phoned I was in my sitting-room. My husband's room is some distance away, and I thought he had gone to bed. When I went to see, he wasn't there. I didn't know he had gone out. I merely didn't care to tell you that, not that it mattered, not at the time, so I said he was asleep. He came in a little while after you phoned—"

"How long after?"

"I don't know—twenty minutes or half an hour. Then, later, when the news came that my brother had been killed, I knew that my husband had killed him."

"How did you know? Did he tell you?"

"Not that night. But I knew, and the next day I talked with him and he told me." Her hand fluttered. "My husband told me everything sooner or later, after he learned that that was the best way."

"When did he tell you that he killed Mr. Moore?"

She shook her head. "I'm not going to talk about that. I have decided that I don't have to." She had stopped glancing at my notebook and was sticking to Wolfe. "I know what this is for and I'm willing to say enough to satisfy you. I realize there are some things I have to tell you or you will turn it over to the police, but I don't have to go beyond that. It is true that my husband killed Waldo, but that had nothing to do with

161

me. He killed him because Miss Livsey had fallen in love with him and was going to marry him."

I wasn't as good as Wolfe was. I jerked my head up at her. Wolfe merely murmured at her, "Jealousy."

She nodded. "My husband had completely lost his head about her—but I suppose she has told you all about that?"

"Not all. I need your version. Go ahead."

"He met her at the company's annual dinner and dance for employees, over a year ago now, and he was a very passionate man. He told me about it, and he wanted to get a divorce. As time went on it got worse with him. She wouldn't let him see her much, and not at all openly. She was extremely clever about it, she wouldn't let him give her a better position at the office, and when I insisted that the only thing to do was to make her his mistress, he said she wouldn't."

Cecily twisted around in her chair to look at Hester. "That was very clever of you, Miss Livsey," she said without resentment, "but it made it very difficult for me."

Hester stayed motionless and had nothing to say.

"He wanted a divorce," Wolfe prompted.

"Yes, and I wouldn't give him one. It would have upset all my life's arrangements—among other things, I had made him president of the firm. He was even willing to forfeit his career for her. So I persuaded Waldo Moore to take a job there."

She nodded, to herself. "You didn't know Waldo. He was the most charming person I have ever known, until he got tiresome, which of course everyone does in time. I doubt if there was a woman on earth who could have resisted him. So I got him to take a job in the stock department, where Miss Livsey worked, and to—well, to divert her. It worked splendidly, as I was sure it would. He had her completely in hand within—I forget, but it couldn't have been—"

"You're lying!"

Hester had spoken.

Cecily twisted to her. "Oh, you have nothing to be ashamed of, Miss Livsey! No, indeed! You're the only woman he ever asked to marry him." She went back to Wolfe. "So there was no longer any reason for my husband to want a divorce, or so I thought, but I might have known, with the drive he had to get anything he wanted enough, that he wouldn't accept defeat as easily as that. What happened was that Waldo Moore was killed. I'm not going to talk about that. It wouldn't do you any good, and I don't have to. Anyway, the blame was not mine, it didn't happen because of any mistake of mine."

"Merely bad luck," Wolfe murmured.

She nodded. "But I had made a mistake, a very bad one. I had confided in my brother. He was older than me, and I had formed the habit in childhood, and I kept it even after we had grown up and I had become aware that he was a peculiar man and not to be taken seriously. That was a mistake too, to think he was not to be taken seriously. I didn't realize how much, clear to the bottom of his soul, he wanted to be the head of the business our father had founded. I was shocked when I learned he was using things, things I had told him in confidence from a sister to a brother, to put pressure on my husband to let him become president. I had taken possession of some letters my husband had received from Miss Livsey, and my brother stole them from me."

"Did you tell him your husband had killed Mr. Moore?"

Cecily looked annoyed. "I said I wouldn't talk about that," she declared to settle it. "But my brother—he thought that, yes. He threatened my husband with it, and me too. That was another mistake, or part of the same one—thinking my brother was not to be taken seriously. I told him he didn't have the ability to direct the affairs of the business and he should abandon the idea forever. Then he—you know about the report he sent in, stating that Waldo had been murdered."

Wolfe nodded.

Cecily fluttered a hand. "It couldn't be simply ignored, because my brother had let it become known and gossiped about by the employees. My husband didn't dare to keep it from the executives, and when most of them were in favor of hiring an investigator he didn't dare oppose it. I think that was extremely clever of my brother; I had never thought he was as intelligent as that. Wasn't that really clever?"

"Very," Wolfe agreed. "It got him killed."

"But he didn't know that," she protested. "It was clever to think of that way to bring pressure on my husband. I was determined, of course, to stop it, and I still think I would have succeeded if you had done what I asked—if you had stopped the investigation. It only stimulated my brother to go on. If you had quit I still think I could have persuaded my brother to give it up. But then he told Archie that he knew who had killed Waldo, and he saw he had gone too far, because what he wanted wasn't to have my husband arrested for murder but to get his job. If Archie hadn't been there he certainly wouldn't have told him that, and he wouldn't have told anybody that. I saw him that day and made him understand what he was doing, and he denied he had said it. But it may have been too late. My husband thought it was. He knew then that my brother had the letters he had received from Miss Livsey, and he thought it had gone so far that my brother couldn't draw back even if he wanted to, and anyway he didn't trust my brother and didn't think he wanted to. So—that night—"

She turned her palms up and lifted her shoulders.

"Yes," Wolfe agreed, "that night. When your husband was not home in bed, and when you learned that your brother had been killed, there was only one assumption for you. How did he do it? Where was your brother killed and with what?"

"I don't know."

"Nonsense. Certainly you know. Your husband told you everything." Wolfe wiggled a finger at her. "Come, madam. You know what this is for."

"Does it matter?"

"Not to you. To you nothing matters. But I'm going to earn my fee, and you know what the alternative is."

"My brother and my husband were much alike in one way," Cecily said. "They were both excessively conceited. When my brother met him that evening, to talk things over, and rode in his car with him, I doubt if he was at all alarmed even when my husband stopped the car in a secluded street. He was too conceited. He thought he could take care of himself. Probably he never thought otherwise, for when my husband reached over the back of the seat to the tonneau to get his brief case, what he really got was a chunk of petrified wood he had put there, and my brother was stunned by the first blow, or possibly killed—my husband wasn't sure, but he made sure."

Cecily's hand fluttered. "Of course," she conceded, "something had to be done, since it was my husband's own car, but only a supremely confident and conceited man would have proceeded as he did. He actually kept the piece of petrified wood and later brought it home and cleaned it and put it back on the desk in his study. Just ahead of my husband's car where he had stopped it at the curb another car was parked—it was the one he had stolen and put there. He transferred the body to it. His reason for driving to Thirty-ninth Street and repeating, exactly repeating, his performance with Waldo's body last December, every detail of it—his reason was that it would be supposed that the same person had killed both of them, and that would be to his advantage because he wouldn't be suspected of killing Waldo. That was the reason he gave me, but it was nothing but a reason. He really did it because

164

he had to do something with the body, and he was confident and conceited, and it was a difficult and complicated gesture of assurance and contempt—for you and me and everyone else." Cecily turned her head. "Except you, Miss Livsey. As far as I know you are the one person toward whom it was impossible for my husband to feel contemptuous. It made me quite curious about you."

Hester had nothing to say.

Wolfe grunted, "About Miss Livsey, by the way, there is a detail. For over an hour, earlier that Friday evening, your brother walked the streets with her, talking. What were they talking about?"

Cecily looked surprised. "I have no idea." She twisted around. "What was it, Miss Livsey?"

Hester was silent.

Wolfe tried it. He opened his eyes at her. "Surely you're not going to stick to that lie now? If you do, I warn you I'll resent it. This will be left with either my witness a liar or you, and I don't intend it to be him. What were you discussing with Mr. Naylor?"

Hester spoke, to Wolfe, emphatically not to Cecily. "He wanted to see me. He asked me to meet him."

"What did he want?"

"He thought I had letters that Mr. Pine had written me, and he wanted them."

"Did you give them to him?"

"I didn't have them. I had destroyed them." Hester swallowed. "He didn't believe me. He had asked for them before, and he threatened to dismiss me—from my job—if I didn't give them to him."

"Good God!" I blurted. I couldn't help it. "Why didn't you say so long ago?"

She was on speaking terms with me, too, for her eyes came my way. "How could I? And have it all come out—about Mr. Pine?"

"Does Hoff know all this?"

"No. He just knows I need help."

"Did you know Pine had killed Moore? And Naylor?"

"No, I—I didn't really know anything. How could I? What I thought—what does that matter?"

Wolfe wasn't interested. He took over, asking Cecily, "What about the letters your husband got from Miss Livsey? Your brother had them. They weren't found among his papers. Where are they?

165

"They were destroyed too," she said. "My husband destroyed them. He got them—that Friday evening." She was frowning. "But isn't that enough? I have trusted you further than I have ever trusted any man. I admit I had to. What assurance have I that it won't go to the police?"

I gawked at her. Was she, in addition to everything else, a ninny?

"None at all," Wolfe said. "You have done what you could to straighten it out, but there is the matter of your husband to be taken care of. Surely you can't expect—"

The phone rang. I transferred my notebook to my right hand and picked up the receiver.

"Nero Wolfe's office, Archie Goodwin speaking."

"Archie, get this!" It was Bill Gore's voice.

"Okay, give it to me."

He did so. It was a straight factual report of an event. I listened, asked a question or two, hung up, and turned to tell Wolfe.

"News from Bill Gore. Mr. Jasper Pine fell from a window of his office on the thirty-sixth floor. Bill has seen him, and from his description I would say that he is in worse shape than if a car had run over him. Dead on arrival."

A little gasp had come from Hester's corner. Cecily made no sound and no move.

Wolfe heaved a sigh. He spoke to Cecily.

"You didn't spend all your time dressing, did you, Mrs. Pine? A telephone call was enough, was it? Naturally I am not surprised. I was quite aware that you would have been much more discreet with me otherwise."

No, it wasn't a ninny that she was. Protect your woman? Not that one. She didn't need it.

35.

Four days and nights had brought us to another Saturday.

There had been on Wednesday, a long session with Cramer. He had left, after two hours in the red leather chair, with as little love for us as when he arrived. He could beef, and did, but that was all, for he had no peg on which to hang anything. He would have dearly loved to see a headline in the Gazette, POLICE SOLVE TWO MURDERS, but he never did.

There had been, on Friday, the day after Jasper Pine's

funeral, a long session with the three vice-presidents, one of whom was acting president. It was strictly off the record and as far as we were concerned that was as far as it ever got. Cecily had talked to them, with her block of stock to back it up, and I suppose her father had too. The Board of Directors never got to see a transcript of the notes in my book. Only one copy of the transcript was made, and it was locked in our safe and is still there.

Saturday at eleven in the morning, when Wolfe came down from the plant rooms I was busy at my desk. There were a couple of little typing jobs connected with the Naylor-Kerr affair, one of them being the bill for services rendered. It included a careful and exact itemization of expenses incurred—Wolfe was always a stickler for that—but the expenses were peanuts compared to the main entry, the fee. I would have been willing to defend the position that he had really earned one-tenth of it, which after all meant only one extra cipher.

I was typing the itemization of expenses when the phone rang and I answered it.

"Archie? Guess who this is!"

"Now, Gwynne darling. That voice? Don't be silly."

"Then you haven't entirely forgotten me? I was sure you had. Aren't we ever going to see you in the stock department again?"

"I guess not. I can't stand the propinquity. P-R-O—"

"Don't be so smart. It's too bad because I have a lot of things to tell you! I never knew so much to happen in one week! Mr. Rosenbaum is the new head of the department, and Mr. Appleton has been made—oh, I just have to see you! I have nothing to do this evening. Have you?"

The fact was I hadn't. I had had a date with Lily Rowan, but she was in bed with a cold.

"I am simply dying," I declared, "to hear about Mr. Appleton. Meet me at the bar at Rusterman's at seven."

"But they don't have dancing there! I thought we—"

"Excuse me for interrupting, but I have work to do. We can move on after we eat and dance all night. See you at seven o'clock, dearie."

I ignored the snort from Wolfe's direction and resumed at the typewriter. When the bill was finished I read it over and checked the additions, folded it neatly and put it in an envelope, and filed the carbon in the cabinet over by the couch. Then I returned to the typewriter, inserted a sheet of my personal stationery, dated it, and started:

Dear Mrs. Pine:
   Last night I went—

   I had to stop to answer the phone again.
   "Archie? This is Rosa."
   "Well, well. You don't need to tell me. That voice. How are the curves?"
   "Now really." She tittered. "How can you find out on the telephone? You know, I went to bed last night at nine o'clock, and I didn't get up till ten this morning, and I feel simply wonderful! While I was drinking my coffee it reminded me of you, and this is Saturday, and I wondered if you were doing anything this evening."
   "Nothing special. Are you?' '
   "No, that's why I called. I thought—"
   "Good for you. Meet me at the bar at Rusterman's at seven o'clock."
   "Oh, that wonderful wine! And steak?"
   "Sure, two steaks. Or maybe three. Seven sharp?"
   "Yes!"
   Wolfe snorted again, and again I ignored it. Anyway, I had to put my mind on my work. This was not a case of transcribing from notes; I had to concentrate on a job of original composition. I proceeded with it:

Dear Mrs. Pine:
   Last night I went to a fortune-teller, which is something I seldom do. What was bothering me was your remark the other day that everybody gets tiresome sooner or later, and I wanted to find out where I stood. She told me that the most I could count on was two months. It seems that I am wonderful as long as I last and then I go tiresome all at once, without any warning.
   I regret to say that under the circumstances it wouldn't be worth it to you, and I am therefore returning herewith the baseball tickets. It is still two weeks before the season starts, so you have plenty of time to dig up another prospect.

                                             Sincerely,

   I was debating whether to sign it just Archie or with my full name, and had decided in favor of the latter when the phone interrupted me again. I picked it up.
   "Nero Wolfe's office, Archie Goodwin speaking."
   "This is Hester Livsey, Mr. Goodwin."
   "Good morning." I cleared my throat. "What do you want?"
   "I know I deserve that," she said. "I want to say I'm sorry

I was so rude to you when you phoned Thursday evening. I—I hope you'll understand. I didn't feel like anything, and I was terribly rude. I wanted to explain—"

"Don't mention it. Feeling better?"

"Oh, yes, much better. I really would like to explain some things to you. Would you care to come over here this evening —you know my address, don't you? It's just a little apartment where I live with my mother."

"In Brooklyn."

"Yes. Twenty-three ninety-four—"

"Yeah, I know. I guess I can find it. How about taking a ride with me tomorrow, in Mr. Wolfe's rackety old sedan, to the country somewhere and see if spring has come?"

"I'm sorry, I couldn't make it tomorrow because my mother and I are going to visit some friends. Don't bother, really—"

"No bother at all." An idea struck me. "The trouble is I'm so uncouth I'm afraid I'd make a bad impression on your mother. I think you ought to know me better before you invite me to your home. Do you know where Rusterman's restaurant is?"

"Rusterman's? Certainly."

"That's a nice quiet place with good food. How about meeting me in Rusterman's bar at seven this evening?"

"Well—that wasn't—I wasn't fishing for a dinner—"

"No, I know, you don't fish. But I think it might be very enjoyable, at least for me. Will you?"

"Well—"

"You will."

"All right, I will."

I hung up, reached for my pen, and signed the letter to Cecily.

Wolfe growled at me, "What the devil are you going to do with all of them?"

I grinned at him. "God knows, I don't. I'm so damn sociable. I can't bear to disappoint people."

ABOUT THE AUTHOR

REX STOUT, the creator of Nero Wolfe, was born in Noblesville, Indiana, in 1886, the sixth of nine children of John and Lucetta Todhunter Stout, both Quakers. Shortly after his birth, the family moved to Wakarusa, Kansas. He was educated in a country school, but, by the age of nine, was recognized throughout the state as a prodigy in arithmetic. Mr. Stout briefly attended the University of Kansas, but left to enlist in the Navy, and spent the next two years as a warrant officer on board President Theodore Roosevelt's yacht. When he left the Navy in 1908, Rex Stout began to write free-lance articles, worked as a sightseeing guide and as an itinerant bookkeeper. Later he devised and implemented a school banking system which was installed in four hundred cities and towns throughout the country. In 1927 Mr. Stout retired from the world of finance and, with the proceeds of his banking scheme, left for Paris to write serious fiction. He wrote three novels that received favorable reviews before turning to detective fiction. His first Nero Wolfe novel, *Fer-de-Lance*, appeared in 1934. It was followed by many others, among them, *Too Many Cooks*, *The Silent Speaker*, *If Death Ever Slept*, *The Doorbell Rang* and *Please Pass the Guilt*, which established Nero Wolfe as a leading character on a par with Erle Stanley Gardner's famous protagonist, Perry Mason. During World War II, Rex Stout waged a personal campaign against Nazism as chairman of the War Writers' Board, master of ceremonies of the radio program "Speaking of Liberty" and as a member of several national committees. After the war, he turned his attention to mobilizing public opinion against the wartime use of thermonuclear devices, was an active leader in the Authors' Guild and resumed writing his Nero Wolfe novels. All together, his Nero Wolfe novels have been translated into twenty-two languages and have sold more than forty-five million copies. Rex Stout died in 1975 at the age of eighty-eight. A month before his death, he published his forty-sixth Nero Wolfe novel, *A Family Affair*.

NERO WOLFE

He's not much to look at and he'll never win the hundred yard dash but for sheer genius at unraveling the tangled skeins of crime he has no peer. His outlandish adventures make for some of the best mystery reading in paperback. He's the hero of these superb suspense stories.

BY REX STOUT

THE THRILLING AND MASTERFUL NOVELS OF ROSS MACDONALD

Winner of the Mystery Writers of America Grand Master Award, Ross Macdonald is acknowledged around the world as one of the greatest mystery writers of our time. *The New York Times* has called his books featuring private investigator Lew Archer "the finest series of detective novels ever written by an American."

Now, Bantam Books is reissuing Macdonald's finest work in handsome new paperback editions. Look for these books (a new title will be published every month) wherever paperbacks are sold or use the handy coupon below for ordering: